Bitch Witch

a novel

Book design by
Blue Harvest Creative
www.blueharvestcreative.com

Bitch Witch

Published by Asher
an imprint of BHC Press

Library of Congress Control Number:
2016900325

ISBN-13: 978-1-946006-74-5
ISBN-10: 1-946006-74-2

also available in eBook and audio

Visit the author at:
www.SRKarfelt.com &
www.bhcpresss.com

ALSO BY S.R. KARFELT

The Covenant Keeper Novels
Kahtar—Warrior of the Ages
Heartless—A Shieldmaiden's Voice
Forever—The Constantines' Secret

Multi-Author Collections
A Winter's Romance
In Creeps the Night
Through the Portal
Call of the Warrior

Table of Contents

For Brian
A fellow night owl.

Absolutely *nothing* in life was free,
and that included favors from the dark side.

S.R. KARFELT

Bitch Witch

a novel

Livonia, Michigan

chapter one

Right on Target

P lastic bags of crispy crust pizza and monthly supplies twisted around Sarah Archer's wrists, cutting off her circulation. She fumbled with her frozen Coke, catching it between a bag and her sweatshirt. The icy concoction oozed out the top of the cup, spilling over her fingers. Resisting the urge to cast them clean and feeling a bit saintly about her amazing willpower, Sarah paused outside Target's automatic front doors to lick the mess off her hand.

A blaring horn made her jump and the drink hit the ground in an explosion of frozen ice, splashing her from bare toes to chin.

Dammit! I wanted that stupid thing! Mourning the icy Coke melting between her toes, Sarah ignored the driver and considered going back into the store for another drink. *But there's no way I can stand in that slow line again without casting to speed things up.*

The horn blared again.

Just breathe. Don't get mad. You dropped it.

And you are standing in the middle of the damn road.

Sarah almost moved. She shifted one sticky wet flip-flop toward the brightly lit storefront when a mom with a cart and little kids shoved around her, heading for the darkening parking lot. The driver laid on the horn and swore at them through an open window.

Sarah changed her mind about moving.

She looked through the windshield, directly into the eyes of the driver. The pretty blonde glared back and lifted her middle finger off the steering wheel. Despite the size of the pickup, Sarah stood her ground. Somewhere in the back of her mind she tried to reason with herself.

Don't, don't, don't.

But Sarah wasn't listening.

It's when she got pissed off that the problems started.

Sometimes she got pissed off easier than others. Like now.

The blonde stared at Sarah across the hood of the shiny white truck and screeched, "Fuck you, fat bitch!"

Customers in the vicinity protested, and someone swore back at the driver.

The vehicle swerved around Sarah, moving half onto the sidewalk in front of the store and almost clipping one of the giant red concrete balls put there to keep cars away. People scattered. An old man holding a cup of Starbucks' coffee dropped it in his scramble to retreat back into the store, while younger people hurried out the doors to watch. The pickup squeezed between a bench and a trash can before bouncing off the curb and fully regaining the roadway.

The encounter would have pissed off even a powerless fat bitch. Sarah Elizabeth Archer wasn't powerless. The retreating truck accelerated so quickly the back end fishtailed as it made its getaway. Too late. The damage was done. There was no way to escape witchy karma.

A ball of heat sparked to life in Sarah's chest, hot against her ribcage, like whiskey torching the esophagus. Tums couldn't help this, but she knew what could. She eyeballed the tricked out pickup speeding away.

"Fat bitch this," she whispered, setting the hot anger free. It felt good not to tap it down, a hot rush of release better than any sex she'd ever had. The spell tracked the pickup like a heat-seeking missile as it shot down the strip mall, catching up with the platinum tantrum trash next to Moe's Grill.

Sarah heard it hit, like a meteorite dropping through the engine and tearing the driveshaft out. An aftershock with a noise similar to a sonic boom blew out the front windows of the nearby wireless store and ricocheted across the parking lot, setting off car alarms in its wake.

"Oh, shit!" Sarah half-walked, half-ran toward her Jeep as people gaped in the direction of the explosion.

What goes up must come down, and for every action there is an opposite and equal reaction. The aftershock headed her way so fast and hard Sarah thought she heard the high pitched whine of its approach. She forced herself to turn and face it. This is what separated the men from the boys, the good witches from the bad. At least she hoped it counted for something. One thing she'd learned long ago was to pay the cost of her own mistakes. She certainly wasn't going to ever be one of those witches that lured cats, or heaven forbid neighbors, to the house so they could pay the piper. Not that she wanted to be a witch at all. She'd renounced it, for Pete's sake! But it was hard to stick to her resolve when she got upset; harder than trying to give up sugar or caffeine.

It's kind of ironic that the road to hell and the road to fat pants are both paved with good intentions.

The aftershock slammed into Sarah, lifting her off her feet and shoving her into the back of her Jeep, against the spare tire. The bulk of the spell's reverberation rolled off her and against the car, pushing it into the car parked nose to nose with hers. Sarah heard the crunch of the vehicles as she hit the ground like a celebratory football slammed from the hands of a scoring quarterback. The impact jarred every bone in her body. It felt like her ribs had collapsed and her spine now rested between her breasts. Lying flat on her back and staring up into the darkening sky she noticed not the panic around her, but the full moon. A blue moon.

"No wonder," she moaned, tasting blood on her lips. She would have known better than to cast if she had taken two seconds to think before reacting. *A full moon, a blue moon, PMS, a witch who hasn't cast in—what—seven months?*

Talk about falling off the wagon.

"Ma'am?" said a voice that made her think of cowboys and rodeos, and people interviewed on the news talking about how a tornado sounded like a train.

"Ma'am?" the accented voice repeated.

Ma'am? Oh, screw you! She didn't look that old! Okay, technically she was wearing flannel pajama bottoms—but they could pass for yoga pants! *Kinda, sorta.* No, she hadn't showered or brushed her hair today but *ma'am?* Who in all of New England said *ma'am?* Although the truck driven by the blonde jackhole had already proven there were rednecks even outside of Boston.

"Ma'am, can you hear me?" A man knelt beside her. "Are you all right?"

Sarah focused on him and the shouts and noise around her seemed to go silent. *Don't, don't, don't! You're in enough trouble!*

She wasn't listening. An actual real-life cowboy leaned over her, complete with faded jeans, a pristine white t-shirt, and a black cowboy hat. A fair amount of tattoos covered muscled arms, and because the universe found her situation so funny, her rescuer wore a necklace with a religious icon.

Ah, I can't just slide to the dark side and be done with it, can I?

Every other moment just has to be a painful learning experience, doesn't it?

Sarah reached up and took the pendant between her thumb and two fingers. It scorched like she'd grasped the wrong end of a stick roasting marshmallows. *Penance.* She held on as long as she could bear it, mere seconds, and let go with a shout that returned the sounds of people and car alarms to her ears.

"Ma'am, hold still. I'm going to call an ambulance," Cowboy said, yanking a cell phone out of his back pocket and running a thumb across the screen.

"No." Sarah shoved to a sitting position, the bag with pizzas still attached to her wrist. The other must have been thrown against the car too. Playtex Gentle Glide Super Plus tampons littered her lap, and the pills from bottles of St. John's Wort and Evening Primrose Oil spilled over the blacktop, peppered with Hershey Kisses and Dove Dark. Some practical part of Sarah's brain noted that the chocolates were foil wrapped and therefore still good.

"You best not move. I'm an EMT and I think you might have a head injury." Cowboy leaned closer as though to study her eyes, giving her a close-up view of the face shaded by his hat. Brown eyes with thick lashes, sharp nose, sculpted lips, stubble—pretty much man perfection. *Please be gay, or married, or really turned off by menstruating single witches who've never had good sex.*

"I'm fine." Sarah yanked the pizza bag off her wrist and wiped her hand across her mouth. She studied the blood on the back of her hand and tentatively touched her lip with her tongue. She'd bitten it, but not too badly. "I just fell," she lied, and added for atonement, "Believe me, there's nothing wrong with my head that doesn't run in my family."

"Can you tell me what eight times seven is?"

Sarah blinked, counting in her head. *Crickey, really? Do all EMTs give pop quizzes? Eight times five is forty, plus two more eights.* "Fifty-six?"

He didn't look convinced.

"Seriously, I'm okay. I have a math deficit that has nothing to do with this. I was an English major. Couldn't you give me a random Longfellow fill-in-the-blank? Or maybe Thoreau?"

Those lips rubbed together, and for a moment *those lips* completely distracted Sarah. Leaning his body weight onto one knee, Cowboy said, "*And seeming to whisper all is well...*"

It took Sarah a moment to place the obscure line from *The Midnight Ride of Paul Revere* and settle her brain on the next line in the poem. But she had gone to school in Massachusetts, so the entire poem about the patriot lived in her brain somewhere. At last she found it, and said with triumph, "*A moment only he feels the spell.*"

No sooner had the words left her lips than the power of them hit, tangling with the residual aftershock of the spell just cast. *Shit!* Magic slipped from her with her next breath and blew over the cowboy as an incantation. He blinked at her as though only now focusing and noticing she wasn't a fat old lady, but a young one, with eyes the color of his faded Levi's and hair as dark as a night sky. He swallowed and his Adam's apple moved with masculine perfection.

Shit! But he spoke it first, I didn't! Sarah fought the urge to yank his cross off the chain and stick it into her mouth, swallow it maybe. She hadn't cast a love spell since one teenage moment of insanity in high school. *Is it only love spells you've cut out? You're not supposed to cast at all!* Surely this cowboy was part of the aftershock of her spell. *The payment is always higher than you imagine! This is what happens when you're in debt to the dark side! Compound interest was invented in hell.*

"Are you two okay?" An older woman gazed down at them, her eyes focused on Sarah. "Oh! You're bleeding!" She straightened and waved to someone, calling, "Over here!"

"No, I'm fine! I'm fine." Sarah scrambled to her feet, dodging the cowboy's hand when he stood quickly to offer it. *Oh, hell no! A touch will seal the deal.* Gaining her feet, Sarah took several steps backward, almost tripping as one of her flip-flops folded in half. If she avoided his touch it would be much easier to break the spell.

Easier? No love spell breaks easily. She looked around, spotted her keys on the pavement and grabbed them. "I'd better get home, I need to…" *get the hell away from you.* She didn't bother trying to finish the sentence with a lie. She had enough penance to do.

"I think we need some help over here!" the lady shouted across the parking lot.

Shut up! "I'm fine!" Sarah grabbed her bags and bent over to stuff the ripped tampon box into one. Cowboy picked up a couple tampons and her credit card. "I can get it. Don't bother," she said.

Ignoring her, Cowboy dropped them into her open bag. Sarah yanked her hand away before they could touch, but accepted his help. She was going to need all the chocolate and probably all the damn tampons after this. Bending to gather more chocolates, she kept an eye on him.

Shouts and someone crying drew Sarah's attention. With her mind on her own problems, she had forgotten the other injuries in the parking lot. Judging by the amount of people standing around in the near darkness, and the flashing lights of an approaching ambulance, Sarah knew she wasn't the only one knocked over.

Shit! This is going to take some serious penance to fix. Seven months of good behavior down the toilet! Again!

"I suppose we're going to need to exchange insurance information too." Cowboy straightened and pulled his wallet from his back pocket.

Sarah recalled the crashing sound as she'd hit the ground, and hurried to look at the front of her Jeep. It rested against the crumpled front end of a BMW Series 6 convertible. *Black, of course. It matches his hat.* It looked like her Jeep had driven across his hood. Even his windows were cracked. Her Jeep didn't appear to have any damage. Sarah's shoulders slumped as she turned to the cowboy. "That's yours?" *Of course it's his. Perfect man, perfect car. He probably adores his mother and has lunch with his sister every week too.*

He frowned, using his wallet to push his hat back further. "Just picked it up today, up in New Hampshire. I swung by here to grab some stuff for the road. Supposed to have that back home by Tuesday morning." He said Tuesday like *Toos-dee.*

"Texas?" *Of course.*

"Oklahoma."

Close enough. "I'm sorry," said Sarah.

He smiled at her with toothpaste ad teeth and was that—Sarah narrowed her eyes at his chin—yep, a dimple in his chin. *Seriously?*

"It weren't your fault." He took off his hat to run strong fingers through dark hair that the universe surely had created for the sole purpose of that gesture. "I thought that was a bomb when it took out those windows, but it sounded different—meteorite maybe? I could hear the whistle before it hit."

"Hmmph," snorted Sarah. Lies had a cost too, not like casting and knocking down innocent people in the parking lot, but enough lies could slowly bind one to the dark side before they ever knew they were going. Sarah figured she was already sitting on hell's riverbank dangling her feet into the river Styx. She certainly wasn't going to tie an anchor to them with lies. Shoving her key into the ancient Jeep door, she creaked it open and said, "Do you have your insurance card then?"

"Yes, ma'am."

If she was going to touch him, it would be to smack him. She wondered if he felt the same urge to touch, to make physical contact. To be safe, Sarah tossed her bags onto the passenger seat, climbed into the driver's seat and leaned over to open the glovebox. "Massachusetts has no-fault insurance. Do you know what that is?"

"Not really, ma'am."

Sarah paused in her digging to look out the driver's door at the cowboy. He leaned against the open door—it was a good thing she'd climbed inside so far—still holding his wallet in hand, fishing for his insurance card while studying her. Sarah wished she'd worn a bra, but at least the frumpy sweatshirt mostly hid that faux pas.

"I think it's supposed to keep things simple, especially when no one gets hurt," she explained.

"You were hurt," said Cowboy in a hushed voice.

Sarah sensed he was going to touch her. She felt him reaching before she lifted her eyes to see the hand, tattooed with what looked like a horse's nose under the bright parking lot lights. She leaned toward it, because she was the stupidest woman who never wanted to be a witch. But no touch came.

"Here." His hand hovered inches above both of hers, offering his insurance card. "Do you have a pen? To copy the information down with?"

That was close! And I wanted him to! She had to get away.

"No. I don't have a pen. Move."

"I'm sorry?" he said.

"Quit leaning on my door."

"Oh!" He immediately moved. "Sorry, ma'am!"

"And stop calling me ma'am!"

He apologized again, and Sarah grabbed the door handle and slammed it shut. Just that much metal and glass separating them hurt her, as if she had been closed off from oxygen inside the car. *Damn! It's strong!* Sarah fumbled to hit the button to roll the window down, which was inconveniently located beneath the radio. As the window slid open her breathing came easier.

Cowboy waited, patiently holding his insurance card out. "I thought you were going to hit and run on me," he teased.

Sarah leaned back against the seat and took a deep breath. His essence came with it. He smelled—Sarah considered a moment, inhaling again, trying to place it—*good.* Not good as in attractive, although he had that, too—body wash, deodorant, and just a slight hint of sweat or anxiety. No, he smelled *good.*

Honest.

Physical, but has a penchant for history.

Soldier.

Fuck.

"I am going to hit and run on you. I've got to go. Here." Sarah tossed her insurance card out the window. It fluttered to the ground.

He tried to hand over his card, but Sarah put the window up so quickly that his hand bumped against the glass. She looked away from him, glanced into the rearview mirror for show—she could already sense the momentary break in activity behind her Jeep—and shoved the gear into reverse.

"Hey! Wait!" Cowboy hollered as she backed out.

His yell came faintly through the glass, but Sarah didn't pause, instead stepping on the clutch and moving into first gear. She needed to put as much distance between them as possible, and do penance for casting the damn spell that tore out the driveshaft of that pickup and bloodied half a dozen people. After that she'd figure out how the hell to break a love spell without casting again to do it.

chapter two

Mazztardz and Cock Fighting

S arah arrived at work a half hour early Monday morning. She hadn't slept last night—not that she ever really did. Witches couldn't sleep long or deeply. Her aunt used to say it gave them more time to play.

Mondays were Sarah's idea of play, and her favorite day of the week. With a box of Dunkin Donuts in hand she swung by the coffee machine in the breakroom on the way to her cubicle. Despite the stigma attached to being female and making coffee for the department, Sarah liked good coffee and didn't mind the stereotype. She made coffee almost every morning, and often brought treats. At lunch she regularly picked up as much takeout as she could carry. Most days she even wore a dress—they hid her penchant for sweets—and she always agreed to work late when asked. She didn't mind being the poster child office worker from the fifties. She enjoyed every minute of mindless drudgery at Mass Power and Light.

Sarah placed an éclair, arranged artfully on a real plate, in exactly the right spot on her desk and slid into her chair. This was what normal people did. People with souls not pledged to darkness.

Sipping coffee with real cream, she gazed at the pale blue fabric of her cubical walls and the muscles in her neck relaxed. Pushing last night's fiasco out of her mind came easy now. A calendar with pictures of New England beaches hung next to a framed poster of inspirational quotes. A fresh flower arrangement sat next to a silver frame with a smiling older couple. An assortment of highlighters lay beside colorful sticky notes, and a huge computer monitor sat smack in the middle of her desk. Normalcy.

Lies.

Sarah grimaced and glanced at one of the quotes on her poster.

Life is what we make it. Always has been, always will be. ~ Grandma Moses

So what if she sent herself the flowers every week? So what if hours shopping for stationery and pens replaced growing herbs and manipulating dark matter? And so what if the couple in the photograph were actually the parents of a college roommate? Sarah had created a normal life for herself, and these props helped enforce that image. What happened to the women in her family wouldn't happen to her, because she had chosen a life without magic.

Mostly, liar.

"If I smell coffee when I get off the elevator I know Sarah's here," a voice bellowed over the cubicle wall. "You're the only clerk who makes it! You have a great work ethic. Don't think we don't notice!"

Didn't do it for you, Mr. Management. "Good morning, Avery."

"Good morning, Sarah. Did you have a good weekend? How're you doing?" Avery Gross, appropriately named, hovered over the fabric wall, invading Sarah's personal space with his bleached smile and Edward Cullen hair. A mid-level manager, Avery had been promoted over Sarah last week. Since then he had managed to mention it daily, with small doses of, *your time will come!* It was always said politely, if self-satisfied, because he really wanted to fuck her.

"I'm just ducky! Yourself?"

The phrase had become Sarah's standard reply, but Avery didn't really need any prompting to launch into his weekend commentary.

Sarah was okay with that. It saved her from lying. She couldn't say her weekend had flown by; it had crawled. Other than casting, blowing up someone's engine and being woven into a love spell, most of it had been spent lying on the couch watching old Meg Ryan movies on mute and rereading novels. Watching or reading anything new might take her mind in dangerous directions, especially during PMS weekend. So Sarah had laid low until cramps and the need for sugar and carbs drove her to make that disastrous Sunday night dash for sustenance.

Do not think about the damn cowboy! Especially not with Avery and his bulging pants now at eye-level. Standing inside her cubicle now, Avery blathered on about Cape Cod, both hands in his pockets. The better to rock back on his heels from time to time and practically shove his dick in her face.

Sarah nodded, trying not to look at the bulge. Although, if she didn't work with him, and if she hadn't instituted a zero sex with other employees policy, she'd be all over that. *Purely for educational purposes. Maybe size does matter.*

Someone down the hall called to Avery that the team meeting was about to start. He looked at his Apple watch. "Gotta fly. Management status meet up every single Monday morning at seven!" He exaggerated the last few words as though weary of it, as though it wasn't only his second meeting.

"Let me know if anyone wants coffee," Sarah said, ignoring a hip thrust.

Avery lowered his voice. "You don't have to do that, you know."

"I don't mind."

"Some people," he darted his eyes around the empty office area before continuing, "might get the wrong idea."

"Wrong idea?"

"Well, you don't want them to think you're brown nosing. I mean I know you're not, don't get me wrong. But you know how people are. Maybe you should take it down a notch. We noticed you're a good employee. We appreciate you, and you'll break the glass ceiling on your own one of these days. There's no need to suck up. You're a shoe-in. You've got the girl-card." He winked.

Brown noser? Girl card?

We *realize you're a good employee?*

Suck up?

Annoyance flared in the pit of Sarah's stomach. They'd offered Avery's job to Sarah first. She'd turned them down. Mindless, meaningless tasks were why she'd taken this job. She didn't want to break any glass ceiling or climb a corporate ladder. All she wanted was to keep her hands busy, her mind preoccupied with the mundane, and not cast any effing spells. If she could do all that, maybe she wouldn't be swallowed up by dark matter at a young age.

"You're not really going to eat that?" Avery indicated the éclair on her desk and patted his perfectly flat stomach. "Just say no! Isn't that what they say?"

Teeth clenched together in a perfect smile, Sarah said, "Breakfast is the most important meal of the day. They say that."

Avery leaned over her, the crotch to face ratio briefly neared to a mere ten centimeters. He crouched down beside her, nabbed the plate and tried a pathetic Scooby Doo impression with the donut as his puppet, "Rut-roh, Sar-rah, I'm rot real reakfast!"

Good gravy, maybe he doesn't want to fuck me. Maybe he wants me to maim him.

"Seriously though, you don't want to eat junk. You'd be surprised how fast a Daphne can become a Velma." Winking again, he plopped the plate down and turned to leave, the bulge in his pants leading the way.

Itchy cock! The spell shot out of Sarah before she could consciously think twice.

It hit Avery near the cubicle opening. That was the problem with casting, one spell always led to another. *And they all feel so damn good!* With euphoria dancing through her, it was easy to take the spell in stride, and even easier to rub Avery's face in it.

"Hey, Avery, can you hold up a minute?"

"Uh." He pressed his thighs together. "I need to get to the meeting. Management responsibilities you know. Ha ha! Or maybe you don't know yet. But you will! Ha ha!"

Sarah scratched at her cheek. *A very itchy cock for Avery!* Double the dose for double the dick. "Just a quick question!" She scratched her shoulder, hoping the action tormented him as she forced him to linger. "I need a manager with admin privileges to approve changes I made to a BHC form. Can you do that for me?" She gazed at him with a pleading expression, not reaching for the mouse. It might take more than a minute. It might take until he scratched the damn thing with both hands in the middle of the office.

Avery jiggled his hands in his pockets. The bulge seemed to have shrunk. "Email it to me. I can't approve anything without looking it over first. You understand."

"It's the 11-17. I only widened the columns so they could fit another decimal point. Mercer wants it this morning, but I suppose I could have you send it to him after the meeting. Would you put a note in explaining why it's late?"

Avery scissored his legs back and forth. "Fine. Hurry up! I can't be late."

"You still have fifteen minutes." Sarah turned toward her computer, slowly clicking at the mouse and scratching the back of her hand with the other. *Itch. Itch. Itch.* Avery didn't need to know she had admin privileges herself. Her boss had said he couldn't be bothered waiting for Sarah to get Finance's approval all the time, but didn't dare give those privileges to all the clerks, as the majority of them spent the day on Facebook and he was afraid what they'd do with it.

Avery rocked from side to side. Sarah sensed rather than saw him try to dig deeper into his pockets to scratch. As Excel finished loading, Avery moved behind her chair and tried to surreptitiously scratch his dick across the back of it. *Really?* Pausing in her clicking, she glanced back at him. He stopped, bent down and frowned at the screen, feigning interest.

Although Sarah spent most of her time on the wagon, when she did cast, it wasn't dabbling small stuff. The Archer women could trace their lineage back centuries and Sarah had no doubt not one of them had ever cast an itching spell that could be relieved by scratching. Scratching would have the opposite effect.

"Oh, hey!" Avery straightened, his entire body twitching, and waved down the hall, responding to an imaginary summons. "Now? Right now? Sure. Be right there!" He backed out of the cubicle. "Sorry, Sarah. Looks like they want me right now!" He turned and ran. Sarah could see his shoulder moving as he clawed at himself.

"Good luck with that," she whispered under her breath.

Bitch, really? Grabbing a pen she clicked it open and shut repeatedly. *Uncalled for. This is his little life. It's like Aunt Lily and her looks. Some people have to feel they're the best or they can't function.*

In the end Aunt Lily's casting with the goal of physical perfection had killed her. Constant casting had a cost, and as her soul blackened her looks reflected an ugliness that no amount of surface polishing could hide. Sarah tried not to remember how Aunt Lily had looked at the end. Wart-covered Kitchen Witches in gift shops were nothing in comparison to what a beautiful face became when it tried to contain that much evil.

Caught up in sad thoughts, Sarah didn't brace for the aftershock of the itching spell. It caught her full in the face and knocked her flat on her back with the chair beneath her.

"What was that?" Mindy Millerton peered over the cube wall. "Sarah!" She darted inside. "Are you okay? What happened?"

The roof of Sarah's mouth itched so severely she sneezed several times in succession.

Mindy laughed. "Did you sneeze yourself over? Sarah! Hey, are those underwear Versace? Those are silk, aren't they? How on earth do you afford all the nice things you wear on our salaries?"

I loot my dead aunt's closet. Sarah rolled out of the chair, briefly displaying the thong side of them. She shook her head, trying to reorient herself. The incessant itching in her mouth was tough to ignore. "H-hand-me-downs," she managed to say. Sitting back on her feet, Sarah untwisted the lavender and gold print dress to hide her underpants and tucked the embroidered strap of lilac bra into place.

Mindy watched with jealousy in her eyes. "From who? The royal family?"

Sarah got to her feet and righted the chair, trying to resist scratching her tongue against the roof of her mouth. It would only make it worse.

"Is your family rich?" asked Mindy.

"I'm not," said Sarah, and it was only partly true. She'd inherited the Archer fortune. None of them had worked, because witches didn't have to. Sarah worked, not touching a penny of their money, not touching even the tempting interest that would easily exceed the salary of any Mass Power and Light executive.

"Did they disown you or something?" A gossipy gleam lit Mindy's eyes. Sarah could already hear the rumors she'd ignite.

"No." Sarah dropped into her seat. "They died." She grabbed the mouse and scooted it over the pad with an image of the Wayside Inn on it.

"Oh," said Mindy, looking uncomfortable. She gazed around Sarah's cubicle. "Oh, hey, did you bring donuts?"

"Yeah. I think there's some left."

"Why do you bring donuts? You suck!" Mindy rushed out of the office, likely to score one before the influx of coworkers decimated them.

ON THE WAY home Sarah stopped by a gift shop in Sudbury to pick up more stationery for her obscene collection. Since it didn't involve dark matter, she couldn't resist a small cast that made other shoppers hurry out of the shop. *A witch needs her space.* If she had to stand in line too long listening to people complain, it would be a lot worse.

Another stop at a local café netted dinner. It took a full fifteen minutes of debate before Sarah made a deal with her fat cells and ordered a low-fat green smoothie and a ciabatta sandwich with sun-dried tomato and raw mozzarella, minus the trademark fresh basil. The idea of fresh basil made her mouth water. She'd been alone for three years now, but it still grew thick in the gardens at home, somehow self-perpetuating despite being an annual plant. Herbs were as bad as baking. It made her want to dance naked under the moonlight and listen to the secrets of the universe.

"Anything else?" asked the cashier.

Careful to avoid eye contact, Sarah shook her head. With the fading delight of two big casts exiting her body, the temptation to cast again slid up and down her torso like strong, tattooed hands might. "Wait. Yes. I'll have a shortbread cookie." Cookies felt good, and they had the added bonus of not escorting her soul to the dark side.

"Dipped in chocolate?"

Well, duh. "Sure. Make it two."

Parking the Jeep along the street in front of the house, Sarah ignored the overstuffed mailbox that no longer closed from all the unopened mail crammed inside. Several plastic-bagged newspapers lay in the street. The grass needed to be mowed. The two-hundred-and-fifty-year-old house sat in the middle of a five acre corner lot on North Street, two stories high with an attic big enough to stand up in. The ivy-covered porch sprawled the length of the house, so deep no light came through the south-facing windows shaded by it. Wicker tables and chairs had once decorated it, but Sarah had gotten rid of them. Not even a rocking chair remained to tempt her into a trance. She'd left the ivy growing over the structure, intertwined with sapphire blue morning glory that bloomed from dawn to dusk in summer.

The antique lead glass in the double doors had changed; once a floral design, it had taken on a spidery look after everyone died. If the forces of evil were into metaphors, and Sarah figured they were, this said: *We've claimed the blooms in our web and await the next blossom.*

"Oh, fuck you," said Sarah, shoving the unlocked front door open and locking it behind her. Inside the thick walls and heavy glass windows, silence prevailed. Home sweet home. No matter that she should sell the monstrosity and get one of those steel and granite condos she lusted after. No matter that this place held horrific memories that no one should have. Like Sarah's oddly dexterous fingers, chubby arms, and dark Archer hair, it was part of her.

There were rooms in the old house Sarah didn't go into. Her mother's room. Her grandmother's room. The basement. The attic. The greenhouse out back. The garden. There were parts of her existence she denied: the dark side, what happened to all the women in her family, and the fact that there were no men. But Sarah knew cutting herself from the fabric she'd been born into wouldn't work. She had to change it. She had to weave a new pattern into it.

That meant a trip to the attic, before the fiasco in the Target parking lot caught up with her. "Tomorrow," she said aloud. "Or Wednesday. This week for sure."

Kicking off Aunt Lily's bright purple Italian leather pumps, Sarah traipsed toward the kitchen. She tossed the bag from the stationery store on the floor next to a bureau littered with other bags. Entering the kitchen, she slid onto a high stool at the marble topped island. Lifting the lid on the old laptop that always sat there, she resumed play on *You've Got Mail.* She ate her sandwich while Tom Hanks did perfectly normal things with Meg Ryan, like put her out of business and realize love didn't come along for everyone if they were stupid.

Sarah imagined her father had been perfectly normal. Despite her Archer witch genes, his were clean. Her mother had claimed he'd been an Olympian, having always attended the games with Aunt Lily. They liked sex with athletes, especially once they'd decided to have daughters. Sarah glanced down at her full breasts, well covered beneath the print dress, her soft arms fully exposed, and her short legs dangling from the high stool. *Yeah, right. He must have been a jockey.* When she'd been stupid enough to ask more about the *donor*, as her mother and Lily had referred to the men who'd unwittingly given them babies, her mother had shrugged and said she never bothered to find out which one did the job right. "What difference does it make, Daughter?"

Giving in to the lure of Cherry Coke over the healthy smoothie, Sarah went to the refrigerator and grabbed the last one. Maybe Amazon delivered soft drinks. She wasn't going back to Target anytime soon. *I wonder if he's at Target today. He should be drawn to find me.* The sudden urge to go there hit her like an unexpected wave of salt water in the desert.

Sarah coughed, tasting salt instead of Coke. "Dammit! I'm not going! Do you hear me?" she shouted at the empty room. "I don't care! I will not! I don't care how tempting he is. I'm holding out for the real thing, so fuck off!"

Turning her attention once again to the stupid movie, Sarah crammed the second chocolatey shortbread into her mouth and ignored the temptation touching her like a well-muscled man beneath a full moon.

chapter three

Oh, Hail No

If Sarah were a regular person she'd never go to church. For starters, getting up early on Sunday morning was for the birds, and for another thing, she hated it. She shoved open the back door of Our Lady of the Light church ten minutes after Mass started and stood there, feet crammed into heels, sans pantyhose, wearing a short summer dress and makeup *on the weekend.*

She hesitated next to a bowl of holy water. She hadn't worked up the courage to go into the attic all week. It was time to man up and embrace penance for the spell cast last weekend. She thrust four fingers into the water, up to the second knuckle.

Searing pain lit through her hand as though the water were boiling. Sarah yanked her fingers out and stuffed them into her mouth. Fingers throbbing with pain she crept into the back of the church to choose a seat.

The last row had already been claimed by loners looking for redemption themselves. Second to last row proved practically as good a place to show the light she was trying to be part of it, but still hide from the priests. This was the place where she usually sat, or stood, or knelt, depending on the parishioners' actions and her mood for mimicry. Sarah didn't understand Mass or Catholicism, but nobody bothered her at this church.

And she'd been to them all.

Evangelicals scared her. They had that look in their eyes. It kind of said *maybe we're crazy, or maybe we know the light intimately. Figure it out.* People at the Baptist church were too damn friendly, in that *are you friends with Jay-sus* way. Too many of them were anxious to die and hang with him. Methodists wanted her to stay for pancakes after, join a committee, or go on a mission's trip. Presbyterians wondered where she lived and who her people were; answers they didn't really want any more than she'd dare give. The Lutherans had been very welcoming, so much so that Sarah had initiated hot nasty sex with the minister while the rest of the congregation focused on an Easter egg hunt. It had been the highlight of her church-going career, but common sense told her not to return. Besides, that minister had enjoyed it way more than she did.

Sex was only fun before she had it. It was more the *idea* of it that was fun, and Sarah worried that's the way it would always be. It was a witch problem. Aunt Lily had always said to *try try again.* Her mother had said casting was far better than men anyway.

Sex wasn't an issue at Our Lady of the Light. These priests didn't do the hot nasty, and from the looks of the people, neither did they. They didn't even talk to each other.

It was perfect.

An entire hour free from the temptation of dark matter.

Even if it was deadly boring.

During the lone moment in the service when everyone shook hands with their neighbors, Sarah stuffed her hands under her armpits and stared at the stained glass windows. Nobody seemed to mind. Most weeks she dodged out when everyone went to communion—something she'd never dared participate in. Not that Sarah respected tradition. She didn't worry that coming from a long line of witches who practiced ritual sacrifice, where souls were offered to the dark side, might make her unwelcome here. Sarah just didn't like suffering and figured the little wafer would torch its way through her body like a tablespoon of drain cleaner.

After doing the sit-stand-kneel-half-burpee routine for a half hour, Sarah decided it was time to go for the big guns in the penance department. She had to atone for all the casting. When an usher backed his way next to her pew and gestured for the row to line up, she stood with the others.

Sarah's heart sank as she inched toward the altar and discovered a serious rite taking place. This really was big guns. The light emanating from these people pushed against the dark matter flowing through her. She didn't have the lady balls to repel it and continue forward. She looked around, anxious for an escape.

A priest stepped in front of her and offered a wafer. It glowed with a light far different than dark matter. Sarah didn't know what it offered to the congregation, but she knew what it offered her.

Penance.

She snatched it with her fingers and stuffed it into her mouth.

Fire.

Time seemed to slow, and the light in the church dimmed.

The priest paused and Sarah realized that the candles lighting the altar had all gone out. He shivered but turned his attention to the next person.

Sarah took three quick steps toward a young woman holding a wine goblet in one hand and running a cloth over the golden rim with the other. She nabbed the goblet out of the woman's hand and sucked down two swallows. Instead of relieving the fire, it scorched her mouth and throat worse and landed in her belly, white-hot. The woman wrested the cup back, glaring, and Sarah ran.

FOR HOURS SARAH lay face down on an old-fashioned, gilt-trimmed sofa. She wondered if kosher food or fasting during Ramadan would cause as much damage, and made a mental note never to find out.

She sensed rather than heard the tune of the ice cream truck three blocks away. Shoving to her feet she didn't bother with shoes, pausing only long enough to grab her credit card.

It took a moment of fumbling with the old lock on a back door to get out of the house. Sarah jogged across the wide back porch, down the steps, and then full-on ran across the grassy backyard. It took her short legs a few minutes to cross the property and cut through trees in the side yard. The grass stood high on this end of the property, and no one maintained the woods. There were no paths, not even deer trails.

No one crossed the Archer property unless forced, except the old guy who maintained the grounds, a casualty of one of her aunt's spells from a couple decades ago. Sarah assumed it had been a love cast, because the man had never once asked for payment in the years since everyone else had gone.

"Pop-Goes-the-Weasel" pinged from the truck's old speaker as it came crawling down High Street. Sarah jogged toward it, waving. She knew mascara ringed her eyes from crying, and that she'd been tossing on the couch long enough for her hair to nest around her head like a witch from a horror movie. The kid driving the truck stopped it in the middle of the street.

"Sup?" The thin, tattooed guy leaned out the window.

Sarah's mind automatically compared those arms to Cowboy's, and realized she'd been dreaming of him at night. In her dreams she knew all his tattoos, but she couldn't remember them, except to know the one on his hand looked like a horse's nose. In her dreams he rode a horse, but something was wrong with it. Shaking her head, she eyed the menu painted on the outside of the truck.

"A dozen Creamsicles and Fudgsicles."

"A dozen?" His eyes swept down her body.

There was no way regular food could pass her lips today. She didn't care what he thought, but his tone still irked her. "Yes, and do you have banana and root beer Popsicles?"

"Yeah."

"A dozen of those, too."

"That's twenty-four treats."

Sarah glowered at him, and the guy scurried to the back of his truck. By the time he'd returned to pile the haul on the small counter, a crowd of kids and a mom had gathered behind Sarah.

"Mom," said one of the little kids, "how come she's buying so many ice creams?"

Sarah handed over her credit card and glanced back at the kid. His mom's eyes widened. Grabbing her son by the shoulders, she turned away and hurried toward the sidewalk. The kid bellowed in protest.

Sarah couldn't place the woman. It might be someone from high school, or an old family from the neighborhood who knew enough. Sarah didn't socialize, nor did she terrorize, but her family certainly had and people had a long memory for some things.

"I don't have any sacks," the ice cream guy said, handing her credit card back to her.

Sarah tucked it inside her lemon-colored bra strap, ripped the wrapper off a banana Popsicle and crammed the treat into her mouth. The ice both soothed and stung the blisters. Holding onto the icy treat with only her teeth, she separated the floaty nylon fabric of her dress from the heavier material beneath. Holding the top layer out like an apron, she motioned with her head toward her makeshift receptacle.

Shaking his head, the guy shoved everything off the tiny metal countertop and into the fabric. Sarah jammed the second half of the Popsicle into her mouth, nodded her thanks and headed home, this time by the road.

Hot pavement warmed her feet, but icy cold soothed her mouth even as her sensitive teeth protested. She wondered if taking communion had mattered at all. Normally she could sense where she stood against dark matter. It had gravity and mass. The weight of evil pressed down on her or lightened, depending on what she'd been up to. Simply being a Shrewsbury Archer left a persistent pressure. Not casting for seven months had definitely lightened it. Going to church, synagogue, or a mosque lightened it too, so she knew that it mattered. But the love cast—the double spoken spell in the parking lot of Target had done something weird. The dick spell against Avery made it worse, although she'd lifted it as soon as she found him in the men's room down on the first floor.

Like it mattered. He'd spent at least a half hour holed up in a stall scratching his dick. You left a mark, bitch.

All of it left a strange vibration surrounding her and made it hard to sense gravity properly. Sarah knew what caused the confusing anomaly. It was the love spell awaiting completion, a double-edged blade, like a weapon with kick that could suck her right into the heart of dark matter and crush her. Breaking the damn spell demanded a trip into the attic, digging through trunks she'd locked up and thought never to look at again. Trunks she'd have burned, if they'd burn. Books she'd never wanted to see again, but hadn't dared lose, in case she needed them. Like now.

Fuck! Evil had an easy job. Evil was delicious and fun.

Better than sex with a Lutheran Minister.

For sure!

A witch could have whatever they wanted. *If they pay for it. Or kill a cat, or hurt your neighbor. Or make some guy scratch his dick raw.*

Absolutely *nothing* in life was free, and that included favors from the dark side.

Angrily Sarah yanked the paper off another banana Popsicle with her teeth and jammed it into her mouth.

Turning left onto North Street, she came to the sidewalk in front of her house. Gnawing her way through the second half of the Popsicle, Sarah almost tripped over the pile of newspapers that had been moved to the sidewalk in front of her Jeep. *I should cancel that thing.* She wouldn't though, because newspapers were a normal thing, unlike the pile of junk in the attic. Although she'd disposed of the worst of it and relegated dangerous artifacts to the basement, important stuff remained, like the book on love spells. All she had to do was find it.

Shit. That's gonna hurt.

Sarah walked halfway up the porch steps before she realized someone stood on the porch, hidden by a riot of blue Morning Glory cascading from the roof. Her mouth full of Popsicle, she found herself looking right into Cowboy's face. Somewhere in the back of her mind she swore she heard evil laughter.

SARAH YANKED THE treats out of her mouth and tried not to drool down the front of her dress. "You are not welcome here." She said it like she was banishing an evil entity and immediately backpedaled. "How did you know where I live?"

Cowboy held up a square of paper. "You gave me your registration, not your insurance card. It has your address on it."

Of course I did! The urge to touch him hit—the spell was stronger already. *Chill! Breathe. Think! You handed him the wrong paperwork because you didn't think!*

Sarah took a slow breath. "Give me a minute. I'll get you the insurance card. Would you mind opening the door for me?" She motioned with her head, holding onto her dress full of ice cream with as much dignity as possible.

Cowboy tugged at the old iron handles, first on one of the double doors and then the other. "It's locked."

"The key is under the mat." She ignored his expression, determined not to look directly into his face.

Jamming the skeleton key into the old-fashioned lock, he laughed. "You must not watch the news. If keeping the key under the mat isn't bad enough, I think I could pick this lock open with a pen."

Sarah rarely locked the doors when she wasn't home, only when she was inside and didn't want to be bothered. It occurred to her if she ever came home to an intruder she'd likely wrap him in a spell to revert his motor skills to that of a ten-month-old child. Or worse.

I've got to pay closer attention!

Big time penance took a long time. How many years could she devote to fixing her mistakes? Thirty approached quickly. The Archer women always said that was the year casting became truly delicious. That didn't leave much time to give up casting for good and stop making mistakes that needed fixing.

Like this one.

Cowboy tucked the key back under the mat and held the door open. Sarah swept through. "Wait here." She shot him a witchy glare, hoping to glue his boots to the front porch. *Because of course he wears cowboy boots.* She needed a moment, or a cold shower.

Because his jeans fit his thighs like that.

Because without his hat his bedhead needs to be on my pillow.

Because he wore an undyed linen button-up shirt with long sleeves that hugged every muscle, and he'd tucked it into his jeans.

Who does that? Sarah wanted to shove her hands down those jeans and yank it out, after exploring for a moment or two.

Wallowing in those delicious thoughts, Sarah rushed across the stone entryway cluttered with shoes, boots, and coats for all seasons, and moved down the dark hallway to the kitchen. Opening the door of the stainless steel freezer, she crammed all the ice cream inside, next to her chocolate and frozen pizza stash.

An arm brushed past her in slow motion. The tattoo on the back of the hand covered in dark hair was definitely a horse's nose. The skin of that hand brushed Sarah's as she tried to yank hers away.

The slightest touch.

Damning them both.

"Mind if I have a Popsicle? Banana's my favorite."

"I told you to stay on the porch!" Sarah shouted at him, unable to believe he hadn't obeyed, that he hadn't been afraid not to. Not only was he not afraid, he was acting friendly and familiar! "Who are you?" She crossed her arms and retreated several steps.

Cowboy withdrew his arm from the freezer without taking a Popsicle and ran his fingers through his hair. "My apologies, ma'am—I mean, Sarah." He offered his right hand. "My name is Paul Revere Longfellow."

Sarah fought the sudden urge to laugh out loud.

"I know," he said. "Why do you think I avoided telling you?" He dropped his hand, smiling with even teeth, a little pointy at the edges of the canines, like a lame vampire—if they really had fangs— or a kid who hadn't worn braces to have his eye teeth trained into place. It made him ridiculously adorable.

Sarah took a Popsicle out of the freezer and handed it to him without making physical contact. She slammed the door shut with her foot. "So your family is from Massachusetts I assume, Paul Revere?"

"Yes, Concord originally. But they went south before the War Between the States."

It took Sarah a beat or two to remember that was another name for the Civil War.

"Are you related to the poet Longfellow?" *The spell came with Longfellow's words. "Listen my children and you shall hear of the midnight ride of Paul Revere." Eff me. This isn't good.* It would make the spell stronger.

"According to family legend we are. I don't think we have the pedigree though."

Sarah glanced at the horse nose on Paul's hand. "But you obviously believe it."

"I want to believe it. I did the tat during my enlistment. It goes up my entire arm, and the tail ends up here." Paul pointed to the back of his neck with the edge of his Popsicle.

"Does it have a rider?"

He grinned. "Just me."

"Of course, Paul Revere. You know there are rumors that he didn't really make that ride."

"So everyone I've met in Massachusetts has mentioned, but the tat is about the poem, not the 18th of April 1775. I hear that's still a holiday here."

"Patriot's Day is the 19th. What's your father's name?"

"Henry W."

"Seriously? Tell me the W stands for Wadsworth, like the poet."

"Henry Wadsworth Longfellow he is. The fourth."

"Good lord. At least you escaped that."

"Thanks to my older brother. The fifth."

Shit, whether the link was blood or not there is definitely a tie to the poet. Reverence and obsession create powerful bonds! It adds depth to the spell. It adds layers of tentacles twisting through time and lives. Binding. Dark witches like the Archers were always women. It was simple genetics. But if Paul was even a dabbler, it would strengthen the spell and she'd never be able to break it on her own.

"Can I see your tats?" asked Sarah. "All of them?"

Paul's brows rose, wrinkling his forehead.

"Please? I'm curious about the horse," she said, putting the smallest amount of force into the request, turning it into a command strong enough for him to obey. She needed to know if he had other symbols on his body, something telling.

Paul chewed through the last bit of Popsicle and put the stick between his teeth while he unbuttoned his shirt. "I'll show you most of it, but it's going to cost you one insurance card."

It took Sarah a moment to focus on the horse. *The spell, dumbass! Here's a good idea, have the hot guy you're tied to with a love spell take his shirt off.* Paul appeared to have zero body fat and the thick hair covering his chest and torso, disappearing enticingly into his jeans, looked like the kind that Sarah wanted to bounce against on her bottom.

She swallowed and forced her eyes to the tattoo. She had to admit it was interesting. The horse raced down the length of his arm, with its rear legs and tail sweeping over his shoulder and neck. But the great bulk of tattoos came from the rest of the poem, which covered the front and back of his torso. The moon broke through clouds on his back, just above the old North Church. The famous lanterns, one if by land and two if by sea, covered his pecs. Sails from the British man-of-war, the Somerset, were visible on his abs. Most of the ship disappeared enticingly into his jeans, obviously sailing across his pelvis, buttocks and thighs.

"Nice."

"My mother said the same thing. But I don't think she meant it." He took the stick out of his mouth and Sarah pointed to the trash can, not daring to touch anything that had come into contact with his mouth. Paul opened and closed the cabinet door hiding the can. "I'd show you the whole thing, but it would cost you more than a Popsicle and an insurance card."

"Dinner and a movie?"

"More." The way he said it did something to Sarah, and it had nothing to do with sex. He looked into her eyes when he said it, and she had a sudden image of him tugging her onto a horse with one hand, the other holding reins and a lantern. *One if by land, two if by sea.*

Sarah moved immediately to the kitchen counter and dug out her wallet, removing the insurance card. Sliding it across the stone counter, she pointed at it. "There you go. Sorry I gave you the wrong thing. I'll need my registration back." It'd be better if he didn't have anything more of hers than he had to.

Paul pulled his shirt on and dug in his pants pocket, exchanging the registration for the insurance card. Sarah caught her reflection in the refrigerator. She'd forgotten about waking up with her hair sticking every which way. She'd forgotten she had cried on the couch the past four hours. She'd even forgotten about the blisters in her mouth. Raising her hand to her lips, she realized they were swollen and she looked like shit.

Be glad! It's bad enough he's here under the power of a spell. Do you want him completely tempted?

The truth was she didn't want any of the spell parts, but she definitely wanted Paul to be tempted of his own free will.

He was watching her curiously as he buttoned up his shirt in the suddenly awkward silence. "Are you all right, Sarah?"

"Not really."

"Is there anything I can do to help? I'm in town for a few days, until the car is fixed."

We could screw. In every single room in this house, including the ones I don't dare go into alone. For once maybe it could be better than casting. "You could leave now."

The brown eyes widened, and he glanced around as though looking for something. His eyes returned to examine her ring finger, her arms and finally her face. At last he said, "Sure thing. Goodnight, Sarah Elizabeth Archer."

Sarah felt his words knit them closer, binding her.

"Goodbye, Paul Revere Longfellow. Sorry about your car." She followed him to the front door and locked it behind him.

chapter four

Labor Slay

Some holidays Sarah still went to work. Since cutting herself off from the witch world, she no longer had family or friends. On Labor Day and the first perfect sunny Monday in September, she had other work to do. She ignored the open door into Aunt Lily's amazing closet and dressed instead in shorts and a long-sleeved t-shirt.

Something brushed against her face as she opened the door to the attic. "Fuck you," she told it, wiping powdery dust off her cheek, almost certain it was a wisp of the dark matter that hung inside the attic, awaiting usage by a witch.

Sarah flipped on the light switch and several bare bulbs lit. The space still seemed too dark. It looked and smelled like ancient trees, dead ones with tall trunks and skeletal branches, clustering together in dark forests and allowing no sunlight to reach the bare ground below. A place where dark matter liked to float.

Taking a deep breath of courage Sarah marched up the stairs, brushing aside dusty cobwebs. "That's normal," she said out loud. "No one has ever cleaned this mess." Two hundred and fifty years of junk cluttered the huge space, including trunks, armoires, bookcases, luggage plastered with old-fashioned travel stickers, and racks and racks of dingy looking old bottles.

Sarah knew exactly what she needed. Aunt Lily had two favorite spell books. One was full of spells to make one more physically attractive. Those spells lifted sagging skin, smoothed wrinkles, made noses smaller, and hundreds of other tweaks. Every morning Sarah tried on Aunt Lily's clothes with Sarah Archer's body, she thought about that book.

The other book Aunt Lily once kept close had a pink leather cover. It wasn't a book about casting love spells. Love spells were like following a diet or fixing your hair. Simple, but unless a witch had experience and the cooperation of the universe, things didn't always turn out as planned. The book Sarah needed contained the basics of undoing love spells. She hoped it wouldn't say *Good Luck with That* and *LOL* a hundred thousand times inside the covers.

Possibly in Aunt Lily's handwriting.

The problem was having to search through boxes and trunks until she found what she needed. The book hadn't been with Aunt Lily's things after she died. Aunt Lily had long ago given up on breaking love spells. She'd stopped caring who she hurt.

"I'll just walk around and look at everything, but not touch anything until I think it over," said Sarah out loud, hoping to dissipate the cobwebby feeling drifting across her heart. Immediately she ditched her own plan by opening the lid of a Tiffany-blue box labeled *Dior.* Inside, folds of pale blue silk shone like new in the light of the bare attic bulbs.

"And I'm right!" Sarah lifted out a sheath dress, pleased by the color. Pale blue repelled spells. It dangled from Sarah's fingertips in one perfectly smooth waterfall of fabric without a single wrinkle. She held it against her and sighed. *Too long.* Aunt Lily had been tall compared to Sarah's short dumpiness.

Unable to resist, Sarah yanked her t-shirt off and slipped the dress on. Oddly enough the outline of her shorts didn't show through. The dress hugged her in what looked like an hourglass shape, but longer and leaner than Sarah had ever looked. She wished for a mirror in the house. It was one item that couldn't be found from attic to basement—who knew what would show up in a mirror when a witch looked in. Sarah spun in a circle, smoothing the dress. She couldn't even feel her shorts beneath the fabric. Impressed by how fit her hips looked, she peered over her shoulder and tried to check out her butt.

"Oh! Dumb! It's got a spell. Shit!" Sarah yanked at the hem to take it off. Although it looked loose, the dress felt skin tight and her fingers had trouble finding the edge. "No! Crap!" Biting her lip, she found it felt fuller than usual. She quickly ran her fingertips over her face and hair. Even without a mirror she knew she looked great head to toe, completely unlike herself. She dropped her hands and looked down at perfectly manicured nails. "Aunt Lily, you cheater!"

Raising her arms over her head and leaning forward she managed to wriggle out of it. Sarah tossed the dress back into the box and peeked inside a matching box beneath it. A suit. For several seconds she imagined Paul in that suit and her in that dress, but shook her head at herself. "Nope. Nothing but the stupid book!"

She pulled her t-shirt back on and moved down a narrow aisle to gaze at bookcases. None were what she needed. Feeling brave, Sarah opened the door to a narrow apothecary cupboard only to discover bottles of wine, and battled the temptation to nab a couple of them. A cupboard with narrow drawers stood open, overflowing with buttons, thread, and what looked like some of the Royal Jewels. Sarah kept walking.

She stopped at a trunk with leather straps and polished silver buckles and peeked inside. Photographs. Shutting it, she sat on it a moment before kneeling in front and opening it again. There were old albums, but mostly random photographs in a deep pile. Most were of Archer women, but no one Sarah recognized. Some had been taken on a familiar Greek island long ago, and some were of people riding in glamorous old-fashioned open cars, or standing in groups smiling at the camera. Everyone looked perfect, well-groomed, wealthy, and desperate to hold onto it. Sarah could tell by looking at them that every one of them had spent most of their lives using dark matter. Dark witches were the ultimate narcissists, because perfection required a lot of time spent thinking about oneself.

Slamming the lid, Sarah stood and rubbed her knees. *How long did I look at those?* She wondered if the love spell was breaking her concentration or if her sudden ADD came from fear of what she'd find.

Sarah spun in a slow circle and eyed the room. They'd died three years ago. Aunt Lily hadn't worried about breaking a spell since Sarah had been about ten years old. The oldest stuff in the attic sat along the rafters. Things were carried up and discarded almost in rings, leaving a telltale timeline like the inside of a tree. The newest stuff Sarah had carted up herself only three years ago, and it sat nearest the stairwell in neatly stacked Rubbermaid containers, looking very out of place. Sarah moved closer to those stacks. The trunks near her things looked newer, less like old steamer trunks and more like Amish-made chests built to rest against the foot of a bed. A black one covered in painted red roses caught Sarah's eye. It matched the quilt still on Aunt Lily's bed.

For a brief moment Sarah stood in front of it and told herself not to be a pussy. She lifted the lid. Right on top sat the pink leather book. "Bee-am!"

Delighted, Sarah dug her fingers around its sides, catching a piece of sheer white silk beneath it. She lifted both up. The book wasn't heavy, but big and bulky like a coffee table book, with silver symbols embossed onto the cover, and what looked like a limp penis outlined on the spine. Sarah grinned as she untangled the filmy cloth from her hand and moved to drop it back into the trunk. For the briefest moment she glanced down.

A mirror lay in the bottom of the trunk, but Sarah didn't see her reflection looking back at her. She saw Aunt Lily and her mother, like the last time she had seen them. Once beautiful Lily ravaged by time and the dark side, as though she were an ancient corpse, with Mother beside her, her dark hair floating in water, her face bloated and blue.

"No," whispered Sarah.

The mirror zoomed in on their faces as though it were a camera lens looking for a better angle. Fear shivered along Sarah's spine. Both women opened their eyes at the same moment and looked directly into Sarah's. Her bowels almost liquefied. *No.* Frozen to the spot, Sarah could do nothing but stare back. Madness gleamed out of their eyes, like it had in small doses at times in life. *They see me.* Sarah clutched the book to her chest, willing herself to slam the lid of the trunk down or *move.* Terror stopped her from doing either. A black tongue slithered from between her mother's lips to wet them.

"Sarah." Her voice sounded like a croak. "We did it for you."

"Yes," said Aunt Lily in her raspy deep voice. "For you." She smiled a pirate's leer.

Sarah manned up and reached out a hand for the lid at the exact moment a mottled arm shot out of the mirror. It looked and felt absolutely real; an icy cold hand grabbed her wrist and jagged nails tore at her skin. Someone shrieked an impossibly loud and long sound of abject terror.

Sarah fought to tug her arm loose, trying to logic it out. *It's not real!*

Promises that it wasn't real repeated through her mind and her ears rang as the ungodly wailing echoed off the rafters. She tried to back away, but the hand held firm, digging nails deeper into her flesh and pulling her closer until her sneakers banged roughly against the trunk and she almost toppled inside.

Stubbornly clutching the spell book to her side, Sarah pressed her backside down in an attempt to sit, but the hand held on and the trunk tipped toward her as though it would fall onto its side and yank her inside that way too. Lights sparkled in front of her eyes. *I'm going to pass out!* Still the hellish banshee scream bellowed in her ears until they itched and her eardrums vibrated dangerously.

Shut the hell up!

Someone wrapped their arms around her waist and lifted her off her feet. Sarah nearly pissed herself. *This is real!* There was no denying the arms were warm and real. Dark spots appeared in her vision.

"Sarah! Sarah!" The arms swung her around and plopped her flat onto the floor of the attic. "Stop! Stop screaming! You're okay! Please stop screaming!"

Paul Revere Longfellow crouched beside her.

I'm not screaming! The sound continued to vibrate into Sarah's bones and she worried what he'd think when he realized the disembodied screaming came from nowhere. One of his hands pressed over her mouth and the screaming shut off.

Oh.

My bad.

"Breathe," he said, lifting his hand cautiously off her mouth. "Come on, you're going to pass out. Breathe in on one, hold it for two, three—DO IT, Sarah."

Sarah obeyed. Paul's face appeared to be covered in scintillating sparkles.

"Again. In. One, two, three, OUT! Pay attention."

Paul looked good in sparkles. *Listen my children and you shall hear of sparkly darkly Paul Revere.* A whispery chuckle took the last of her breath.

He patted her cheek roughly. "Do it!"

Sarah closed her eyes. Her head ached. Her throat ached. She still clutched the book to her chest as Paul wrapped both his arms around her, to hug her against his body. Definitely sealing the deal.

Everything went black.

SUNLIGHT FILTERED IN through an open window. Someone was mowing the grass. It smelled good. Sarah turned her head in that direction and saw heavy turquoise draperies. *My mother's room!* She sat up, still clutching the spell book in her arms. *Not good!*

Fear descended in a rush even as her eyes frantically searched the room. Since they'd gone, she'd occasionally worked up the nerve to come in here and hunt for a dark item that had gone missing.

A shivery breath escaped her when she didn't find it.

"You don't look much better," said a familiar voice. Paul sat on the edge of the bed beside her. He leaned forward and brushed hair off her face. "You should have sat up slowly." He used both thumbs to wipe the tears from under her eyes.

Tears. My tears are on his skin now.

Sarah let the book thump to the bed beside her. Dark objects were the least of her worries. *There's no point in worrying about the past now. None whatsoever. Not when the future is nothing but dark matter.* He'd surely carried her downstairs from the attic.

"Why are you in my house?"

"I made a copy of your insurance card and brought yours back. You said you wanted it. I could hear you screaming from down the street. I thought someone had broken in."

"Why do you keep coming around here?" She knew why, but wondered what he thought.

"I'm staying nearby until the car's ready. What happened, Sarah?" he asked.

Her mind raced for a truthful answer that would be acceptable. "I thought I saw something creepy inside a trunk. I guess I had a panic attack."

In the full on sunshine Paul's eyes were the softest brown. Trust-me eyes. Black lashes ringed them, so thick it looked like he wore eyeliner. Sexy eyes. Those eyes were studying her own rather intently. Sarah cleared her throat.

Paul frowned. "You should have a cup of tea with honey. Your throat must be raw after all that screaming."

"How did you get inside my house, Paul?" She always locked the doors when she was on the inside.

"The key under the front mat," he said. "You know, that's just not safe. I was certain you would have moved it since I saw it, but there it was." He rubbed his neck with his horse-tattooed left hand.

That neck was thick. Why did men have big necks? Why was it so hot? The horse's tail was visible on the back of Paul's neck, and his hair curled down over it a bit. He moved his hand from his neck to slide it beneath her hair, touching her neck and stroking the fine hair that grew there. A sudden urge to purr hit Sarah.

Stop it, dumbass! I'm as pathetic as the neighbor guy Aunt Lily cast on, and he used to pluck her chin hair!

"I've never heard anyone scream like that and I told you I'm an EMT. I've pulled burn victims out of car wrecks. You were terrified. Is someone threatening you?"

A little laugh escaped. *Yeah. You are. Dark matter too. The blood in my veins. The blood in yours.*

"That hah sounded like a yes. Is an ex bothering you? Did he do something in your attic to scare you?"

Sarah swung her short legs toward the edge of the bed and scooted in his direction. "No, nothing like that. Look, I'm okay."

Paul took her left hand and extended her arm to peer at it. There were so many bruises and gouges it looked as though she'd been pounded by a hammer with nails in it.

"You didn't do that to yourself. I know what abuse looks like. Sarah, you can tell me the truth. I know you don't know me, but sometimes it helps to tell a stranger."

Something in those words echoed in Sarah's head. *What if I did?* Sarah had seen plenty of men afflicted by love spells. Some ended up in jail. A couple killed themselves. One mowed the grass outside right now, unable to leave the house that Lily had once lived in, drawn to her even after her death. Did any of them know why they acted like they did? Would it have mattered?

What if she told him?

Today Paul wore a polo top, leaving a lot of the horse visible. Placing her fingers on the horse's head she patted it in a friendly way, as though attempting to ingratiate herself to a real horse before jumping on its back.

"Do you have an open mind, Paul?"

He considered this. "I'm almost always willing to hear both sides of a story, but I'm pretty firm about right and wrong." He glanced at her damaged arm. Sarah wondered what the EMT would think if that arm healed itself right in front of his eyes. She took a breath. Every family had secrets, but she doubted they held a candle to witch family secrets.

"Do you believe in fate?"

He licked those amazing lips of his. "I suppose I'd like to, but I fought in Afghanistan."

"And?"

"And it seems a first world luxury."

Sarah took her fingers off his tat and ran one across her lips, gazing into his eyes. "Do you understand physics?"

"To a community college level maybe."

"Mmm. Well, you mentioned right and wrong, could you sum that up as light and dark?"

"As long as it's still politically correct to do so."

"I'm a witch."

Paul's expression remained blank. "As in Wiccan or devil worship?"

"Oh, for pity's sake. Neither."

His gaze swept her face as though searching for signs of imbalance he'd previously missed, but he gamely asked, "Harry Potter?"

A whisper of a laugh escaped her. "Oddly enough, you're getting warmer if you're thinking Voldemort. I'm a dark witch by birth. It's passed down in blood, and we do tend to stick together. The reason I asked you about physics is because scientifically that's what witchcraft boils down to. It's easier to keep religion out of it, but it has to do with right and wrong or light and dark. Dark witches have a genetic predisposition to manipulate dark matter for our personal benefit. Are you familiar with dark matter or dark energy?"

"Are you going to tell me that dark matter did that to your arm in the attic? Because if you are, I'm going to suggest we head for the emergency room and an MRI."

Sarah sighed. *And this is one reason we don't tell. Nobody wants to hear it.* She rubbed her hand over the bruised and shredded skin of her arm. It didn't hurt because she chose not to let it. "Nobody hurt me, Paul. I saw something that brought back a very bad memory, so bad that dark matter flowed through me. Because I didn't manipulate it or cast it back out into the world, it hurt me like this." She could very well have pulled it deeper inside, into her heart. That's what her mother and Aunt Lily had done. The pond they'd ended their lives in had probably been to make it easier for her when the outside world looked for cause of death. *We did it for you.* Sarah shuddered.

"So dark matter has a hand and fingernails? Because I know a handprint when I see one."

"It can take any form." Sarah held her hands toward him, palms up, and opened a channel from her core to them. Two handfuls of red and orange fire took form as though her hands were the logs of a campfire. Against bare skin some of the flames leapt close to a foot into the air.

Paul shot off the bed, backpedaling straight to the floor and onto his backside. "Holy cow!"

Sarah pressed her hands together and extinguished the flames.

"That's dangerous! I don't know if you used chemicals or what, but that is downright stupid in this old house! You could burn the whole place down."

"Like this?" she asked. She held her palms outward for the briefest second, and half the room burst into flames around them. Flames licked the curtains and canopy above the bed, smoldered against the floral wallpaper, and then vanished. Not even the smell of smoke remained.

Paul had crab-walked backward a few more feet, and dropped to his backside on the floor, his long legs outstretched. Opening his mouth his lips formed the word "How," but no sound came out and he closed it again, staring at her.

"It's as easy for me as it is for you to make a fist, but it comes from here." Sarah pointed at the area of her heart. "It's a limited capability, like strength or energy is to you." She gestured toward the wooden wardrobe. "You know you can push that armoire over, but not a car. We have no real limitations like that thanks to dark matter. Dark matter itself is unlimited, and witches can access it for additional power, but, let's just say it's very expensive to use. There is always a cost for casting with dark matter."

"I don't know why, but I half believe you," he managed in a thick voice.

"It's true. The night I met you in the Target parking lot, that bomb was me."

Again his mouth opened and closed.

"I try not to do that. I had PMS."

A faint huff of laughter shot out of Paul's mouth.

"I guess it sounds kind of funny, but really it's not. When dark matter flows through a witch, it increases in volume. Causing dark matter to expand in the universe is a very bad thing, and there are consequences."

"Like with gravity or anti-matter?"

That must have been a really good community college. "Even more immediate problems. There's always a backlash for casting. That woman in the pickup was rude to me, so I did something to her. The cost for it came due. We call it an aftershock. I tried to pay it myself—that's why you found me flat on my back on the pavement—but I'm afraid it got you too."

Paul looked at his forearm as though he expected to find it black and blue and shredded like hers.

"I wish," she continued, "that what it did to you had been as simple as bruises. Dark matter is as intelligent as light, but it looks for weakness and takes advantage."

"Are you telling me this dark matter stuff is evil?"

"Yes, and it wants me."

He widened his eyes. "It doesn't already have you? You're not evil? Voldemort sure was."

The comment hurt. She blinked, hoping her eyes wouldn't water, and glanced away from his candid brown ones. "I'm trying not to be, but I am a dark witch."

"No," he said. "I'm sorry. That was rude."

She met his eyes. "Call it like it is, Paul. Don't be polite to evil. It gets a good foothold because people don't want to be rude."

"Sarah, this is the oddest conversation. You're not pulling my leg, are you?"

She bit her lip and considered how to respond. She settled with flicking two fingers at his black cowboy boots. A force slid Paul two feet closer to her. He shoved to stand immediately and backed up to the door.

"Believe me now?"

"Don't do that again."

"Okay," she said. "I won't." He appeared to be taking it well, although it seemed his logical brain kept trying to protect him and convince him it wasn't real. A lot of people did that, pretended what they saw wasn't real. It made them more comfortable. It made them feel safer. That's why there was so much dark matter.

Paul shoved his hands into the pockets of his jeans and kept a safe distance. "Why are you telling me this?"

"Because the dark side wants you too."

He glanced around the room. "What do you mean?"

"That night in Target my spell reverberated onto both of us. It tried to bind us together. You made it worse with your poem, tightening the noose. I tried to loosen it with that icon of yours." Sarah pointed at the pewter cross on his neck. "I left hoping distance would weaken it, but you keep coming back, Paul. And you touched me now. Several times."

Turning his hands palm up, he looked at them. "Are you saying I'm going to start making fires?" He moved his fingers as though attempting it.

"No, I didn't say you were a witch. Dark witches are always women and we're born to a bloodline, not made. I'm saying you and I are bound to each other as a payment to dark matter. Collateral, if you will."

Paul dropped his hands and tilted his head to the side, frowning. "Bound, like a love spell?"

"Bingo."

"Now I know you're playing." He glanced around the room as though looking for hidden cameras. "How'd you do that pulling thing? I know! My boots are steel toed! It's magnets, isn't it?"

Sarah rolled her eyes heavenward. "Yeah, Paul." She moved her hand as though lifting something and Paul rose two feet into the air, sliding up the wall. "It's magnets."

"Stop! Put me down!"

Sarah made sure he landed gently, but his brows drew together and he glared.

"You said you wouldn't do it again!" he protested.

"I'm sorry. But you won't believe me for more than two minutes."

"Maybe I don't want to believe you."

Sarah crossed her arms. "I only told you because I thought maybe it would help!"

"Help?"

"Yes, help you understand why you'll spend the next twenty years making excuses not to go home so you can stay here and stalk me. You won't be able to stop yourself."

"Oh, wow, really? You basically hit and ran on me, and I needed to make an insurance claim. The body shop wouldn't even file with your insurance because I didn't have the right paperwork."

"Why'd you come back today?"

"I was being nice returning your insurance card!"

"Yeah, right. Why were you being nice?"

"I don't know, Sarah. Maybe because I'm from Oklahoma."

"If you say so. But wait until you try to leave. You won't be able to. You won't be able to stop thinking about me. You'll want to do anything to spend time with me."

"Seriously?"

"You know it's true! If right this minute I asked you to pluck my chin hairs, you'd do it, wouldn't you?"

"You have chin hairs?"

"That's not the point. It was a gross example. My point was that you can't bear to leave! Thoughts of me will consume your entire life. Anything that was important to you before will disappear. You'll think only of me."

"Okay, well, watch this." Paul walked out the bedroom door and Sarah followed.

"I figured if you knew the truth, you'd understand what was happening to you, and maybe we'd be able to figure out what to do about it together."

Paul hurried down the wide staircase. "If you stay here, and I get the hell out of Dodge, I'd say we're off to a good start breaking this love spell of yours."

"But you're not listening, because it isn't my love spell." Sarah followed him to the front door. "It's from the dark side and you won't be able to resist."

"You do realize I think you're insane, right?"

"No, you don't."

Paul yanked the front door open. "Goodbye, Sarah. Watch me resist coming back, okay?"

"Just try calling instead of coming over next time the urge hits. Let's see if distance helps. My number is all 7's and 1's, you know, 7-1-7, 1-7—"

"It's been real." Paul galloped across the front porch and down the steps as Sarah shouted her number after him.

chapter five

Spelled Out

Sarah called off work on Tuesday, in case Paul came by. It was her first sick day in two years of working for Mass Power and Light. They sent her flowers. For the first time in her life she received flowers that she hadn't ordered herself. They came in a little yellow cup with a smiley face on it, all daisies and greenery. *The coffee sucks without you. MP&L Billing Dept.* For a brief moment Sarah was the happiest woman alive. She wondered if Paul was the kind of guy who'd send flowers, and checked her phone again for missed calls.

She hadn't slept last night, preoccupied with watching her phone. Twice she'd called 611 and asked them to call her to make sure nothing was wrong with it. By four in the morning, she had looked up hotels in the area and called them looking for Paul. She hated her stupidity for not asking which one he was staying at. Two of the hotels had hung up on her when she'd asked for Paul Revere Longfellow.

She'd taken a bath instead of a shower that morning, because standing in the shower with water running in her ears might make her miss his phone call. Wet hair dripped down her back because she couldn't risk the noise of a blow dryer. Sarah wandered aimlessly around her house, phone in one hand and flowers in the other.

Ugh! I have it so bad! She kissed the mug and slammed the arrangement onto an end table. Flipping open her laptop, she turned *Sleepless in Seattle* on with mute. Grabbing a copy of the novel *Outlander*, which she'd read approximately two hundred times, Sarah checked again she hadn't muted her phone and that her phone ringer was still on high. She tucked it under her bra strap, and tried to read with the movie in her peripheral vision. Thoughts of Paul kept flashing through her mind; their conversation, his expressions, his comments. He was the first person she'd ever told. There was something thrilling about it. The scenario replayed in Sarah's mind as it had over the past twenty-four hours and it occurred to her that:

> A) Paul was staying away.
> B) After the way she'd acted, he had to think she was either a needy lunatic or a needy lunatic witch, and really, what was the difference?
> C) If he could put her out of his mind, and she could put him out of her mind, wouldn't that in fact break the spell?

"I mean, duh!" she said to Tom Hanks on the screen. "I have to want to break it, right? I'm the one with the background to do it, and if he can put me out of his head I can put him out of mine! Right? Duh, duh, duh!" She thumped the laptop shut and marched upstairs to her mother's room. Darting inside, Sarah snatched the pink leather book, slammed the still open window shut and followed it with the bedroom door seconds later. Sitting on the top step she opened to the first page of Aunt Lily's old book and began to read.

Sometime after midnight Sarah shut it and leaned forward, resting her head on the book. Not one of the spells would stop a witch from wanting someone. If a witch wanted someone, she took them. The spells were all designed to make the other person go away. From wiping the witch's address from a mind, to causing another person to forget how to walk, it was all about making certain the love-struck person didn't bother the witch.

It made Sarah nauseous.

That's why that guy still mows the grass. Aunt Lily never even tried to set him free.

Sarah wondered if her aunt had made him tend the yard on purpose. She opened the book again and reread one of the pages. The longer a spell went unchecked, the stronger it became. There was no way dark matter would allow her to set the guy free now. *And I'm not half the witch Lily was.*

Sarah studied the bruises and gashes on her arm and ran her hand over it. They vanished. Standing, she went directly upstairs to the attic and faced the trunk, still ajar from her earlier visit. Grabbing the white cloth off the floor she dropped it over the mirror where her mother and Aunt Lily still looked out at her.

"You didn't do it for me," she told them, knowing that they couldn't hear her. They were long gone, part of dark matter now, but she needed to say it for herself. "You did it because you couldn't have everything you always wanted anymore and you didn't know how to cope with that life."

Sarah had decided the day that she'd stood on the shore of the mill pond and watched the police search for their bodies that she wouldn't end up like that. She was no longer so young and strong that casting came easy and without cost. Now she battled the temptation of dark matter every day. As a young witch with plenty of dark matter flowing through her, she'd rarely needed to pull dark matter from the universe around her, unless she was feeling particularly greedy. And even when she'd been greedy, Mother and Aunt Lily had so much power they'd taken care of most of her wants and needs before she recognized them. Aunt Lily had even taken care of the boy she'd cast the love spell on in high school.

Thinking of how that might have worked now made Sarah's stomach drop. *I was a stupid selfish brat. I still am, but I'm trying!*

Sarah tossed the book inside and slammed the lid of the trunk shut. "I miss you both."

She glanced around the attic. This was all that was left. A bunch of stuff. Her eyes fell on Aunt Lily's dress box and she bit her lip as an idea hit her. It wouldn't require a drop of casting, and if it worked, it would help break her draw to Paul. Sarah darted across the attic before her good sense could argue and grabbed the box. She raced toward the stairs, certain she could hear other items calling out to her: *Look at this! You're missing good stuff! Try me on! Did you see this box? You could have fun with this! You'd look great in this!*

At the top of the stairs she realized she had the suit box too and flung it away. She hit the stairs at a run, ignoring imaginary voices. "Oh, fuck you all!"

THE NEXT MORNING Sarah brought muffins instead of donuts to the office, and made vanilla hazelnut coffee. Purists bitched whenever she did, but she loved it. This week's flower arrangement had been delivered yesterday, and someone had put it on her desk for her. Yellow tea roses in a crystal vase sat next to last week's wilted arrangement. She set that one in her trash. The new roses had no scent and didn't compare to the gifted daises, even if they had come from an office fund. Someone had thought to send them. It cost her over three hundred dollars a month to send flowers to herself, and on her clerk salary that was a lot. Refusing to touch the Archer fortune wasn't easy, but since she drove an old vehicle and lived rent free, she managed.

"Oh. My. Wow!" Mindy stared at her over the cubicle wall. "That dress is *insane*."

Sarah smoothed the blue silk. According to the ladies room mirror it looked every bit as good as Sarah had assumed it would. The pale blue matched her eyes, and she'd crammed her feet into a pair of Aunt Lily's ridiculous designer stilettos. The temptation to cast on those shoes and make them comfortable was fierce, but Sarah had worn flats in from the parking lot and knew breaking the love spell was more important than comfort.

"Tell me that is a hand-me-down and I'll scratch your eyes out!" Mindy came through the cubicle entrance and put her hands on her hips. "I hate your guts."

"Thanks," said Sarah.

"I'd sell my soul to look like that," said Mindy.

Sarah's heart fell. Aunt Lily had.

"I was going to ask you out to lunch, but I'm not going anywhere with you looking like that. Go fuck yourself." Mindy marched back out of the cubicle.

Encouraged by this response, Sarah played social butterfly instead of spending the morning hibernating in her office and pouring over forms. She helped the two newest clerks with the archaic computer system and delivered folders to Document Control. She spent one hour in her boss's office filing his paperwork and genuinely listening as he talked to her about career path opportunities inside the company. From ten until noon Sarah attended a meeting in Personnel dubbed "New England Women Lighting the World." She managed not to fall asleep, resisted the temptation to cast on a fly terrorizing the conference room, and felt saintly not giving the speaker the taste of a real buzz word.

After the meeting Jackie Hamilton, a blonde drone from Personnel, squished six people into her old Mercedes sedan and drove to Papa John's for pizza. Sarah sat in the backseat wedged next to Avery Gross and his big package. For once she thought she held her own next to his annoying perfection. Every time he shifted his finely sculpted legs to make more room for his junk—which seemed to have healed up nicely because he was definitely back to waggling it at people—Sarah amused herself crossing and uncrossing her now magically long-looking legs. She could tell Avery noticed.

The dress had transformed her. Sarah's toenails, ragged from a summer spent in dire need of a pedicure, appeared polished blue. Chubby and ghost white limbs looked lean and tan. Unshaven legs didn't need pantyhose. A comfortable sigh slid through Sarah, the rare kind of an average woman enjoying a pretty day. Her contentment had required zero casting and none of the actual sacrifice of a worker drone, unlike mani-pedi-facial-spa-chick, woman-in-business Jackie. Now that Labor Day had passed, Jackie had apparently given up her carefree summer navy suit for brown and strapped on a tan Fitbit bracelet to match. The woman wore a size two, because thin was in for female executives and she had her career path and life by the gonads, goddammit.

Crammed in the hot backseat with her head against Avery's shoulder, Sarah tried to get a read of him, allowing the drone of voices and the background music of ABBA to lull her into a bit of a trance. If she was going to try Avery on for size, and possibly weaken the spell pulling her to Paul, it seemed like a good idea to find out some things, like if he had a wife at home. But the start and stop of Jackie's car traveling up Boston Post Road pushed her life into Sarah's head instead of Avery's.

Family of mill workers. *Lots to prove.*

Divorced, working mother. *Big surprise, Jackie has bigger balls than most men.*

One daughter who'd been taking her SATs since middle school. *Poor kid.*

Determined to override Jackie's boring facts about her wretched kid being primed for an Ivy League college—*any New England Ivy League college because Jackie would show them all*—Sarah turned her face against Avery's arm and sniffed him. Axe body wash. *Seriously, dude?* Plenty of aerosol deodorant. *Cares zip about the ozone.* Freshly ironed shirt. *Maybe he lives with his mother.*

Jackie parked almost half a mile from the restaurant, explaining she needed to get five thousand steps in by noon. Everyone in the car grumbled, and Sarah agonized in Aunt Lily's heels. She regretted not cramming the fly up the woman's perfectly powdered nose when she had the chance.

Seated at lunch across the table from Avery, she took revenge with every bite of her extra-cheese, stuffed-crust pepperoni pizza and large Cherry Coke. Jackie had to earn her dress size with a side salad and no dressing. *So, hah, and I went to Brown.*

While Avery blathered on about working out, Sarah pondered the different ways she could wear this same dress if she invested in suit jackets, sweaters, belts, and vests. On the car ride back Sarah realized she'd only thought about Paul thirty or forty times all morning, and maybe she should leave her office once or twice a month to hang with these people during lunch. They weren't as deep as Tom Hanks and Meg Ryan, and they weren't as hot as a bunch of 18th Century Outlander Scots, but they hadn't made her want to cast flames into their genitals—the fly hardly counted—and pizza definitely tasted better with conversation.

Avery walked ahead with Jackie, who had to park at the back of the lot because she could score another five hundred steps. Twice he glanced back at Sarah bringing up the rear in her stilettos. She managed to keep them on and hadn't cried once, although she had a feeling that tonight when she took them off and put her feet flat she might.

The second time he looked back Sarah knew their conversation was about her. It didn't take any pull from dark matter to know that, or to move in with her finely tuned witchy senses and eavesdrop on their conversation.

"You're kidding, she went to Brown University?" said Jackie.

So boring, but yeah, suck it.

"What kind of grades did she get?"

"Pretty decent I heard," Avery said.

Come on you loser! I aced everything, and I didn't cast to do it either! Funny thing about witches, when they did anything by hand they wanted accolades and a parade.

"Why is she still a clerk after two years? I've never seen her put in for a single new position, and everything internal comes over my desk."

"That's the question," said Avery. "Maybe she has no ambition."

You asshole! I like the job!

"If she graduated from Brown she has ambition."

Swoosh! Skinny bitch knows it.

"Does she always dress like that?" asked Jackie.

Sarah smoothed the sides of the sheath dress down. *She dresses awesome, but today is nothing but net.*

"We-ell!" Avery dragged the word out and ended with a cough as an exclamation point. "I'm not sure what's gotten into her today."

Total hotness. Sarah waved at the guards sitting inside their shack near the entrance to the building. She flashed her badge and swayed her hips. *Am I right, guys?* The female guards looked at each other and rolled their eyes. *Oh, fuck you both, bitches.*

Jackie never once looked back, clomping alongside Avery in her sensible loafers. "That's probably why she's still a clerk. It just shows a lack of class."

What?

"I bet it's expensive. Most of her clothes look pretty high-end."

You all are more obsessed with money than a coven of witches.

"Yeah, but that looks like it belongs to her wealthy little sister. I'm surprised she can sit down in it without blowing the seams out. I couldn't bear to look when she climbed in and out of the car."

Bitch!

"In her defense I've never seen her wear anything like that before."

"Maybe Mercer can get her into one of my Dress for Success classes. I'm embarrassed for her, but I could help her out."

Ugh! An angry noise shot out of Sarah's mouth and she surreptitiously pointed the tips of her fingers at Jackie's back. Avery held the door open for her, but of course Jackie couldn't have that. Her iron gonads might drop off if she let a man help her. The spell hit her as she reached to hold the door for him, forcing her unwilling body over the threshold into a face plant in the middle of reception. From outside the doors Sarah heard the squeaky sound Jackie's skin made as it slid across polished floor.

Sarah could have handled a rude remark, but not pity. Genuine embarrassment made her meaner than she might have been, especially since a niggling realization hit her. *It would have to be one freaking powerful spell to cast on everyone looking at the dress years later, but it wouldn't need to be near as strong if it was cast only on the wearer! This dress is casting on me!*

Sarah tromped past Jackie and Avery as he attempted to help the woman to stand, while still respecting her independence as a woman to help herself up. *Oh, it sucks to be a man in the 21st Century! Talk like a Cinderella Mouse, Avery!*

Sarah let that spell fly too. It had little strength, and wouldn't last, but she knew he'd said something in a high squeaky voice when everyone gathered around Jackie's prone form burst out laughing, including Jackie.

Whatever! The aftershock of both spells hit Sarah as she stomped up the stairs, and she tripped up the last one, hiccupping a high-pitched helium sound.

"Did you guys drink at lunch?" Mindy Millerton stood above her, brows raised.

Sarah hiccupped the sound again and said in a high-pitched voice, "Do I look like a fat pig in this dress? Tell me the truth!" The last word was punctuated with another hiccup, but Mindy didn't laugh. She stood clutching a large Pendaflex file, wearing a cheap, shapeless off-the-rack dress in probably a size sixteen. Considering Mindy stood barely over five feet tall, Sarah's remark couldn't have been directed at a worse person.

"Did someone say that? I keep a shank in my purse if you need it."

"Come on, Mindy! Why did you say it looked so good?"

"It does." Mindy gazed at her, complete sincerity in her expression. "I'd fuck you."

Sarah laughed the hiccupping mouse sound. "Liar. I think we could be friends though."

"Yeah? Maybe if you lost ten pounds and gave me all your hand-me-downs," said Mindy, "and stopped eating baby mice at lunch."

"Seriously girl-crushing on you right now," Sarah said as her normal voice returned.

Mindy waved bye with her middle finger. "You left your cell phone on your desk. It's been ringing for the last two hours. What nerd outside middle school uses Taylor Swift's Shake It Off as a ringtone?"

Paul! Sarah's mind shot to him like a compass returning north.

"I might have looked at it and noticed you have calls from the Shrewsbury Police Department. Second hand clothes, huh, shyster?" Mindy marched off, tossing over her shoulder, "If they give you the chair for stealing, will me your clothes? I'll pretend we were friends posthumously."

chapter six

Jail is not Prison

Sarah, thank you for getting me out!" Paul's voice faltered as he swept his eyes over her dress, but he wisely said nothing about it. The cops didn't seem to notice. Paul signed his release papers and Sarah ran her debit card to pay the fines, and they stepped out the front doorway of the station.

Sarah grabbed his arm and hauled him off to the side. "Now will you admit you feel the draw? Or do you have another reason for sleeping in the park by my house?"

Paul couldn't quite meet her gaze. "Actually, I had nowhere else to sleep."

"Why didn't you get a hotel room?"

He waited for several cops to pass them and go inside before replying in a low voice, "Not enough cash."

"What? You drive a BMW convertible! Why can't you afford a hotel?"

"The car is my father's. I was supposed to pick it up for him. I have no money because I left Afghanistan four months ago. Apparently nobody wants to hire an EMT who spent the past three months in a psychiatric hospital in Dallas."

Whoa.

Psychiatric hospital? And I showed him I was a witch!

"Why were you in a psychiatric hospital?"

"Are you going to judge? I mean as a woman claiming to be a witch, who thinks she's caught up in a love *spell,* I don't think you should be casting any stones."

"I'm not judging. It was because of the war, wasn't it?"

Paul didn't answer. He still wore the polo shirt and jeans he'd had on the last time she saw him, and dark circles ringed his eyes.

"How about I feed you? You don't have to talk if you don't want to."

"Nothing weird? I am ravenous."

"No. I promise."

On the way home Sarah swung by Chick-Fil-A and picked up too much food. They ate sitting on the sofa with the Weather Channel on mute. Paul devoured two sandwiches and two orders of waffle fries. He picked at Sarah's fries until she surrendered them, wondering when he had eaten last. He fell asleep on the couch without having said much more than, "Do you have any more ketchup?"

It was eleven o'clock in the evening before Sarah remembered to change out of the wretched dress. Ten minutes later she stood in the backyard in her favorite pajamas and lit the dress on fire. It took three bottles of charcoal lighter to get rid of it and left a two foot in diameter scorched circle in the grass. When she turned around, Paul stood on the back porch leaning against the railing, watching.

"Didn't like that one so much?" he asked.

"No."

"Yeah. Me neither. Thanks for dinner, Sarah, and for bailing me out."

"You're not leaving?"

"Yeah. I have a bus ticket to get back up to New Hampshire. I'm pretty sure I can change the date on it, and I'll wait for the car up there."

"You're welcome to stay with me, Paul. You'll get arrested sleeping in a park up there too." *Am I in-fucking-sane? I can't have him staying here!*

"I thought you were trying to limit our time together. I'm supposed to call instead of coming over, remember? Don't feel sorry for me, Sarah. My family has money oozing out the ears, oil and fracking kind of money. All I have to do is toe the line for my share. I'm just not a cooperative man."

It sounded familiar. The murky origins of the Archer fortune were far worse than oil and fracking, another one of the reasons Sarah wouldn't touch it. Sarah crossed her arms and studied Paul. At this particular moment the obsessive draw to him took the form of a need to make sure he was safe. The term *three months in a psychiatric hospital* had done a lot to twist the pull toward him into something close to maternal.

"Are you honestly not drawn to me?"

Paul crossed his arms and leaned against a pillar on the porch, gazing down at her. "You seem really nice."

Sarah laughed. "I'm not. You don't have to try not to hurt my feelings. Be candid. You're not dreaming about me? Or having obsessive thoughts about us? Desperate to—you know?"

"Do men ever do those first two, even when they are in love?"

The other witches in her family's coven used to refer to Aunt Lily's men as groupies or love slaves. Sarah nodded. "Yes, definitely. So not the first two, but the third? Despite these pajamas you find me attractive?"

"Ugly PJs don't hide the pretty." He pronounced it *purdy*. "But I'd say that about a lot of women. No offense."

"None taken. I just want to be clear about this. When it comes to hot nasty sex with me you could take it or leave it?"

Paul shifted uncomfortably. "Yankee women say exactly what they think, don't they?"

It was weird. Maybe she should tell him to go; it would make life easier on her. The fact that she could suddenly tell him to go was uncanny. The fact that Paul felt no pull was downright bizarre. Sarah knew the bindings of a love spell had wrapped them both that night in the parking lot. But if it hadn't bound him to her or her to him for very long, what had happened to change it?

"Stay. Please? I'd like to figure out what's going on. There's plenty of room." Sarah skipped up the steps and led the way through the back door. "There's an apartment right off the kitchen. I think it's nice."

Sarah had never been inside it. Housekeepers had lived in it, quiet unobtrusive women who rarely spoke. She had a moment of anxiety before she flipped the door open and hit the light switch, half wondering if she'd find a cinderblock cell. But the space was roomy and bright, with a wet bar and small refrigerator. A window even looked over the side yard.

Relieved, Sarah led the way across thick carpet as though she'd been there before. "It has a bathroom."

The bathroom startled her. It opened into the far side of the room. A mirror as wide as the double sink reflected Sarah and Paul as they approached. Apparently no one in her family had ever been in the room either, or it would have been destroyed. Sarah eyed it uneasily, but the only scary thing she saw was the mirror image of her wearing baggy pajamas.

Digging through drawers, Sarah found new toothbrushes, soap, and towels. The last woman had left immediately after news came of Aunt Lily and her mother's deaths, but apparently she'd cleaned her room first. Other than three years of dust and some rust in the toilet bowl, it wasn't bad.

"You sure?" Paul asked, already eyeing the toothbrushes.

"Positive," said Sarah. "There are just a couple house rules. Stay out of the attic and basement. I'd rather you didn't go into any of the bedrooms upstairs either, at least any of the rooms with the doors shut. Feel free to root through closets for anything you might need downstairs, but don't open any clay pots or glass jars that are sealed shut. Um. I don't cook, but I guess you can. Be careful not to use any cast iron or copper pots if you do. Oh, and they grow everywhere, but don't use the fresh herbs. Also, don't let anyone inside. In fact if anyone knocks at the door, don't answer it no matter what they say. And the guy who does the yard work, don't try to talk to him if you see him."

"Okay, that's more than a couple house rules. Is it all right if I run the vacuum and do some laundry?"

"Oh, hell, I might really fall in love with you if you do."

Paul lifted his brows.

"You know that's a joke, right? The laundry room and vacuums are down the hall to the right. I'm going to bed now. I have to be at work early. Call me if you have any problems during the day." Sarah walked out the apartment door, then turned around and stuck her head back in. "Goodnight, Paul."

IT TOOK A long time to fall asleep. Sarah had locked the bedroom door against Paul, just in case he had some sort of delayed love spell attack. *Like I'd have minded.* But in reality she might have minded.

The majority of the night passed with Sarah tossing and turning, worrying about Paul as though he were her child. *What happened to him in Afghanistan that left him in a psychiatric hospital for months? What is the story with his family? Does the guy sleep in parks often?* The dark circles under his eyes haunted Sarah's dreams when she did fall asleep; consuming her thoughts more than the love spell gone astray. Whatever the spell had done, it had surely been festering and growing this whole time. Yet her feelings for Paul were no longer anything like any love spell she'd ever seen.

Paul didn't come out of his apartment before she left for work. Sarah rooted through cupboards and found a lone box of Cream of Wheat that hadn't expired. She left it on the kitchen counter with a note that there was milk in the fridge. *Just in case he doesn't recognize milk when he looks in there.*

Sarah entered the breakroom at work at the same time as Mindy. Someone else had already made a pot of nasty coffee.

Mindy swept her dark eyes over Sarah's lavender blouse, black skirt, and sensible shoes. She glanced at the countertop in the breakroom. Sarah mentally cringed; she had forgotten donuts.

"I've never been so disappointed in you," said Mindy. "We're finished."

Sarah used her lunch break to run to Natick Mall and get the cookie store to frost Cinderella mice onto a large chocolate chip cookie cake. She rushed back to work, located Mindy's cubicle, and opened the box to display the treat.

Mindy raised her eyebrows. "I was joking about fucking you. I didn't mean to get your hopes up."

"I figured."

Mindy shut the lid on the box. "Sorry. I'm not sharing my rat cookie with you. No offense, but you're getting fat."

Sarah made a mental note to find something in Aunt Lily's closet that Mindy could wear.

FOR THE FIRST time ever Sarah's work day dragged. Despite the dozens of texts Sarah sent to Paul's phone, he only responded to one.

Sarah: *What do you want from Olive Garden for dinner?*
Paul: *I cooked.*

Did that mean he'd cooked for himself? For her? Since there were no groceries in the house Sarah considered stopping and getting herself something, then worried that he'd eaten Cream of Wheat all day. *Maybe I should get him something anyway. No. He said he'd cooked.* In the end she figured they could always make her frozen pizzas and went directly home.

It rained on the drive home, the kind of rain that blew down in sheets and nearly pushed her car off the highway. The kind of rain that swallowed umbrellas and turned them inside out, and followed Sarah to her doorway, spilling water down the back of her blouse, daring her to cast it away like all the Archer women had done for centuries. Sarah endured it and reached the front door feeling like a martyr, put upon and angry at the universe for making life so damn difficult.

The front door was locked and the key under the mat gone, which pissed her off. She had to dig through her purse and find her house key because kicking at the base of the door and swearing didn't make Paul open it. Did the moron have no clue how impatient a witch was? A variety of minor but amusing spells flitted into the back of Sarah's mind.

Make him speak in Pig-Latin for a day.

Or force him to walk everywhere like he's on a balance beam.

Maybe the talk like Bob Dylan thing. Aunt Lily loved to do that to guys. She was so good at it that Sarah used to think that Bob Dylan might have been her aunt's first victim.

Fortunately for Paul, once she got the door open the smell of homemade lasagna wiped away every trace of annoyance. Paul met her in the vestibule wearing a pair of blue gym shorts and a navy t-shirt, more of his ship tattoo visible on his thigh.

"I hope it's okay that I used dried herbs. You said no fresh." He took her dripping pocketbook and hung it on a hook. "Are you cold? Come into the kitchen and stand by the oven. I'm a thirty-bowl cook, as my momma says. I've been cooking for hours and it's hot as hades in there."

Sarah followed Paul through the clean vestibule, kicking off her damp shoes. All her bags of stationery had been unpacked and the supplies were stacked neatly on a bureau next to the coat rack. She could smell lemon oil and vinegar beneath the delicious layer of Italian cooking.

Steam seemed to cloud the kitchen, and dishes and pots crowded the sink. The first thing to draw Sarah's attention was the fresh breeze blowing through the room with the scent of basil on it.

"You opened the windows!"

"Don't tell me that's a rule too? This place needs fresh air. It took hours to clear the cobwebs and dust out of this room." Paul opened the convection oven and took out a loaf of bread.

"You made bread? You shouldn't make bread here!"

"Oh, come on! That's a rule? You said I could cook."

"Yeah. Not bake."

"I made chocolate lasagna too. It's in the fridge for dessert."

No, sir. Seriously. That has to be the most sexually attractive sentence in the history of mankind. It made Sarah's mouth water, but only for food.

"It's as good as it smells. One thing I can get right is dinner."

Sarah's gaze swept the kitchen countertops. Piles and piles of cash covered them. Paul had set crocks on some of the stacks to keep the cool breeze from blowing money around.

"Please tell me you didn't rob a bank."

He chuckled. "I know you had to bail me out of jail, but I'm not a criminal. I've been in jail a couple times, but definitely not prison."

"There's a difference?"

"Please! Yes. Jail is for mistakes, prison is for criminals. What's the story with all that cash? I found it everywhere. My room had it stuffed into practically every drawer. There's probably ten thousand dollars in euros I counted jammed in the cubbies of the coffee table in the living room. I found Canadian money too, and what's the old Greek currency? Drachmas? All sorts of Asian types. There's close to a hundred thousand in American. I hope you don't mind I spent some on groceries, but I paid for the taxi to bring me back from the store."

"I didn't realize that was here. You can use it for taxis or whatever you need. You can have it."

Paul frowned at her and turned the oven off. Using pot holders that looked new, he took lasagna out of the oven. The glass dish it sat in looked new too.

"You went to Target."

"Yeah, I have a credit card there. I couldn't find any pots and pans that weren't crockery. You didn't say not to use crockery, but I had a feeling maybe you meant to."

"Thank you, I did. Paul, you seem to have a sensitivity. Does your family dabble in the craft?"

He set the dish down and turned to look at her. "You've got to be joking. The Longfellows are staunch Methodists. You should hear them making excuses just to open a bottle of wine. If any of them even believed witches were real they'd think you're a bunch of Satan-worshipping lunatics."

It occurred to Sarah that Paul's sensitivity and intuition might have nothing to do with magic. Maybe he was simply a nice guy, like he'd said. Witchcraft would have been easier to deal with.

She helped carry food to the kitchen table, thankful he hadn't set the dining room. That room had too many memories for her to enter, but they'd rarely sat at the kitchen table. Paul had set it with new yellow and blue stripped placemats beneath old white plates that only looked vaguely familiar. Large glasses of iced tea floated slices of lemon and spearmint leaves. Her eyes went directly to his.

He scratched the back of his neck. "Is the spearmint too much? I know you said no herbs, but, Sarah, it seemed a crime not to make it right. It's not from your garden though. I bought it at the grocery store."

Unable to resist, Sarah took a sip and melted into her seat. Sweet, peach and Ceylon. The mint made it. She blinked back tears. It made her homesick for her family. Paul scooped lasagna onto her plate with a side of cucumber and tomatoes. It looked and felt new. It might have been the first big Italian meal ever cooked in the Archer house. None of it tasted of the dark side; it tasted like the other side. Good. Except it didn't burn her mouth.

There were things that needed to be said. "Is it okay to talk witch weird now? I don't want to stress you out."

Paul scooped lasagna onto his plate. "I have good days and bad. Today's a good day and to be honest I'm curious. Other than the house, you seem pretty normal."

"Thanks, but I'm not. For the record I've never known a witch who worshipped Satan, or anyone other than themselves. I told you before; it's more a matter of light and dark. We have an innate pipeline to dark matter. It's like Amazon Prime to the universe without a credit limit and not only can you have stuff, but you can have everything go your way too."

His dark eyes swept her face as he put the plate in front of her. "That sounds dangerous."

"And it feels good when you place an order. No, not good. Fucking great. I mean better than sex—not that that's much fun for witches anyway."

Paul lifted his brows but didn't comment.

"The thing is, once you start getting what you want you tend to want more and more. After a while you change and nothing is enough. Eventually dark matter uses you up."

He nodded.

"That's why I'm trying not to cast. It's so easy to slide to the darkness. I've watched people go there, and am trying to figure out how not to do it myself." Sarah took a bite of lasagna and closed her eyes to chew.

"What did you come up with?"

"Hmm." She swallowed and looked at him. "I'll have to get back to you on that. I do know that it's an all or nothing thing, and that I suck at self-deprivation. Did you really make chocolate lasagna?"

chapter seven

The Blue Guy

By Friday Paul and Sarah had a routine that involved an almost unrecognizable dust-free downstairs and no takeout for dinner. Friday night's dinner almost disappointed Sarah when Paul set a simple bowl of soup in front of her, but the Pasta Faggioli and homemade cheese bread made up for its looks at first bite.

"I like being here with you, Sarah," Paul said.

She put her spoon down.

"Don't get worked up. I still don't want you any more than the blonde who works in the bakery at the supermarket. Actually less. You know what? The more time I spend with you the more I like you, but the less I want to—you know."

"Thanks." Although she had to admit to herself she felt the same. "Do you mind if I cast in a small way? It won't do anything weird to you."

Paul chewed on his bottom lip, narrowing his eyes at her. "What about the dark matter deal?"

"Oh, nothing like that. I mean I can do plenty of stuff without pulling more dark matter in."

"Really? Like what?"

Sarah shrugged. "Like everything I did that day I showed you fire. Plus."

"What are you going to do?"

"Just a little thing to see if I can figure out what we are to each other."

"We're friends, Sarah. It isn't hard to understand."

Sarah turned her head to hide sudden tears.

"Haven't you ever had a friend?"

Taking a quick breath, she shook her head and blurted, "You know, not really I don't think. I mean I've loved people, don't get me wrong. My aunt and my mother. They died." She swallowed. "There's a lady at work—I think we're friends, or we will be someday. Do you have lots of friends?"

"No. Not anymore." *They died too* slipped unspoken from his mind to hers, and she thought he felt it go because he stopped looking into her eyes.

"Okay, lick your spoon. By lick I mean suck it and leave some spit on it," Sarah instructed.

"You know that's gross."

Nodding, Sarah shoved her soup spoon into her wide mouth and sucked on it. This would be erotic if she was to do it with any other guy. Paul sat catty-corner to her, his fit legs spread in torn jeans, and his horse tat sticking out of his tight grey t-shirt, yet all she could think was that he looked adorable with a big spoon jutting out of his mouth. Not hot guy adorable, but *Aw! Cute! How sweet! I'd like to pin this on Pinterest next to a Beagle or kitten picture.*

He yanked it out of his mouth the same time Sarah did, only his had a line of spittle attached.

"You're vulgar. That's perfect." Sarah knocked the back of their spoons together and allowed a small whisper of a question to race through the room, through the house, through the ceiling and attic and up into the September sky. When it seemed enough time had passed, she mentally tugged the question back. A faint silver light shimmered above the spoons, like starry dust motes joined together. Sarah stared at it for several moments, her heart thumping erratically in her chest. *Could it mean something else?*

"Do you see something I don't?" said Paul. "Because I only see dust."

"Yeah, a unity symbol. I don't get it. Everything still points to us being bound in love—except the part where we're not."

"Is that the whole deal? We're not going to suddenly take flight are we?"

"That's it."

Paul rolled his eyes. "After that big build up, I thought you were going to do something interesting, like you'd conjure up a rabbit or cat or something impressive."

"No. For starters I can't just conjure anything. I live in the same universe you do. If I could conjure anything at any time I wouldn't be into Las Vegas Magic. I'd get some gourmet brownies and inhale them every night before I went to bed. That's when I'm at my most impulsive," Sarah confessed. "I'd probably die of brownie poisoning by the time I'm thirty."

"You can't get *brownies*? Not even with dark matter?"

"Oh, hell. I could get all the brownies I wanted, but not without following the usual rules."

Paul grinned. "What are the usual brownie dark matter rules, Sarah?"

"Well. I could make someone go get me brownies, or make me brownies. I could allow dark matter to lead me to the best brownies on earth, and once I got there I could make everyone give them to me and crown me Queen of all the brownies if I so chose to do it."

"But then you'd die of brownie poisoning?"

"Not if I put some effort into it. I could—if I was really pulling from dark matter—make it so it didn't hurt me right away. I could even not get fat if I worked that angle. Think plastic surgery with your mind, and the dark side as the doctor. But, and here's the kicker, once I started, eventually I'd need those brownies. And conjuring them and eating them would be better than the best sex you could imagine. It would be great. I mean every single bite, even the smell, would be nirvana. I'd be the gorgeous brownie-eating queen of the world. Then one day I'd need more dark matter to hold my crown. Then the next hour, more. Then the next second, more. It would start to fall apart, but my desire wouldn't. All the dark matter I'd used would demand more of me. You have to *pay* the dark side, and eventually it takes everything and leaves you dying for a brownie fix and no way to get it." Sarah shoved down an inappropriate urge to cast on Paul so he'd make her some brownies right now.

"Sounds like drugs. What is dark matter's currency?"

"Us. Me. Oh, at first it would take cats, or puppies, or other people. It's just like in old stories. It eats life, essence, blood, energy. Sooner or later it comes for everything you've got though. A witch's ability to increase dark matter is finite, whereas dark matter is infinite. At least I think it is. In some ways my plan not to use it is both ludicrous and hopeless. "

"God. I'm never going to eat another brownie."

Sarah threw her napkin at him.

"Let me take you to the movies," Paul said with a smile. "Not Netflix. Let's go to the theater and see that new Marvel one. I have enough of my own money left to buy you a Cherry Coke too."

FOR THE FIRST time in her life Sarah sat inside a real movie theater, complete with stadium seating and large reclining chairs. Paul made good on his Cherry Coke promise, and bought himself a Dr Pepper. Sarah insisted on a large buttered popcorn to share, and felt guilty when he had to hand over his last twenty to cover it. She'd have to find a way to give him money. Just because she wouldn't spend Archer money didn't mean Paul couldn't.

He had seemed okay using the haul he had found his first day cleaning, but only for groceries and household purchases, which this week had included ordering new locks for all the doors. But when she had suggested he get some new jeans at True Religion, he'd acted scandalized and insulted.

Paul crossed one leg over a knee of his ancient holey jeans. "I love these movies," he said over a mouthful of popcorn. "Did you see the last one?"

Sarah had to admit she'd never seen any. During the previews anxiety crawled through her stomach and dark matter gathered in her peripheral vision like living dust motes, awaiting opportunity. Scenes of mindless violence flickered across the screen and in the dark Sarah could see dark matter swirling around the heads of people in the audience.

Once the movie started, Sarah relaxed into her cushioned seat. The violence seemed cartoonish and the characters made her laugh. Dark matter receded as though growing bored, drifting outside her line of vision. Several times Paul leaned close to whisper backstory into her ear, and Sarah poked him on occasion to hiss questions.

It didn't occur to her that they were bothering anyone because the theater erupted into comments and laughter and protests from time to time. The interactive feel of the audience made it more fun than sitting at home and watching a movie alone, and Sarah was glad they'd come. She poked Paul's leg during a fight scene and whispered, "Who's the blue guy?"

A teenager in front of them stood so fast she startled. He shouted at her, "Bitch, really?"

To her amazement, easy-going, polite, Oklahoman Paul Revere Longfellow nearly shot over the seat to get in the kid's face. "After the movie, little boy. Outside!"

The stupid kid with glazed eyes and flecks of dark matter roosting in the irises pounded his chest like an animal in the zoo and said, "Why wait, asshole?"

"Because I'm watching the movie, Opie," said Paul, settling back into his seat as people called for them to settle down.

"Yeah, that's right. You sit down with your dumb-ass *who's-the-blue-guy-dumb* bitch."

Paul shot out of his seat so fast clouds of dark matter parted and swirled. He grabbed the kid's long pale hair, hauled him half over the back of the seat and punched him squarely in the jaw. Sarah felt the blow land as dark matter flowed from the air around them, taking form in Paul.

"No!" She grabbed onto his elbow but he pulled free, landing another punch. "Paul." She allowed power to slide into her next word. "*Stop*." His fist froze in mid-swing, and he glared at her with an expression not his own. Sarah recognized the look of disappointed dark matter roosting there. She pushed him back into his seat.

"Yeah, you better stop, motherfucker!" the kid wheezed, regaining his footing.

"Hold your dick," Sarah said, keeping her voice low. He obeyed, grasping it with both hands. "Don't talk. Not a word. Hold your dick and your words." The dark matter flowed into Sarah now and only the audience stopped her from making the spell worse, forcing her to speak quietly and calmly. "Hold your dick and your words until you cry with regret."

The kid squeezed himself and mouthed something vulgar at her.

Sarah smiled at him, whispering, "So for a while then, jackhole."

"What's going on here?" Accompanied by unhappy audience members, two ushers shone flashlights into Paul and Sarah's faces. "Take your seats, everyone! The sooner you sit down, the faster you can get back to your movie."

Sarah waited until they had climbed over seats and past legs to where she stood glaring at the skinny dick holder. "They started it," she said with power in every word. "They should go to jail. Look what that kid is doing."

The kid yanked at himself as though trying to pull his hands away, but it only made his movements look obscene.

"What about him?" said an old man to Sarah's right, pointing at Paul. "He punched that kid."

The dick holder nodded.

"Paul's a vet," said Sarah, as though that explained or excused it. With a small cast it did. More ushers came and escorted the dick holder and his complaining friends away. Talking eventually died down and attention returned to the screen.

Paul glared at Sarah as she settled in for the rest of the movie. Neither of them touched their drinks or popcorn or whispered again. The theater took on the strained ambience Sarah would have expected from the first. Dark matter kept her from focusing on anything but Paul. It swirled around him as though it had found a new residence and only needed a way inside.

Braced for the aftershock, Sarah never expected the full force of her very own spell to rebound and slam against her. It blindsided her, shoving her further against the comfortable seat and knocking her soft drink to the floor. Unnatural heat warmed her thighs and she slid her hands up the length of them. Only sheer witch stubbornness kept her from embracing the spell and exploring between her legs. Paul watched her from his peripheral vision as she slid her hands up her body and brushed against her own breasts. She managed to jam both hands beneath her armpits and trap them there, fighting the spell as it bore against her in its entirety. Dark matter stabbed angrily through her breasts and crotch, protesting her lack of cooperation.

I will NOT play with my own tits!

Spells didn't often rebound. Fuming, Sarah tried to think why this one had. That kid sure as hell wasn't so full of light he could repel a spell so quickly. *Maybe someone of light prays for him—a lot!* Whatever the reason, she knew that wherever he was he no longer clutched his dick, since her fingers now longed to clutch a non-existent penis of her own. Swearing mentally, Sarah no longer noticed the movie.

Unable to keep her hands trapped beneath her arms, she wrestled in her seat until she managed to sit on them. Paul crossed his arms and turned away, his focus pointedly on the screen. His obvious anger made the tears in Sarah's eyes run down her cheeks and, just that fast, the spell broke. *Until you cry with regret.* Her own words set her free, but instead of relief Sarah wanted to stomp her feet and swear in frustration.

The movie ended at last and they followed the crowd out into the lobby. Without a word Paul went into the men's restroom and Sarah queued up for the ladies' restroom. She kept her hands beneath her armpits, prepared for the overdue aftershock, and waited impatiently. There was zero temptation to cast her way to the front of the line.

A familiar voice sounded from behind her. "Hey, lesbian girlfriend."

Everyone looked, and Sarah turned to grin at Mindy from work, her mood lightening.

"Hey."

"Was that your boy-toy I saw pounding on some twerp in the middle of my movie?"

"It was."

"That's good. We were all getting bored just watching our sixteen dollars a person movie that we paid for."

Several of the women in line shot unhappy and judgmental looks in Sarah's direction. "Sorry."

"Whatever. Can't believe you don't know who the blue guy is. I'm probably breaking up with you for that. If I'd been sitting in front of you, I'd have punched you myself."

Sarah grimaced. "See you Monday?"

"Not unless you're holding donuts and you edu-ma-cate yourself about who the blue guy is." Mindy got out of the unmoving line, lecturing as she made her way to the door, "Reabsorption. It's a thing, happens when the line is long enough. Makes blue eyes green, because yellow mixed with blue makes green. Did you know that? See what color mine are? Yeah? Not green, are they?" Mindy tried to make her way past the crowd of women clogging the entrance to the ladies room. "You might want to move so I can get out of here before something worse blows out."

PAUL DROVE HOME. Sarah didn't mind. She scooted low in the passenger seat and put her feet on the dashboard, pretending that his silence didn't hurt, but it did. The aftershock had finally hit and cut up the inside of her mouth. It bled a bit.

Miles before the house Paul steered the Jeep off the main roadway and parked it beside a still black pond with an old gristmill on the far bank. A bright moon hung silver and low over the trees. The last time Sarah had been here, the cops had been dragging the pond.

"We shouldn't stop here."

Paul took a sip of his giant Dr Pepper. "I want to know why it was okay for you to do what you did, but not me. Because I probably would have punched that punk a few times and he'd have shut his mouth. What you did—Sarah, people are going to think he has either a mental condition or that he's some sort of sex offender. You went too far."

"I didn't want you to get arrested." The truth of Paul's words hurt, but she kept her answer short.

"Why do I have the feeling you're not telling me the truth? At least not the whole truth?"

Sarah shrugged, staring through the Jeep's square window. There didn't seem to be any point in telling him that the spell hadn't affected the kid for long, nor in explaining a rebound. Not unless he'd noticed and asked why she'd watched the movie for a while with her hands beneath her jacket, tucked up inside her bra. After a moment of quiet she swallowed a bit of blood and said, "See that ring of light around the moon? It looks huge tonight, but the truth is the night sky is made up of dark matter with only that much light to hold it at bay until morning."

Paul leaned forward to squint over the steering wheel. "There's too much light pollution here to really see the night sky as it is. This is practically an optical illusion. There are so many stars in the Milky Way that in many places the sky glitters with light at night."

Sarah recalled nights spent with her family when they'd traveled to other places. She'd seen the skies Paul spoke of. But there was a saying witches liked to quote. *"Dark always wins because there's so much of it."*

"You can't think like that. It isn't your job to win the war, Sarah. It's only your job to win the battle."

"Are you quoting me soldier advice?"

"I'm quoting you logic. What's wrong with your mouth? You're talking funny." He leaned forward to gaze at her in the faint light of the dashboard. "Your lips are swollen."

"It's the price for casting."

Paul widened his eyes and hit the light on the ceiling, turning it on. "Open your mouth. I want to see."

Sarah obeyed, watching his expression. His dark brows pulled together and he growled, "God, Sarah. It looks like someone took razors to your mouth." He hit the light again to shut it off and put the car in gear. "Let's go wash that out with salt water. Does that always happen?"

"Mmphf. It varies."

"Does it last long?" Paul pulled the vehicle onto the main road.

"That varies too. Depends on how big I cast." *And what torment dark matter is in the mood for.* Sarah watched the woods flit past the window as the car sped down the road. She blinked back tears of pain. Choosing to ignore aftershock pain wasn't an option. Dark matter didn't make anything that easy.

ENTERING THE FRONT door while juggling the mail, newspapers, and his large soda, Paul tried to tug his key out of the new door lock and dropped his Dr Pepper. The edge of the giant cup hit the marble of the foyer as Sarah turned her eyes toward it and automatically corrected the mistake. Willing liquid and ice back into the cup and the lid onto the rim came second nature. The cup shot back through the air in an arc and came to rest in Sarah's hand. It wasn't until she turned her eyes in Paul's direction that she realized how shocking it might be for him. "I'm sorry. I'm so comfortable with you I didn't think."

"No," he managed, his eyes wide as he managed to dislodge his key and kick the door shut behind him. "That's actually incredibly cool. I guess you really are a witch."

Sarah laughed. "Are you just figuring that out?"

Paul led the way into the kitchen, flipping on light switches. He turned on the hot water tap and went to the cupboard, selected a small glass and grabbed the salt shaker. "Come here," he said, motioning to the sink. "I'm making salt water for your mouth." He tested the heat of the water on his wrist, filled the glass and unscrewed the top of the salt shaker.

Sarah cringed at the amount he poured into the water. "That's going to be disgusting."

"Wo-man up, witchy-woman," he said, swirling the water in the glass to mix it. He handed it to her. "Swish it around, and use all of it."

Scowling, Sarah took the glass. The first mouthful burned, likely more than it would for the average person. Salt had light properties and her mouth had so recently been full of dark matter. Eyes watering, she spit the first mouthful into the sink. Paul leaned against it, watching the blood-tinged water swirl down the drain as she took another mouthful. It surprised Sarah to sense that the sight of that little bit of blood upset him.

"I had a really bad time in Afghanistan."

Sarah didn't dare look at him. This was the first information he'd ever offered.

"After it was over I kept having a bad time. I'd dream about it, but sometimes in my dreams things went differently. Nobody died. We won the battle. I wanted it to be true. Some days I'd pretend that's how it had been. I'd pretend so hard that when doctors talked to me about it, I'd refuse to admit the truth. I got so good at pretending there was a time I couldn't tell what was real and what was what I wished."

Sarah spat more pink-tinged water and set the glass inside the sink. Paul continued to lean against the sink, both hands squeezing the edge of the granite counter. She put a hand over Paul's, her fingers covering the horse's nose.

"When that explosion hit that truck at Target I thought it was a bomb. You were on the ground and when I spoke to you, I don't know. I knew it wasn't a bomb then. You were so matter of fact and the things you said were almost funny. It took the edge off for me. Even after you left later I kept looking at the front of my dad's car, reassuring myself that you'd been real. I did have to come back and see you, because I wanted to make sure I hadn't imagined you.

"The first time I came here you were so off the wall with the Popsicles and all. I made a copy of your insurance card and came back again as an excuse to see you..."

Shit. Sarah still didn't dare look at him. It *was* the spell.

"That time I came I heard you screaming—I was shaking by the time I got upstairs. I don't know what I thought; you sounded terrified. But there you were standing over a box just *wailing*. I think I've done that myself, when I've heard a loud noise and flashed back. I knew I could help you. It felt good. It felt real. It reminded me of when I used to be capable, when I was an EMT. I was good at it. Once. But then you did all that weird stuff, and I had to get away. I thought maybe I needed to go back to the hospital. That my mind had completely snapped."

Sarah looked at him then. "I'm so sorry, Paul. So sorry."

"I didn't want to go back. I blocked everyone from calling my phone and thought maybe if I just took a break, you know— anyway, that's why I stayed in the park. I mean, I didn't lie to you. I didn't have enough money, but I could have called someone. It's just that ever since the hospital my family has been really protective. It was a big thing for them to agree to let me come pick up the stupid car. They gave me prepaid credit cards, so I couldn't get taken advantage of, they said. But I had to use all that to get the car repaired. Sometimes it feels like they're more worried about their money than me."

"Damn." Sarah almost hugged him. She moved to do it, but changed her mind and quickly backed off.

"Anyway the only reason I called you when I was in jail was yours was the only number I knew." Paul laughed, a whispery sound. "Since I'd deleted their numbers. And I like being here. It's peaceful. There's no pressure on me. I thought maybe we could do each other some good. The truth is I figured you were a little bit nuts too."

Sarah leaned against the sink beside him. "Yeah, well, I think you have that right, Paul."

He let go of the sink and dropped an arm across her shoulders. "Tonight at dinner when you did the spoon thing, I was worried. But then I saw nothing unusual. I mean some dust I guess, but I *knew* that was real. Then at the movie theater, that kid. Man, he made me mad. You know I see punks like that who are just looking for trouble while good men die. It's such a kick in the—you know some people give everything, and they don't expect anything in return, except maybe a little human decency." There were tears in his voice. "I'm glad you stopped me though. I might have really hurt him. I don't know. But when you did what you did to that kid, in front of all those witnesses—well, I knew then that I wasn't hallucinating that unless the entire theater was. Shoot. You blew my mind."

Sarah covered her face with her hands. *See how stupid it is to tell? Idiot!*

Paul moved in front of her and wrapped both arms around her, pulling her not into a romantic embrace, but a simple hug punctuated by a rough sob on his part. "Don't. It helped. The Coke spill clinched it for me. I *saw* that. I *saw* you reverse that spill like I might grab something I dropped out of the laundry basket. It looked as normal for you as it would be for me to nab a sock before it hit the floor. I'm not crazy."

"I'm sorry, Paul. It's kind of an unspoken rule not to tell regular people. I shouldn't have."

"No! Everyone needs help and a friend, Sarah. I'm not saying I'm okay. That kid at the theater, man. I need to get those feelings under control. You do too, though, you know? You shouldn't just make some dude grab his junk and hold it in public."

"I know."

"But the Coke thing was cool. Can you do it again? It's one of those things you can do without using dark matter, right?" Paul let go of Sarah, grabbed the glass of half-used salt water out of the sink and whipped it across the kitchen. It hit the fridge and shattered all over the floor.

After a moment of stunned silence she said, "You are so cleaning that."

"You're not very good," he said. "I thought you'd stop it or maybe you can put it back together or something."

"I didn't know you were going to do it!"

"So time travel is out?" Paul said, chuckling. "Or can you take us back a few seconds and nab that glass before it hits?"

"Yeah, right."

"Dang." He scratched his cheek. "For a second I thought it was cool to have a witch friend. Now, not so much. Kinda lame."

Sarah smiled at him. "Everyone's a critic!"

"Good night, Sarah." Paul gave her a half hug and kissed her cheek. Sarah closed her eyes, smiling even wider. It wasn't until they'd departed, Paul cleaning broken glass, and Sarah heading upstairs to her room, that she realized that kiss was sweet and needed, but Paul's lips didn't feel like anything more than her aunt's once had.

chapter eight

The Blind Side

Sarah slumped in the church pew, trying not to worry the sore spots inside her mouth with her tongue. The salt water had helped. This morning she had used it again and it hadn't burned as badly.

The congregation moved to kneel and Sarah scooted forward onto the cushioned kneeler. A guy in the pew in front of her kept half his butt on the seat. *Cheater.*

Since she'd scored the last row this week, Sarah scooted back a bit and copied him.

Yesterday Paul said he'd go to church with her, but when she stuck her head into his room this morning he'd answered everything with "Huh-uh." Except the hike. He gave a definite "Mmmm" when she asked if he'd want to go back to the gristmill in the daylight and hike around. *Maybe it's time to put that much behind me. It's not like I believe in ghosts.* The thought made her snort. The guy in front of her glanced back and Sarah looked around, pretending it hadn't been her.

Eyeing the sunshine lighting up the stained glass windows overhead, Sarah contemplated the love spell. The thought of Paul leaving—and he would leave once his dad's car was fixed—and going back to Oklahoma made her sad. It wasn't because she would be broken hearted and need to follow him, but because every day she looked forward to spending time with him.

Face it. He's my first real friend.

Maybe I could find him a job here! He said he couldn't get an EMT job after being in the psychiatric hospital, plus the sight of blood upsets him. But I bet I could—

That sounds exactly like obsessive casting to keep your boyfriend close, doesn't it, stupid?

She groaned. An old lady and the guy with his backside half on the pew in front of her turned to look. Sarah stared at the missal, pretending to read along with the priest's droning.

This is so boring!

Like witch ceremonies aren't?

Maybe that's why I'm so at home here...

Of course dark matter didn't congregate here. It dusted over several people, and a few handfuls waivered around one of the altar boys. Some lay on the floor around the confessionals, and a small cloud of it hovered over one of the shrines full of candles, but nothing like at a witch ceremony. The entire purpose of those was to draw dark matter closer to use. Aunt Lily had hosted them at vacation destinations. The witches who came would cast on themselves and each other and leave looking like they'd been to a discount plastic surgeon in a foreign country.

By the time the congregation started their slow progression toward the altar for communion, Sarah had had enough penance and snuck out the back with half a dozen other sinners. A quick swing past a couple drive-thru's netted breakfast, chai lattes, and sandwiches to take on the hike. Sarah got two of everything. If she was going to eat like a hog, so was Paul.

Twenty minutes later she pulled up in front of her house and parked her Jeep behind a Shrewsbury police car.

No!

She looked up and down the street, but nobody parked in front of Sarah's property unless they had broken down or were going there. She took her time getting out of the Jeep in her dress, tugging her purse over her shoulder, and gathering the food and drinks, allowing her mind time to race over what this might be about and should she or shouldn't she tell the truth about whatever they wanted. Sarah made it halfway up the sidewalk before she could see through the greenery growing over the porch. Two cops stood by the front door.

Dammit!

This would surely take a big cast to get out of.

And I just went to church!

Sarah couldn't get a good look at them until her feet were almost to the steps. What she saw made her almost trip.

It wasn't two cops. It was one cop with Paul.

Shit! What did he do? Both men turned away from the door and waited for her. The cop took a step closer, but Paul simply watched her, dressed to the nines in a suit.

Oh, he better NOT have gotten that out of the attic!

But she knew he had to have.

Placing only one foot on the bottom step she said, "What's going on?"

The cop said, "Ms. Archer? Do you know a Paul Longfellow?"

Sarah put another foot on the step and paused to look at Paul. *What the heck?*

"Yes," she said. "I know Paul."

"Thank, God," Paul whispered. "Do you know where he is?"

Sarah frowned at him and shot a glance at the cop. *Is he pretending to be someone else? Crap. What kind of trouble did he get into?*

"I'm not sure where he is," she said, holding Paul's gaze. *Help me out here. A clue would be nice.* "I just got home from church." It was worth going just to sound so damn innocent.

"When did you see him last?" the cop asked, eyeing the cardboard container with two chai lattes.

"Ah, we went to the movies last night. Is this about that?"

All innocently Paul said, "What happened last night?"

Sarah glared at him. *Really?*

"Ms. Archer, it's crucial that we locate Paul Longfellow. Did you see him this morning?"

Sarah didn't think she could manage another lie to that cop, but she sure wasn't selling Paul out no matter what kind of trouble or weird he was up to at the moment. Even if he had snuck into the attic and taken that suit after she specifically told him not to go up there. He looked as ridiculously hot in it as Sarah had *thought* she looked in the matching dress.

"How about you tell me what's going on?" she asked the cop.

"He's missing, that's what's going on," answered Paul. "I've been trying to find him for the past two weeks."

Good acting. She wouldn't sell Paul out, but when they got inside he was in trouble.

Sarah walked up the rest of the porch steps and spoke to the cop, allowing the ball of energy in her middle to slip out in her words, "As you can see, officer, everything is under control here. You can leave *now*."

The cop galloped down the stairs to the sidewalk and to his cruiser without another word.

"You are so irritating," said Sarah, shoving the drinks at Paul to hold.

"What?" he said. "I can't believe that he's leaving. Look at him! He's getting in his car!"

Sarah grabbed the front door knob and twisted. It was locked.

"Really?" She spun toward him to impart another glare and fished in her purse for the new key. "I can't wait to hear this story, but more importantly, I told you not to go in the attic. That suit has a spell on it."

Paul glanced down at it. "A spill? From what? Where?"

Sarah unlocked the door and held it open for him. "Be obtuse, and I seriously do not want you up there! Well, get in, what are you waiting for?" He scooted over the threshold and Sarah kicked her shoes off. "Okay, I told you not to open the damn door if someone came. Between that, the effing cop deal, and going in the attic after I said not to, don't whine about me doing this." She turned toward him, hands still full, and motioned with her chin.

Paul shot backward under her power, shoving the door shut with his body. He remained pressed against it, his feet dangling a couple inches off the ground. He swore and dropped the lattes.

Sarah reflexively caught them with her essence just as they hit the marble, repeating the simple spell from last night with another flick of her chin. The lids and liquid arced through the air into their containers and the plastic lids snapped firmly in place. The recycled cardboard carrier landed neatly on the bureau Paul had cleaned and organized last week. Plopping her bags and pocketbook beside them, she tugged a cup out of the carrier and took a sip of the still hot tea.

"This shit is so good," she said, eyeing Paul. He looked terrified. She waved a hand and he slid down to his feet. "I'm sorry. You just really pissed me off."

He lifted a trembling hand to his face and pressed it against his forehead.

"Oh, crap. I'm so sorry!" Sarah set her drink down and ran over to him, wrapped her arms around him and hugged. "It was a joke! I thought you were doing better!"

He wrapped his arms around her and held on, his freshly shaved cheek pressed against the top of her head. It was different than their other hugs. Suddenly she was very aware of his body beneath that suit and a freshly ground coffee, ironed shirt, expensive soap smell she'd never noticed before. Today he smelled completely different. He smelled right. In fact, he smelled perfect.

It reminded her of that night in the Target parking lot, only better. He tightened his arms and it felt right.

Sarah twisted her head to inhale another breath of him and saw his neck. Something in her stomach twisted. "Paul, where's your tattoo?"

"I'm not Paul," he said, his voice a low rumble against her body.

From behind Sarah, Paul's voice said, "Henry, what are you doing here? Sarah, why are you hugging my brother?"

SARAH MANAGED TO let go of Paul's brother. Everything in her wanted to hold onto that man, but she blindly grabbed the drinks and breakfast instead and marched perfunctorily into the kitchen without a word.

"Why are you here?" Paul asked behind her.

Henry cleared his throat and Sarah knew he was craning his neck, trying to see her. She could feel it as easily as she could feel the shape of the bagels in the bag clutched against her stomach. She set the items on the stone countertop, grabbed three plates out of a cabinet and yanked open a drawer for a knife.

"I'm here because we've been looking for you. Are you surprised, Paul? You didn't call anyone, but the insurance company did. They called Dad and said you'd been in an accident. We've been worried sick! Dad hired a private investigator to find you. I took a leave from work. Mom had to go on Xanax!"

Paul followed Sarah into the kitchen without replying. He had on his gym shorts and grey t-shirt, his hair mussed in his typical bedhead fashion. Henry followed, an almost exact replica of Paul, but with neatly combed hair, no tattoos, and a James Bond-style suit.

Sarah put half a bagel onto each plate and cut a pastry in half to share between her and Paul, giving Henry the whole one. For the first time in three years she moved to the espresso machine and set about making a cup of coffee.

"I'm not a child," said Paul.

"You're their child," said Henry. "And you prove you're responsible by acting like it. You could have called!"

Sarah poured cold water from the tap into a metal container.

"I'm fine," said Paul. "The accident was a parking lot fender bender. I wasn't even in the car. I've been waiting for the dealer to fix the damage. They're ridiculously slow."

"We didn't know that!"

Sarah ran her fingers over fresh roasted grounds. Some stuck to her skin. Their scent smelled like Henry. She blew gently to dislodge them into the filter. Around her, every atom in the universe swirled into a gentle dance of perfection.

"Now you know," said Paul. "Tell them I'll be back when the car is ready. That was the deal the whole time wasn't it? I'm handling picking up the car exactly like I said I would."

"You didn't say you were going to disappear for weeks."

Sarah added cold water, hit the button to begin brewing and tapped out a rhythm against the machine. She could feel it through her entire body. *One, two, three. One, two, three. One, two, three.* She wondered idly how the love spell had transferred from Paul to Henry.

"I said I wasn't going to call, and I'd text if I needed something. It wasn't necessary. Don't treat me like a child, Henry. For starters, you're only seven minutes older than me."

Twins. Of course.

One, two, three. One, two, three. One, two, three. The universe hummed a distant sound of approval. Sarah watched the liquid dispense, weaving her spell into every drop. *It's the only way I'm going to keep my wits, though if I have to be in a love spell, I've hit the jackpot.*

"You don't consider an accident as needing something? We knew you didn't have much money on you. It looks to me like you got lucky here. Are you going to introduce me to your benefactor?"

Sarah spun away from the machine with a cup of coffee in a small white stoneware cup. She put it into Henry's hand and closed his fingers around it. "Black, strong, the way you like it. I'm Sarah Elizabeth Archer, Paul's friend. I'm a witch." Guiding Henry's hand, she lifted the cup to his lips.

He took a sip willingly, his eyes locked on hers.

"Sarah, what the heck?" Paul hissed from somewhere, but Sarah only had eyes for Henry.

Henry swallowed a mouthful of coffee and something in Sarah's gut spun with pleasure. Her cast for facts about him could only work if she was completely honest too, so she told him the truth. "That's the first thing I've made in three years. I think I've been waiting for you. Sorry I shut the door with you. I thought you were Paul. He never mentioned a twin brother." With her thumb she swiped moisture off his bottom lip, then turned and hoisted herself to sit on the counter. Grabbing her latte, she refocused her gaze on Henry and took a sip.

Paul looked back and forth between the two of them, but Henry never took his eyes off Sarah.

"Oh, hell," said Paul. "The spell. It tied you to my brother somehow, didn't it?"

"So it would seem," said Sarah. Her new spell took hold and facts about Henry passed through her. *Fastidious. Determined. Intense. Enchanted with me.* She smiled.

"You touched him," said Paul. "Several times. You made him something to drink!"

"I did," said Sarah. "And eat." She held his plate up. "Well, technically someone else did but I brought it to him. I'm pretty sure it still counts." Using her witch senses she checked the atmosphere around her and her smile turned into a grin. It counted. The love spell had grown so powerful she couldn't fight it. She didn't want to. Somehow it had moved from Paul to Henry, and the only thing she could do was accept it with one caveat, by weaving a new spell. Fact. No matter what the love spell did now, her spell would keep her aware of the cold hard facts.

Henry took the plate from her and walked around the counter as he took a bite of the bagel. He set the plate down and took off his suit coat, draped it over one of the tall stools and sat down.

"So you're bound together?" said Paul.

"Deliciously," said Sarah.

"Why didn't you fight it? I thought you didn't want it?"

"It appears I was wrong about that." *Deliciously.*

chapter nine

Prickle in the Middle

The fact that Sarah was a witch who'd slammed Henry against the wall and bound him into a spell didn't seem to bother him much. They sat together on the sofa, on the same cushion. Still in the thin dress she'd worn to church, Sarah's soft thigh pressed against the side of Henry's hard one. If it felt as good to him, she understood why he'd been so quick to forgive the slam. He'd removed his shoes and tie and rested an arm around Sarah's shoulders, placing a sock covered foot over hers. He left it there as though claiming her. She could have purred with pleasure.

Their blood may as well have been magnetized to each other. Facts from her spell floated through Sarah's mind, but they consisted of things like the cleft in Henry's chin, the way his eyes crinkled at the corners when he smiled, his absolute devotion to his younger brother. All things that made him more attractive.

If that's possible.

"This is ridiculous," said Paul, still sounding disbelieving. "You two don't even know each other." He leaned an elbow against the fireplace mantle and watched them. "Sarah, you do realize this isn't my brother. I mean, of course it's my brother, but he's acting like an idiot."

Henry tugged Sarah closer without responding.

"Not that he doesn't act like an idiot on a regular basis, but he definitely doesn't act like this kind of an idiot."

Sarah's spell offered information with less bias than Paul. *Weighs 180 pounds. Allergic to Sulfa drugs. Has never had a cavity.*

Sarah rubbed her palm over the surface of Henry's. The motion produced heat from the friction of smooth skin to smooth skin. The heat entered Sarah's core, the area she cast from, so warmly that sparks shot from the sides of their hands. Henry seemed fascinated by it, chuckling every time it happened. His breath against her face reminded her of stepping inside a coffeehouse.

"Sarah!" Paul leaned forward and clapped his hands together. "Earth to Sarah! He's an oil executive!"

Sarah blinked at Henry. For a brief moment that bothered her, but she couldn't think why, because she lived in a world that needed oil. Henry watched her reaction with faint creases of worry on his forehead. "My car uses oil," she declared, and was rewarded with a delighted chuckle.

"They all do!" said Henry, and more sparks shot from between their hands.

"That was deep," said Paul. "You two are making me literally nauseous. Henry is also pro-fracking, Sarah. He's on one of my father's committees to get it approved in New York State."

"We need to be independent energy-wise, as a country I mean," said Henry.

Sarah nodded. He was right. That was a fact. She wished Paul would shut up. A swoon-worthy humming zinged through her bones and Paul's complaining knocked into it like a buzz saw, killing her vibe.

"He smokes!" said Paul.

"Just a pipe," said Henry. "Cherry tobacco."

"I *love* cherries," said Sarah. Aunt Lily had an old-fashioned smoking jacket in her closet, with price tags still on it. It had always seemed too formal to Sarah, but she had a feeling Henry would like that.

"I've been thinking about quitting."

"And," Paul raised his voice to an annoying level for his next pronouncement, "he is against gay marriage!"

"I was," Henry admitted. "But who cares? It passed."

"Yeah, it passed," parroted Sarah. "Besides, we're straight." She shot Paul a dirty look.

Preoccupied with pacing, he didn't notice. He stopped to glare at his brother, crossing his arms over his chest. "I'm telling her."

"Behave." Henry tried to shove him away with his foot, but Paul dodged it.

"Henry is engaged."

Sarah's hand froze on Henry's palm. Why hadn't the spell told her that fact? *Because you're too busy deifying his face to think.* Nobody who looked like Henry could be single.

"No," he said. "Well, I mean yes, but I haven't given her a ring or anything."

"That's only because you have to get Mom's ring resized, and gather a flash mob of hot-air-balloon music video dancers for your *impromptu* proposal."

Henry slid the ring finger of Sarah's left hand between his fingers. She felt it everywhere in her body. "That ring would fit your finger perfectly as is."

Sarah's face warmed with pleasure. *Fact and karma.* "Really?" Her voice came out with a little squeak in it.

"Oh. Are. You. Kidding. Me."

"Really," Henry replied, ignoring his brother. "It's in my suitcase in my car—which is at the police station. I'll have to go back there and get it."

33" waist. 34" inseam. 16" collar.

Sarah slid her legs into his lap. "Someday I might let you off this sofa, but first why don't you tell me about your drilling equipment?" She winked at him without any embarrassment.

"Huh-uh," said Paul. "This is not happening. Sarah, I'm going in the attic."

She ignored him, placing her palm over Henry's again.

"I'm not kidding. I'm going into your freaky-deaky attic and I'm going to figure out what to do about this."

She wished he'd just go already, and felt nothing but relief when he stomped out of the room in the direction of the staircase. Before she could completely relax again, and before the humming could build up in her bones again, Paul marched back and jammed his finger under her nose, looking from her eyes to Henry's.

"Do. Not. Have. Sex."

Sarah felt a flush bloom over her face and saw one on Henry's cheeks as Paul marched off again.

SARAH DIDN'T KNOW how much time passed. Henry lay beside her on the sofa, an arm under her neck. They continued to rub their feet and legs together, pressing palms and touching noses. Random facts kept fluttering through her mind, most of them about his physical attributes. *Six feet tall. Size twelve foot. Runs a mile in seven minutes.* Sarah undid three buttons on his shirt and asked, "No horse tattoos?" *No tattoos. Scar on left thigh. Has teeth whitened.*

"Hah, no. I think Paul was only making the best of his name with that."

"You need a necklace," she said, running a finger over the spot where one seemed to be missing.

"I gave mine to Paul. It's been in our family for ages. It's a first son thing, but I gave it to him when he got home from Afghanistan and was having...trouble."

"He told me. Not about your necklace, but about the hospital."

"He must trust you." Henry brushed his lips over Sarah's and a thrill shot through her. He pushed against the back of the sofa to roll her beneath the length of his long body. Sarah felt small beneath him, petite instead of squat. Somehow important areas lined up just right.

Average sized penis. Shaves legs. Battling nail fungus on one toe.

Her spell was incredibly annoying. Sarah stared into his eyes and tried to ignore it.

"You're lovely," he whispered. The intensity in his golden brown eyes made Sarah very aware that her dress had scooted up somewhere around her panties. She smiled. He felt good, each touch as delicious as a small cast.

A loud thump startled them both. Back from the attic with a stack of books, Paul proceeded to toss them onto the coffee table one by one.

"I *will* get the hose," he said.

Henry sat up, pulling Sarah into his arms. "Get used to us, little brother."

Paul focused on Sarah's eyes. "Your attic puts the creep in creepy."

"I know, right?" she said, but turned her eyes back to Henry's.

"She's definitely a witch, Henry. Just in case you missed it when she pinned you against the front door with your feet dangling in the air."

Henry frowned.

"I am sorry about that," said Sarah. *Dry heels. Regular manicures. Drinks expensive wine.*

"I've seen her pull fire out of thin air."

Henry's frown deepened. "Would you show me?"

"Sure thing," said Sarah. "Hold your palm over mine and don't panic. This kind won't burn." A small handful of flames leapt from her hand to Henry's, dancing between them.

He grinned. "Now that's something else. It tickles. How do you learn to do this stuff?"

"My aunt taught me this."

"But you never took any classes?"

Sarah laughed. "No. I'm a natural."

"You're not in show business are you?"

"No! Definitely not."

Paul came closer and slapped their hands together, putting the flame out. "It's not Criss Angel magic! They're Salem witch— *witches*, Henry."

"No, now, that mess was not the Archers," said Sarah. "I mean not entirely. The Puritans were ridiculous."

"They're the kind who sacrifice cats and sometimes people to the dark side," said Paul.

Henry's eyes widened.

"Not me!" said Sarah. "You know, nobody can help what family they're born into."

"That's true," said Henry, still looking uncertain.

Cracks his ankles. Sleeps five hours a night. Drinks protein shakes for breakfast.

"Last night she cast a spell at the movies so some teenage boy couldn't stop holding onto his dick."

"You did what?" Henry let go of Sarah's hand and frowned up at Paul. "Come on! You don't really believe that stuff is real, do you? Don't make me worry about you even more."

Sarah interrupted. "I *was* mean to the kid because I was afraid he was going to get Paul into trouble."

"You are so thoughtful," said Henry, smoothing her dark hair away from her face and draping his arm around her shoulders again. "You have the most beautiful eyes. They're so light, the palest blue I've ever seen. It's striking against your skin and dark hair."

"Thank you! I like yours too. Brown eyes with black lashes is deadly sexy."

"Nobody has ever said that to me before."

"It's very Hollywood." *Uses monogrammed handkerchiefs. Caught pink eye at the gym earlier this year. Keeps track of his illnesses in an Excel spreadsheet.*

"Just stop talking. I am so embarrassed for you both," said Paul. "So, Sarah. I found all these spell books. This is some cray-zay. Can you use these on normal people? Like there's this one," he dug through a thick black book, "that will make other people do what you say. I think it affects your voice. But I thought if you could do me a favor and put this on me, Sarah, maybe I could make you *get a clue* and quit drooling on my brother—who until a few hours ago was actually drooling in love with another woman!"

Sarah looked into Henry's eyes. *Does he really love someone else?* Why couldn't that fact come to her?

Paul leaned over to grasp her chin and force her to look at him. "Focus, witchy-woman. Can you put this spell on me?" He tossed the heavy tome into her lap, opening it to the page he wanted.

Sarah glanced at the spell. "It would require you to drink the blood of a singer."

"Well, what about this one?" said Paul, tossing a leather bound book on top of it and thumbing through pages of parchment. The writing looked old, like calligraphy. "This one helps you see things from a logical perspective. You and Henry could both use a glass of that."

"I'm logical," said Henry. "When you enlisted you told me you were doing what you'd always known you should do. Well, as soon as I saw Sarah I knew—something. That never happened with...

uh...." His voice trailed off as he seemed to search for the name of his girlfriend.

"Right," said Paul. "It's logical to fall in love with a woman you just laid eyes on, who you know zip about. She might as well be a different species than you are. She's. A. Witch. You had a problem with Kathleen because she's Catholic and Irish."

"I'm Catholic," said Sarah, frowning at him. *Agnostic. Goes to church on Christmas and Easter. Hates chicken.*

"You are?" said Henry.

She shrugged. "Well, not technically." *Jogs on a treadmill in his office. Loves sushi. Hates cats.*

"All right then."

Sarah leaned her head against his shoulder, perusing the handwritten logic spell. It helped distract her from the random facts about Henry. Oddly enough none of the details made him less appealing, not even the toenail fungus. *I'll just make him keep his socks on.* He appealed to her so strongly that if it weren't for Paul, she would drag Henry up to her bedroom right now.

Which would only increase the strength of the love spell.

The logical spell seemed like a good idea. It would require making a potion and breathing it. She was already so deep into dark matter; it would make little difference in the penance department. "I need a slice of sour dough bread, a cup of well water, a sheet of blank parchment paper, a shingle from the roof of a man with his priorities in place, a sprig from an evergreen tree, a piece of undyed linen, a splinter from stocks, an earthen bowl to mix it in, and an abacus. We have most of this stuff right here. Paul, didn't you make sour dough bread a couple days ago?"

"Yes, and there's some left over. Does it matter if it's stale?"

"I think that would make a better potion. The only problem is getting the shingle from the roof of a man with his priorities in place."

"You don't know anyone?" Henry winked at her.

Paul groaned. "What about from a priest's house?"

"A rectory? That's a matter of debate in my opinion," said Henry. "I'm not sure a man who gives up women fits the bill of having his priorities in place."

"I'm sure that it would work," Sarah said, and nodded to Paul. "I could make this."

chapter ten

Toil and Trouble

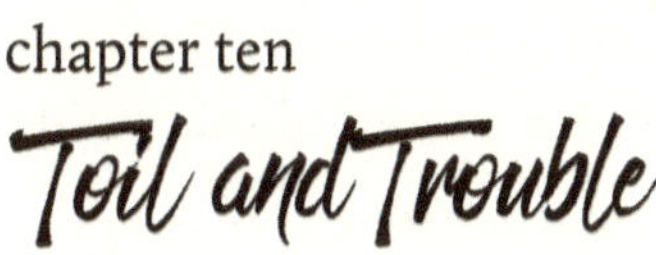enry flat out refused to get out of the Jeep to steal a shingle from the rectory of a church.

"Sorry, kitten. I'll get you all the shingles you want at The Home Depot, but I can't steal for you, especially not here. If we got caught I don't think I could do a credible job explaining why to my stockholders."

Cautious in real life. Ruthless in business. Protective of family.

Paul crawled over his brother from the backseat, a hammer in the rear pocket of his jeans. "You know I can't remember for sure, but I have a vague memory of him using that exact excuse when we were six and sneaking chewing tobacco out of Gramp's toolbox."

"Seems to me we both got a whomping just the same," said Henry.

"Well, you were the older more responsible one." Paul grinned. He gestured with the chisel in his hand toward the old man sitting on the front porch of the rectory. "You're up, Sarah. This part was your idea. Remember? You'll pay a little visit while I do the dirty work. Maybe you and Henry do have something in common. Anyway, get a move on. Operation Get-A-Clue commencing in three, two, one!" Laughing, Paul jogged across the lawn to the back of the old house.

Sarah's heart slammed against her ribcage as she marched up the sidewalk toward the priest. *Why do I listen to Paul? Why do I need another spell? If I have to be stuck in a love spell, Henry is the perfect man to be stuck there with. Really, where's the harm?*

Kathleen. The name echoed in her head. *And spells aren't real.* Sarah shoved the thought of Henry's old girlfriend out of her head. If Henry could do it, she sure could. As far as real went, Henry was the most attractive man she'd ever met. He'd dropped everything to come find his little brother. Despite being wrapped into a love spell, he'd even had the fortitude to call his parents in the car, and make Paul apologize to their mom for worrying her.

Just because there's a love spell doesn't mean he's not perfect.

Right. Perfect OCD businessman with toenail fungus.

I don't care about that stuff!

Since when?

The logic spell was definitely a good idea.

Plus, since we are perfect for each other, it'll make Paul see that!

"Hello, Father," said Sarah, extending a paper bag toward the priest sitting on the porch swing. "I brought some ice cream for the priests." It was all she had. A pile of treats from the ice cream truck that she'd spent a fortune on.

"Oh!" The priest leaned forward, his wrinkled smile displaying a mouthful of worn teeth. He looked ancient, with wisps of silvery hair stuck to his smooth, freckled head. "What flavor you got?"

Sarah forced herself up the first porch step. "Um, well, all different kinds. Fudgesicles, Creamsicles, and root beer Popsicles." She'd kept the banana for herself.

The priest clapped his hands together. "That sounds wonderful! I haven't had a Creamsicle in years! Do you have orange?"

Sarah studied him, planted and tucked into the swing with a robe on his lap and a Bible beside him. Determination settled through her, mostly to be finished and get back to the car where Henry waited. She stalked up the steps and handed the bag to the old priest. "They're all orange."

"Sit with me right here." He patted the wide swing. "Share one too." He lifted the Bible and extended it toward Sarah. "Put this on that little table over there for me."

Sarah froze. The cover of the book had been worn smooth in places, the edges frayed from use, and bits of colored silk markers jutted from between the pages. If it weren't a thing of power to begin with, it had become one from years of devotion and prayer.

Once on a dare, Aunt Lily had touched an old copy of the Tibetan Book of the Dead. It had taken her a month to figure out how to repair her blackened hand. Sarah suspected if she took that Bible from the priest her entire hand would catch fire.

"Oh, I don't have time to stay," she said, holding the bag out. "You enjoy them with the other priests."

"Do I know you?" He peered over the top of wire-framed reading glasses, blinking rheumy pale eyes. "What's your name?"

He was still holding the Bible out. "Sarah," she said.

He raised his brows. "Sarah?"

She cleared her throat and said quickly, "Archer."

"Sarah Archer, I'm Father McCloud. You look familiar. Does your family go to Our Lady of the Light?"

"They don't. I do, but I'm new."

"Will you take this Bible for me, Sarah Archer?" Something knowing glowed in his eyes and Sarah took a deep breath.

It would be good penance. She glanced around. A bird bath full of rainwater sat against the porch railing; it might work. She reached for the book and the priest's left hand snaked out and grabbed her right one with surprising strength.

"I see what you are, Sarah Archer. Why are you here?"

She closed her eyes and battled tears; his fingers scalded her wrist. She wondered if her skin burned his too. "I'm trying not to be that anymore," she said.

Father McCloud let go and set the Bible beside him, resting his hand on it. Sarah wondered if it soothed his blisters. His eyes briefly took in the red welts on her wrist.

"You have to give up your dark ways, if you mean what you say."

"I'm trying," she said. "I keep backsliding."

The priest nabbed the bag of treats from her other hand. "Who doesn't?" He peered inside the bag and smiled. "These look good." He looked up at her, taking his glasses off and folding them. "Have you tried *asking* for what you need instead of taking it?"

"You'll say no."

Father McCloud dug a Creamsicle out of the bag and tugged it out of the wrapping. "That's how the world is meant to work. Free will and all. Ask anyway."

"I need a shingle from the roof of your house. I'll bring it back."

"What on earth do you need a shingle for?"

"I'm trying to break a spell, I guess."

"You guess?" He took a bite of his ice cream.

"Well, it's a love spell, and I think—no, I know—or I'm pretty sure I want to break it. I think I would love him anyway, so maybe it doesn't even matter. But if I do this spell, I'll know for sure if it's real."

"The church doesn't hold with witchcraft and spells."

"I didn't do it. It was an accidental cast."

"Accidental?"

Under his sharp gaze, Sarah shifted from foot to foot. "No one did it on purpose. It was kind of a mix up because of another spell."

"Huh." The priest gnawed on the ice cream bar. "The trimmings and trappings, spells and casting, are to get your head in the right place you know. It's dark matter toying with you, moving your soul into position for acquisition. You're being foolish."

Sarah knew the priest was right, but she also needed to understand what to do. She needed clarity. "It's a small thing. I mean, it's not a dark cast, but I still need the shingle."

Father McCloud rolled his eyes heavenward and sighed. "You don't, and the spell won't work because they never do. I'm not giving you permission to use my shingle for witchery, but I am asking you to remember to bring it back when you take it anyway. I don't want a leaky roof. Someday, when you ask for something you want, and it is denied you and you don't take it anyway—that is a day you've walked away from dark matter. That is the day you've stopped *trying* to change and have changed. You may go, Sarah Archer."

"THERE ARE STOCKS in the basement, and an abacus," Sarah told Henry as facts about the hair care products he used buzzed through her brain.

"I think I might like a peek into your basement myself. It sounds like a museum buff's dream."

Nightmare maybe. Standing upstairs in the open doorway, Sarah listened to Paul rooting around in the bowels of the deep, dark cellar. Far below her, the beam from his flashlight shone through the darkness as he searched. Puffs of dark matter billowed from the open door and shivers raced up her spine. Henry's hand running up and down her back did nothing to soothe it.

"Don't worry," he whispered, his breath warm against her cool skin. "It's just a basement. Paul can handle basements. I'm protective of him, but this is nothing compared to what he's been through."

No it's not! "Paul, are you all right?" she called down the rickety stairs.

"I'm seriously creeped out, Sarah," he said from the darkness. "Is that a guillotine in the back?"

"Please let me go too!" begged Henry.

Bi-monthly facials. Weekly massage. Uses organic moisturizer.

She shook her head at him and yelled, "Yes, Paul. Try not to look around. You're searching, not exploring. Does your pendant feel warm on your neck?"

"It's my cross, remember?" said Henry. "I loaned it to him, and I can promise it's not supernatural." He chuckled against her ear.

"No, well, a little, but it's cold down here," came Paul's answer. "This is one deep skanky basement. I think there's water dripping. This isn't just dirt is it? I mean the floor is, but the walls are stone, right? I feel like I'm inside a mine that might collapse."

"Hurry up, please. The abacus is right by the first post near the stairs, inside a pile of old laundry baskets. It's red and white, see it? The stocks are about three posts back. They're just the board where the head and hands went through and they're leaning against another post. Just use your knife to dig a piece of wood out, and get back here."

"Oh! Well, I see the abacus. Seriously, why isn't there electricity down here? Of course, why would there be electricity? This was designed for creep factor, right? I think there's a cardboard box of bones down here." His voice sounded shaky.

"They aren't human. Don't freak. Just get the splinter. It looks like old weathered wood with three holes in it."

"Yeah, really? That's no help. A lot of stuff looks like that down here. And you gave me one crap flashlight. Give me a second."

"Have you ever thought about growing your hair long?" whispered Henry against her ear.

Never again. Sarah had cut it after they died.

Running his fingers over the thickness, Henry smoothed the ends against her shoulders.

Wears silk boxers. Has chest hair waxed, and swears at the aesthetician every time. "Henry, please focus. Paul is in danger."

"In an old basement?"

"It's not just any old basement. Dark matter is a real thing. Haven't you ever been anywhere where you could just feel the wrongness? The potential for something bad to go down? That basement is so full of it I can hardly see down there."

Henry pulled a face that suggested he didn't believe her, but he hollered down the stairs, "Paul, are you all right, man?"

"Just give me a fucking minute, okay, Henry? You're such a pain in my ass! I'm moving as fast as I can."

"Don't get worked up. I just wanted to know you're good."

"I don't need you breathing down my neck while I dig through a pile of crap. Go back to licking Sarah's ear."

"He's not usually like that," whispered Henry against Sarah's ear, and she felt his tongue move lightly against her lobe. She shivered.

"For the love of fuck, you're really doing it aren't you?" shouted Paul. "Kathleen is going to kick your ass."

Henry laughed, his teeth grazing Sarah's ear. She put her hand against his chest to push him away and focus on Paul, but ended up leaving it there.

"I'm glad you think it's funny, two-timing your girlfriend." In the basement Paul slammed something, and a crash echoed like a woodpile being knocked over. "Dammit. I think I've got your fucking wood from the damn stock thing buried in my hand."

"Come back, Paul," said Sarah. She couldn't say why her unease intensified. Maybe because she'd never heard him swear like that, or maybe it was because less dark matter puffed out the open doorway now, choosing instead to stay downstairs with Paul.

"I'll come when I'm finished. I can't see a damn thing down here." The faint light of his flashlight vanished from Sarah's view and she heard him thump it a few times.

"You're finished, please, Paul. Head toward the light of the stairwell."

"Come back, buddy, don't push yourself," said Henry.

In the basement Paul threw something and the sound of breaking glass crashed. "Would you give me a goddamn break, Henry? You think I'm weak minded because I lost it after what I went through? You go to war and see how you handle it! You watch your friends blown to pieces so small you have to wash it out of your hair. You listen to grown men scream for their mothers while they die and then we'll talk!"

It was getting to him. "Hold onto me and don't let go!" Sarah grabbed Henry's hand and raced down the steps. "Fuck the dark, Paul! Just fuck it, you know? Look for the stars. Remember you told me you can't always see them but they're there?"

The old stairs creaked and bowed and the only light Sarah had shone from her cell phone. Henry's fingers slipped away, then he clutched at the back of her blouse.

"I'm fine." Paul's voice came from several yards ahead. So much dark matter surrounded him Sarah couldn't see him at first. "I just cut myself on whatever the hell this glass ball is. I think I'm bleeding."

NO! Not down here.

As soon as Sarah's feet hit the dirt floor she relaxed. Dark matter moved through her like caramel through chocolate. *So good.* Sarah felt taller, stronger, more capable, and powerful. This was her domain, why had she worried?

Paul stood next to the old stocks, his arm extended. Drops of his blood dripped onto the dirt floor. Each one of them increased the strength in Sarah's body, warming her in interesting and wrong ways. Henry's hand on her shoulder made her mouth water. She hadn't even kissed him yet. Not really. He smelled good in the dark. The material of her dress pressed against her breasts and cool air blew up under it, icing between her thighs.

The facts ticker-taping through her mind took a sudden turn. *Favors sex in airplanes and showers, likes to dominate.* The last one left her sizing Henry up in his Italian suit and loafers. *Hmm.*

"Sarah, are you all right?" he asked, squinting in the direction of his brother. "I think Paul's hurt. Paul! Hold your arm above your head. It'll slow the bleeding."

"I think I know what to do with a cut!" said Paul. He sounded angry, combative.

Henry slid his arm through Sarah's and tried to move her along. She let go, allowing him to go ahead without her. She didn't want to hear anymore facts. Dark matter glided along the floor like rising water in a flood. It warmed Sarah's feet and ankles as it moved upward.

"Mmmm," she said as it caressed her legs and drifted higher. Stretching her arms above her head she closed her eyes, wanting to feel it *there*, wanting to feel it everywhere.

Someone jerked her arms down. "What are you doing?" asked Paul. She opened her eyes and smiled at him, though surely he didn't see in the darkness as well as she did.

"Stretching," she said, and reached to run her fingers over his lips.

He slapped them down. "I'm Paul."

"I know who you are," Sarah purred.

"Something's wrong with her," said Paul to Henry.

"Nothing Henry can't fix. Kiss me," she breathed.

Henry obeyed, bending down and pressing his mouth against hers, twining strong fingers into her hair to tip her head back roughly. Sarah touched him, her hand moving across the zipper of his pants to squeeze.

"What the hell are you doing?" said Paul, pushing against them. "Sarah, what are you doing?"

She pulled away from Henry's mouth to look at Paul with fresh eyes. In his old jeans and familiar linen shirt he looked delicious, too. "Come here and find out," she said, reaching for him. Around her the dark matter seemed to snap to attention, transmitting exactly what she wanted to Paul. He glanced down at her hand on his brother and slapped her across the face, hard.

Sarah's head snapped on her neck, and she saw stars.

"What are you suggesting in this disgusting hole? Get upstairs, Sarah Archer! And don't you dare cast filthy ideas on me!"

Sarah dropped her phone and ran for the steps, the stars still sparkling in her vision. She tripped up the bottom step and fell forward. The light from the open door above waited as she crawled up the stairs as fast as she could go. Behind her she heard Henry shouting at Paul and the sound of a punch being thrown.

No! Horror churned through her middle and the urge to cast vibrated deliciously in all the best spots. Some ugly part of herself liked that Henry would defend her from Paul's anger.

"Fuck you!" Sarah shouted at the dark matter, horrified at herself for embracing it. Scrambling up the last steps she allowed a small cast, completely devoid of dark matter, to burst from her. "Starlight!"

Sparkling light lit her peripheral vision and she crawled through the doorway onto the landing before turning around. The entire basement had lit up like a tiny galaxy. Paul and Henry's silhouettes moved against the swirling stars like shadows with Paul forcing Henry toward the stairs, an abacus in one hand and the entire top portion of the stocks in the other.

Sarah crawled across the floor and leaned against the wall, hiding her face against her knees, too ashamed to look at them. As they reached the top step she knew she couldn't bear to face either of them and shot to her feet. She dashed around the corner, ran up the curving stairway and down the hall to her bedroom before slamming and locking the door.

chapter eleven

Logically Speaking

There was no way Sarah could face either man. Humiliated, ashamed, and furiously angry with herself she refused to open her bedroom door. Paul pounded on it and gave up with the parting comment, "You should be ashamed, Sarah, but I know that wasn't you."

But it was.

Maybe it was a fantasy that many people wouldn't engage in, but stuff like that did happen to Archer women. Sarah could remember multiple men exiting Aunt Lily's bedroom on different mornings. As a child she hadn't thought much of it. Witch normal wasn't regular normal and Aunt Lily normal wasn't even witch normal.

But what's your normal?

She thought about Paul, his brokenness and kindness.

She thought about Henry and his curious attraction.

No. Never. She hadn't meant to suggest anything objectionable to the brothers. *That's not true. I meant it when I said it.*

Tugging her white comforter down, Sarah crawled under it and pulled the blankets over her head to hide.

At three o'clock in the morning Sarah roused and took a shower, dried her hair, and dressed for work. A blue and green print dress with a gold blazer, long pilfered from Aunt Lily's closet, went perfectly with blue heels and a pink silk scarf. Taking a deep breath, she opened her bedroom door.

Henry slept on the floor outside. *Sends all his clothes to the dry cleaner. Makes his personal assistant run his errands. Listens to opera.*

Sarah stooped and put her hand on his shoulder. "Henry, I'm sorry. It's like being drunk and drugged and king of the world all at the same time. Last time I went in the basement I ordered a pizza just to hit on the delivery guy."

Henry sat up and rubbed a hand across his face. "No, it's okay—uh—what did you do with the pizza guy?"

"Well, nothing, but only because he was sixteen and weighed close to three hundred pounds."

Henry blinked at her, bleary-eyed. Even rumpled and sleepy he looked like he could command a boardroom or maybe tour a winery in his custom-made suit sans tie.

"Which stopped you? The pizza boy's size or age?" asked Paul, coming up the stairs wearing his usual gym shorts and t-shirt. "I was on the couch. Heard your door open."

Sarah straightened. "I'm sorry, Paul. I don't know what else to say. I know not to go down there."

"You didn't answer the question." He handed her the cell phone she'd dropped in the basement.

Sarah shrugged. "Likely the combination of factors saved him."

Paul looked at Henry. "Are you hearing her, brother?"

"At least she's honest."

Paul sighed, returning his attention to Sarah. "Why don't you hire someone to come clean that crap out and have the basement remodeled into a movie theater or something? Or maybe, I dunno, get walls and a floor?"

"I might need some of that stuff. I've got to keep it somewhere."

Paul arched a brow at her. "If you say so. Well, obviously I've put last night's dinner away by now. I can nuke it for you, or make some pancakes. You're going to work ridiculously early aren't you? It's four o'clock in the morning."

"I figured I could try my hand at that logic spell first."

Paul's face lit up. "Really?"

Standing, Henry took Sarah's hand and threaded his fingers through it. *Republican. Has never dated a Democrat. Only pretends to recycle.* "If that's what you want, kitten, I'm in too. I know what I feel is real, and I don't believe in this spell stuff anyway."

THE PIECE OF wood from the old stocks rested against the kitchen island. The abacus sat on the counter, an ancient calculator made of wood with red beads strung on white thread. Sarah touched it and sensed an old connection to her Archer blood. Skins of olive oil and goats had once been counted with it. She didn't have to touch the wood of the stocks to know an Archer woman had once been shackled there.

Paul neatly laid out other ingredients: a dried slice of sour dough bread from the loaf he'd made, a cup of well water, a sprig of evergreen, blank parchment, the shingle he'd detached from the rectory roof. The shingle wasn't stone or ancient, but composite and slightly damaged from the retrieval process. Sarah hadn't yet mentioned he'd need to put it back. She had a bad feeling he'd make her do it.

Paul slid a large clay bowl across the counter with a few threads in it. "I hope that's enough linen. It's from my shirt seam. I didn't want to have to really cut into it. It's my favorite shirt."

"It's good. Did you dig that splinter out? The one you got from the stocks yesterday?"

"Yeah, look," he said and held his hand out so she could see the swollen red wound. "That stupid thing was two inches long, and thick!"

"I'd like to use that. There're several things here from you and me. If I let Henry's necklace soak in the middle of this too, it'll make it stronger."

Henry ran his finger over the list from the old potion book. "It doesn't say a cross."

Collects wine, mostly as an investment. Knows how to Tango.

"Oh, it never would," said Sarah, "but it's tied to you both and it would give it a lot of oomph."

"Well, I threw out the splinter," said Paul.

Sarah shot him a stink eye.

"Seriously, like you keep yours? Tell me there's a collection of Archer women splinters in that stupid basement. Not that I'd be surprised."

"Where did you throw it? I can see it was pretty large. You didn't flush it, did you?"

"Fine!" Paul turned on his heel and stomped out of the kitchen toward his apartment.

Henry chuckled. "You two fight like my fiancée and her brother."

Sarah turned her stink eye on him.

"I meant my ex-almost-fiancée."

Tries to be politically correct, but doesn't often mean it. Flosses after every meal.

Henry's smile vanished. "If you knew how I felt, you'd never worry about her."

Sarah fought the urge to throw her arms around him and forget about the stupid spell. She knew exactly how he felt because she felt the same way, but she also knew it might not be real. "You know, Henry, if this logic spell works properly you might want to catch the next flight home. The truth is, maybe you do want Kathleen to be your fiancée." It hurt to say it, but she managed, confi-

dent it couldn't really be true. *I'm a witch! If this attraction was pure-*
ly a spell, surely I'd know!

But even if it was real for her, that didn't mean it was real for him.

Henry sat down on a kitchen stool, the look in his Jack Sparrow eyes pained. "I'm going to be brutally honest with you, Sarah. I don't really believe in this witch stuff. I mean I'm not stupid; you shoved me into the air somehow and suspended me up there. I felt what happened in the basement yesterday. And those sparks between our hands when we touch—I'm not a stupid man. I realize you're somehow other, though I'm leaning toward Siegfried and Roy skills. Last night Paul explained to me what happened the night you met. I don't mean to discount your beliefs, and certainly not your telekinesis, but to me this potion is a lot of mumbo jumbo. Everything unusual about you can certainly be explained by science. But I know what I feel for you is real. My mother always says love is the only true magic in the universe."

When Paul came back, Sarah was on Henry's lap, kissing him. Paul poked the bathroom wastebasket against her arm to get her attention. "Earth to Sarah. You have a job to do!" He turned his attention to the earthen bowl on the counter. "Is everything in here? I feel a bit of vomit coming up if you think that would help."

"Suck it up, little brother," said Henry.

"Toss the splinter in and Henry's necklace, the one around your neck," instructed Sarah.

"Shouldn't you do it?" asked Paul, unclasping the pewter cross.

"It won't matter." Sarah extricated herself from Henry and gave him a last peck on the cheek. *Cheats on his taxes. Owns boots made of stingray. Plays piano.*

Paul picked something out of the trash and shook the splinter out of a wad of tissue. He dropped the necklace into the bowl, chain and all.

I don't know what half the spell books in the attic are bound in, so the stingray boots shouldn't be a big deal. Sarah set the earthen bowl on top of the priest's shingle and laid the abacus over it. She leaned over the counter and stared, unblinking, at the concoction. Titles of books on economics and the stock market, books Henry had read, rambled through her mind. She shoved the useless knowledge and the niggling stingray fact aside to focus.

"It looks like you threw some random junk in there and tossed in water. Won't it turn into a paste or bubble or something?" asked Paul. "So far all the spell stuff you've showed me is a bit of a disappointment."

Sarah ignored him too, staring at the ingredients through the slats in the abacus. A little four note tune found its way inside her and she hummed it. "Hmmm, hmm, hm, hm." Around her, the reassuring buzzing she'd come to love took up the tune.

After a moment so did Henry, his humming a rich tenor. Paul seemed to resist for a while, satisfied with tapping the rhythm out with his fingers against the edges of the shingle. Eventually he seemed to remember the whole thing had been his idea and hummed it too. Sarah blinked. Her vision seemed clearer and from somewhere a whispered reassurance entered her mind. *"You go together."* She noticed Henry blinking too and grinned at him, wondering if he'd heard it too.

He winked.

I knew it! The attraction between them would have been there even without a rebounded spell. She sensed it with the same certainty that she sensed outside birds flew over the house, and squirrels argued in the trees. A humming surety caressed her bones, and surely Henry's, too. *All is as it should be.*

But there is work to be done.

Sarah removed the abacus and put her hand into the bowl, lifting out Henry's necklace to dry on a tea towel. *That is enough of that.* "You should make pancakes now, Paul. I like to get to work early."

"We'll go with you," said Henry, "and drop Paul off at the police station to get my rental. He can drive it back here and I'll take you to work in yours."

Paul stared at Sarah. "Wait! Didn't it work on you? It didn't, did it?"

"Did it work on you?" Henry arched a critical brow and Paul crossed his arms.

"Don't look at me like that. Something happened. My vision is so clear I think I can see through time. I definitely can *see* all the cobwebs I missed in here. It's obvious you never dust, Sarah. But don't you two feel any different? You don't, do you?"

"Yes," said Sarah. "I do. It worked. The choices I need to make are perfectly clear. And I think you're right about the basement, Paul. I'm going to hire someone to clean that stuff out and dispose of it. If I'm going to put the witch behind me, that's a good place to start." With the spell coursing through her, the idea of going back down there didn't seem frightening.

"My father sits on a museum board out of Boston," said Henry. "Some of that stuff may have historical value. Bet they'd send a curator to take it off your hands. It would be a good tax write off."

"I don't want any publicity," said Sarah.

"Of course not. You'd be another anonymous donor." Henry smiled.

"Great!" Paul interrupted. "I'm so glad you realize you're some sort of a hoarder witch. But I meant do you two feel any different about each other? Sarah, are you still in love with Henry? Henry, how do you feel about Kathleen?"

Sarah returned Henry's knowing smile. No wonder he did so well in the business world; people would do a lot for a smile like that.

He wrapped his left arm around her and fished in his pocket to pull out his cell phone. "Now that I've participated in one, I can safely say that I still think spells are a load of garbage," he said as he texted with his thumb. "But I know exactly how I feel about Sarah, and—uh—the ex too!"

Sarah peppered Henry's cheek with kisses.

Paul groaned, glaring at the mess on the counter. "Something went wrong! It didn't work! Sarah, did you do it right? I mean you dumped all this junk into a bowl and what? You didn't even stir anything."

"It worked," she said. "I know exactly what I have to do."

"Me too," said Henry, laying his cell phone on the counter. "It has nothing to do with that bowl of junk, but I sent a message to Kathleen, and I'm taking Sarah out to dinner this weekend. I have an important question to ask her."

"What? Are you high? You just met!" shouted Paul, throwing his hands into the air.

"I'm being logical, Paul. Isn't that what you wanted? There's no point in leaving Kathleen dangling. She's a good person and she deserves to know what I'm doing here. And life's short, you know that. I'm thirty years old and Sarah and I want to be together. Don't be upset, be happy we found each other."

Paul began to pace. "It's not real!"

"Let's say you're right," said Henry. "Let's say what we both feel is a spell. So what? We feel the same about each other. Be happy for us."

"It's true, Paul," Sarah agreed. "Who does it hurt if we're together?"

"Me."

Sarah searched his face as he stared at her, not sure what he meant.

"I have a sensitive gag reflex," he said.

Sarah rolled her eyes and Paul sighed. "See, you can't name one person it would hurt!"

"Yes I can! Kathleen. Yourselves. The truth. Reality. Your future miserable selves. I could go on. Are you going to move to

Dallas, Sarah, to become an oil baron's wife? Join the Daughters of the American Revolution? Start getting Botox? Or is Henry going to move here and help you kick your witch habit? Maybe he can wet vac the dark matter out of the basement for you, or help you burn enchanted clothing in the backyard by moonlight. Which is it going to be?"

"Either way," she said, certain the love spell couldn't do any harm when their feelings were based firmly in reality.

Henry smiled. "Kathleen can take care of herself, Paul, and I don't see why Sarah and I can't summer in New England and spend the rest of the year in Dallas or at home. She'll love Oklahoma."

"Oh, screw it. Make your own damn pancakes, Sarah." Paul knocked the box of pancake mix flat on the counter. "I'm going back to bed!" He stalked to his room and slammed the door.

chapter twelve

Work Out

Henry's hair dripped with rain as he hopped into the passenger seat and jammed a small overnight bag into the back of Sarah's Jeep. He returned his attention to Paul running across the parking lot of the police station. "He's in a pretty bad mood. I didn't think he was going to come get the car for me."

"Yeah," said Sarah. She didn't need her witch senses to tell her that Paul was pissed at both of them. Steady rain blurred her vision through the windshield, and she turned the wipers on as fast as they'd go. "Paul's pretty disappointed we didn't come around to his way of thinking."

Lucidity hadn't upset Sarah. Clarity had freed her. The morning's logic spell had made the facts clearer. It made perfect sense, she told herself. The love spell was only a boost to the truth both Sarah and Henry felt. What did it hurt if they were bound together? For once a love spell only added flavor to the truth.

She frowned as Paul slammed the door of Henry's rental car too hard and sped out of the parking lot, tires squealing.

Henry sighed. "Last night while you were holed up in your room I asked him what his problem was with us. When we were in high school we had this rule where we never dated each other's friends. I don't mean only old girlfriends either, I mean hanging-out-with-friend friends. The rule kind of faded away as we got older. In fact, Paul dated my fiancée—I mean my ex-fiancée—once before he was deployed. So I asked him if this was like that, that I was stealing his friend."

"I'll always be Paul's friend."

"He said it wasn't that. He said we just don't belong together." Henry shook the rainwater from his dark hair. It beaded on his good suit jacket and he brushed it off, splashing Sarah. He noticed too late and his lips twisted into a smile very different from Paul's. Sexy.

The logic spell kept Sarah from reacting to that smile in the middle of the police station parking lot. It also made her focus on what Henry had only moments ago taken from the suitcase in the trunk of his Mercedes. Maybe part of Paul's anger was because he'd also noticed the small box Henry held in his hand.

That Sarah could understand.

"Henry," she said as she slid the Jeep into first gear, her mind still clear and logical, "you're not seriously going to give me that ring, are you? Paul is right about the fact that we've just met. I'm not ready to think marriage. In fact, you should probably know that the only Archer women I've ever heard of who got married were back in the day when they did it for property ownership." She looked at Henry for his reaction.

He seemed unfazed. "No, I haven't lost my mind, just my heart. I think we should start with a date or two." Henry grinned at her. "I didn't want to leave the ring in the trunk. It's a ten carat diamond, and it's been in my family a long time. My mother would have my head if something happened to it."

Knows all the verses of Jingle Bells. Secretly sings it year round. In the mood for sushi.

"You had me worried there." She turned the Jeep onto the main road and accelerated.

"If I was going to propose to someone I just met it would be you."

"I feel the same way. But I don't want Paul to get more upset than he already is. Maybe after some time he'll come around." A slight wave of relief went through her as Henry tucked the ring box into the interior pocket of his rain spattered suit jacket. "So what are you going to ask me Saturday night then?"

"Hey, don't try to ruin my surprise. You know, I don't believe in this spell stuff, but I stick by what I said to him this morning. I wouldn't even care if Paul is right. I really wouldn't. If this is a spell, leave me right here."

Sarah smiled and turned into the drive-thru of the Wayside Bake Shop. She ordered fresh baked scones over the intercom.

"Your co-workers must love you," said Henry, and reached over to squeeze her knee.

Twenty minutes later in the Mass Power and Light parking lot his warm hand remained there. Sarah slid the gear into neutral and pulled the parking brake as thunder rumbled and rain battered the windshield.

"You know the worse part of what happened in the basement yesterday?" he asked.

Sarah couldn't quite meet his eyes.

"You went to bed early," he said.

"Early?"

"Alone. Maybe neither of us was up to much after that basement. I don't know what's wrong with that place—frankly I think it's some sort of hallucinogenic fungus or something—but it affected me too. Only Paul kept his head. But, anyway, I want to say that tonight I don't want to sleep alone—and I sure don't mean bunking with my brother." Henry focused his intense gaze on her.

Cheeks flaming and heart pounding, Sarah grinned. Leaving the keys in the ignition she took the bakery box from Henry and reached for the door. A jolt of panic shot through her at the same time Henry slid one long leg onto the driver's side and grabbed her shoulder.

"Do you really have to go?"

"I do."

"Why?" He leaned close until his minty breath blew on her face, his deadly handsome eyes pleading. "Can't you take some time off?"

She could, but it wasn't a good idea. "I'd better not right now."

"I wanted to wait until Saturday to spring this on you, but I can't wait. I have to go to Dubai for six months. I want you to come with me."

"I—I can't!" *Oh my gah! Traveling the world with Henry!* She'd never wanted anything more, but it could cost her soul.

"Don't take this idea wrong, but I could find you a hundred different jobs in my company if you're uncomfortable just going with me. You should see the place we're building there." Henry shot a dubious glance at the old brick building. "Please say you'll think about it."

Anxiety shivered through Sarah at the thought, and the temptation to agree practically overwhelmed her. She hadn't traveled anywhere in the three years since her family died. "No." She rushed her words, almost garbling them together. "I need this job, I need to work here. This place, it helps me, it keeps me—well, I mean—it helps me keep it together. I like—I like the repetition of it, if that makes any sense." Without work to calm her, she'd never be able to control the temptation to cast.

Henry leaned so close his face looked blurry. "That makes no sense," he whispered, and kissed her. "Think about it."

Sarah wrapped her arms around him and didn't realize the bakery box was being crushed between them until a rhythmic tapping interrupted. Henry pulled away and wiped smeared lipstick off her mouth with his thumb. "Someone's knocking on your window."

Sarah's heartbeat doubled at the thought of leaving. "I have to go," she said without moving.

"So you said." Henry continued to run a finger around the edges of her lips, ignoring the persistent tapping. Sarah felt the heat of a spark sizzle from his skin. He smiled. "Eight whole hours is too long. When do you have lunch?"

"Eleven."

"I'll be here waiting."

Hates your Jeep. Would buy you one in Dubai. Wants to spend hours with you in bed, now.

Sarah forced herself to turn and grasp the door handle. She stepped out into the rain before she realized the person knocking on the window had been Mindy. Her friend swapped her an umbrella for the box of scones.

"Hold it over my head too," Mindy grumbled, walking close and peeking inside the box. "Was that guy you were licking the same boy toy from the movie theater? Because I have a thing for troublemakers too."

"It's his brother."

Mindy did an about face to stare after the retreating Jeep. "What! Are you kidding me? Do you have access to a clone army? How many of them are there? Can I have one?"

"There's only two. They're twins." Sarah checked her lipstick with her fingers. She could still feel Henry's touch. The selfish witch in her wanted to cast and make him come right back. Another part of her wanted to get some distance and think.

"Can I use one for a few days?"

"No."

"A couple days?"

"Mindy!"

"Selfish slut. That awesome Hermès scarf makes you look fat."

Laughing, Sarah unwound it from her shoulders. "I brought it for you."

"From the rag bag?" Mindy took it and draped it around her neck. "I'd rather have the boy toy. You need to learn how to share. Bet you were an only child."

THE RAIN NEVER let up. All morning it pounded against the windows and roof of the office building until the sound of it vibrated through Sarah. Some primitive part of her wanted to kick off her shoes and run outside in it all the way to Henry. She knew what September rain felt like against her skin, warm and soft. Despite the boring repetition of her job, nothing could drown out the temptation of freedom beckoning from outside, or the thought that Henry would be back soon. The logic spell faded away until Sarah could barely focus on her job. *I could have taken the day off! I'll bet just being with Henry would keep me from casting!*

Avery Gross set a flash drive on her desk, explaining it contained forms in need of review edits. When Sarah didn't look away from her screen or respond, he cleared his throat.

Sarah kept one hand on the mouse, hoping to look busy enough that he'd go away. Her other hand worked back and forth over a bare patch of wooden desktop. The velvety smooth texture of that wood reminded her of the brief groping she'd given Henry in the basement yesterday.

"Sarah, are you all right?" Avery persisted.

She wanted to say yes to Dubai. She wanted to be the kind of woman who could. "I am all right. Are you?" she answered without thinking, and residual magic from the aftershock went with her words. She smiled. The cost from the morning's spell felt harmless. It bound Avery with one message: Sarah was all right.

"I—I am all right too," he faltered. His gaze flickered to her mouth and he swallowed. "Um, do you have lunch plans? Because Jackie Hamilton and Mercer invited me out, and I thought maybe you should come too."

"No, Avery. Not today. I have plans."

"If you could change your plans—I mean, it's your boss and Human Resources, you might want to think about it."

That's so never going to happen. "You might want to think about what you want, not them," she replied. Her eyes went to the clock, and her mind returned to the thought that Henry would be back in forty minutes for her.

Avery was standing too close. She felt it with every pore, and unexpectedly Henry's presence moved through space like a vibration and she knew he'd come early, and already waited for her in the parking lot. Sitting up straight, Sarah grinned. The need to see him crackled through her and she got to her feet in one smooth move, bumping against Avery.

"Sarah." His voice sounded gruff. "So you're okay."

"I've never been better," she sighed, suddenly feeling magnanimous. "Or I will be once I get to the parking lot." She smiled, not caring about the obvious innuendo in her words. What she did on her own time wasn't Avery's business. The Mass Power and Light parking lot suddenly seemed as romantic a destination as any beach she'd been to. Half of Sarah's mind listened distractedly to the rain as she waited for Avery to move his hulking bulk so she could get downstairs and see Henry.

From behind Avery, a sharp female voice disturbed Sarah's distant thoughts. "Excuse me? Am I interrupting?"

It took her a moment to place it. *Jackie Hamilton from Human Resources, the one who doesn't eat and wants her kid to go Ivy League.* Sarah glanced up at Avery and realized he stood too close.

"Jackie," Avery said, "we'll meet you downstairs in ten, if that works for you?"

Sarah stooped to dig her handbag from beneath her desk, ignoring the woman's perky droning and determined to resist whacking her bag against Avery's stubborn head. She waited for the sound of Jackie's sensible loafers shuffling down the hall before straightening to inform him again she wouldn't be going to lunch with them.

Avery didn't seem to be listening. He wrapped big arms around her, and smacked his mouth against hers so hard one of her teeth cut the inside of her mouth. Somehow Sarah had never realized before just how huge Avery was. She pounded a fist against his chest and he backed off immediately.

"What are you doing?" She wiped the back of her hand across her mouth and checked it for blood. "Are you nuts? I'd like to keep my job!"

"Sarah, I'm sorry. I guess I got carried away."

"I guess so. Didn't you hear what I said?"

Avery smiled, looking somewhat abashed. "About the parking lot?"

"Yes!" She poked a finger into his chest. "And I'm sure as heck not talking about going anywhere with Mercer or skinny bitch!"

"Oh," he said. "Gotcha."

"Good! I'm glad we're *finally* on the same page. Took long enough!" Tucking her purse beneath her arm, Sarah marched away.

HENRY WAITED IN the Jeep right outside the guard shack. Sarah could see him waving as she exited the front doors of the office building. She ran through the blinding rain and puddles, water soaking her clothes and filling Aunt Lily's shoes. She yanked the driver's door open, crawled right onto Henry's lap and kissed him, pulling his bottom lip into her mouth and biting. He chuckled against her mouth, wrapping an arm around her and slamming the Jeep door shut with the other.

Travels first class. Only reads non-fiction. Has never cheated on a woman before.

"There's not enough room for both of us in this seat," he complained between kisses.

Sarah grasped a lever near the floor and the seat crashed backward, almost laying Henry flat.

"Ooph!" he said against her busy lips. "You're soaking wet."

Sarah laughed.

Henry brushed the damp hair off her face and kept his hands there, kissing her properly. For several minutes Sarah focused on little besides not getting her leg stuck in the crack between the driver seat and the door, not getting her backside wedged too tightly against the steering wheel, and undoing the buttons on Henry's shirt.

Likes a woman's legs wrapped around him, and keeps eye contact during sex. Bites.

"I brought you lunch," he whispered.

"It's delicious," she said against his lips. "Thank you."

He laughed again. "I'm talking about the sushi in the back. I brought a bottle of wine too. I was hoping the weather might clear up for a picnic."

"It's not, and we're not going anywhere anyway." Sarah pressed her body against his. "Not until I finish every bite of you."

"Whoa, kitten. Don't forget we're in a parking lot in a Jeep full of windows."

Sarah glanced up at the steamed glass and giggled. "Are you shy, Henry?"

"I don't want to get arrested."

"I'm willing to risk it. Besides, no one can see in!"

Henry tried to sit up, but Sarah didn't let him. She tugged the top of her dress down until she exposed far more than cleavage. "How about now? Are you willing to risk it now?"

Judging by the reaction of Henry's body beneath hers he'd gotten past his worries.

At that exact moment the passenger door swung open. Before Sarah had a moment to fully turn her head in that direction, Avery Gross hopped into the passenger seat. "Wow, Sarah! Are you starting without me?"

Sarah stared, trying to make sense of him being there.

"What the hell!" Henry shouted. He flipped the seat lever, sending himself flying upright and wedging Sarah's rear against the horn.

"Get off her!" Avery shouted.

I'm definitely the one on top. Sarah continued to gape at him; certain he was the slowest man she'd ever known. She reacted too late as he swung a fist toward Henry. "No!"

The sickening sound of fist on jaw seemed louder than the horn blaring beneath her backside.

"You bastard! Sarah, did he hurt you?" Avery crawled over the console, trying to hit Henry again and elbowing Sarah's face in the process.

It hurt like hell. "Stop it!" Sarah grabbed a handful of Avery's hair and yanked as the driver's door swung open.

All three of them turned to look. A flushed and tousled Henry clung nose to nose with Avery, an arm around his neck. Sarah held both men, her bare breasts pressed against them in the confines of the little Jeep while her backside continued to blare the horn.

Jackie Hamilton stood in the rain, her mouth hanging open. Behind her, Sarah's boss Mercer and several security guards looked on.

chapter thirteen

But, Kitten

*P*aul laughed. He slid off the edge of the sofa and onto the floor and laughed until tears ran down his cheeks. He laughed until he had to press a hand against his stomach to control his wheezing. Sarah and Henry's problems seemed to have gone a long way toward cheering him up.

"Stop it!" Henry wasn't amused. "I got arrested!"

Sarah hadn't known until that day that getting arrested didn't always involve handcuffs. They'd been issued citations to appear in court, but according to Henry their crimes would be listed in the local newspaper. He'd shouted into his mobile phone the entire way back to the house.

Somehow Paul managed to laugh harder.

"You think it's funny? I'm CFO of the goddamn company, Paul!"

Paul collapsed, pounding one bare foot against the carpet as he gasped with breathless amusement.

Fear thundering through her, Sarah swung her hands above her head and brought them down hard. "Both of you stop!" The entire house vibrated with her anger; windows and dishes rattled and something upstairs thudded to the floor. "I lost my job!"

Had a pet hamster in third grade. Made a tape of breasts cut from movies in college. Earned his first $10,000 with it.

"Sarah, I told you not to worry! It's an easily replaceable job!" Henry frowned at her. "You're a clerk! I could get you a dozen jobs in my company alone—at least until this all gets back to Dallas. Dammit, don't overreact!"

Paul sobered in an instant. "Don't swear at her, Henry."

"Fuck that! This is going to cost us millions!"

"Don't be absurd," said Paul, wiping his eyes. "Even if word gets back to the stockholders, so what? You made out with—well, it's going to look like the other woman I hope you realize, since everyone knows you're engaged to Kathleen. But still, it's hardly the crime of the century to attempt a hook up in a car!"

"There was another man involved!"

"What? Who?" asked Paul, hoisting himself back onto the couch. "Just what were you two doing?"

"It was a misunderstanding!" Sarah protested. "The stupid logic spell caught this guy at work in the aftershock. He thought— shit, I don't know what he thought! It was so long coming and subtle I didn't realize how it was affecting him!" Sarah stalked back and forth, frantic. She *should* have seen it coming. It made perfect sense the aftershock would suck Avery in. She buried her face in her hands. "I thought it was a small aftershock! I should have known better! It's never small!"

Dozens of spells ticker taped through her mind. It would require major casting on a dozen people to fix the mess at this point. She could almost feel the dark matter in the basement pressing against the floorboards beneath her feet, anxious to help. "Shit! What am I going to do? I need that job!" Sarah pressed her hands against her mouth, fighting the sobs building up in her chest.

"Come on, kitten! I'll find you a job. Even if I lose mine I can find you a clerk job," said Henry. "If you need money, I can help you with that too. Don't worry! Please, don't cry!"

"It's not that simple," Paul told him. "She needs repetition to soothe herself. It's like that autistic kid you have in the mailroom at the Dallas office. You couldn't stick him in any mailroom, he fits into yours. Sarah needs *this* job." Paul pushed to his feet and went to her, offering a hug. "Hey, you'll figure something out."

"Yeah," she said through tears. "Sure I will. I always do. That's not it. Don't you understand? I could make it go away in the next hour by casting. The dark is always there waiting to help. I can't get away from it, not for long. I'm doomed!"

"No, you're not. You're not going to have to cast to fix this. Tell me exactly what happened and who was involved. We'll figure this out together. I'll help you."

"There's no way. My boss, H.R., and security made that perfectly clear. I'm out."

"You've already made up your mind, haven't you? You say you want to give up casting, but it's your first line of defense. If you don't want to cast, Sarah, you have to find other ways to get what you need."

"There is no other way!"

"Fine! Don't even try. Give up. Cast away. It's your choice and your life."

"Wait," Henry interrupted. "Ya'll are serious, aren't you? You both believe a bunch of mumbo jumbo—just words that you say from here could change what happened?"

"No," Paul answered. "She can't change what already happened! Don't be ridiculous. She can only change what will happen."

"Do you really believe this stuff, Paul? You actually believe Sarah can change the future?"

"Is that really so hard to believe? We can all affect the future. You say you're in love with her and you don't even believe she's really a witch! Did you not notice the entire house shook because she swung her arms? Did you not see what happened in the basement yesterday? Did you not participate in a spell this morning? How deep in denial are you?"

"I'm not saying she doesn't have telekinesis. She did staple me to the door! I'm not pretending to understand it. I saw it! Still, come on, Paul, there's no such thing as witches! No offense, kitten," he added to Sarah, then looked back to Paul. "Sarah simply believes what she was taught. It's a mindset that she's been programmed to believe. I can understand that, but you have no excuse."

"So are oil barons a mindset. Henry, who else has a box of bones in the basement and spell books in the attic? You claim to love her, brother, but you can't even accept what she is!"

"Stop arguing over semantics!" said Sarah, extricating herself from Paul to pace over an antique Persian rug. Her hands shook. "Call me what you will, but there's a war going on in the universe between darkness and light and I don't want my soul going to the dark side. It is winning you know! This fight isn't just about me! You're all part of it no matter what you believe!"

"Hey!" Paul kept pace beside her. "You're not in this alone, and you don't need to go into battle right this second. Go upstairs and take a hot bath, have a nap, and come have dinner in your pajamas. Then we'll plot and plan over my lasagna."

"Witches don't take naps!"

"Try. Listen, they cannot fire you for kissing your boyfriend in your car." Paul looked at his brother. "Can they, Mr. CFO?"

Henry made a face. "She had her top down. So maybe."

Paul glared at him and said evenly, "Wardrobe malfunction. While Sarah takes her nap, you'd better go ice your face, bro. You look like you were dragged behind a horse. I hope you at least punched the guy back."

POUNDING WOKE SARAH. The first thought that came to mind was Paul hadn't gotten her out of bed for lasagna. She sat up and turned on her bedroom light to check the time. The clock flashed ten minutes after midnight.

I haven't eaten for an entire day almost. It felt like a medical emergency.

The second thing that came to mind was the memory of Mass Power and Light security guards taking her badge.

Sarah threw herself against the pillow. A few tears escaped down her cheeks and into her ears. She rubbed her eyes furiously, and realized too late she was grinding mascara over her face.

The pounding continued to thunder through the house. Sarah sat up, threw the covers off, and crammed her feet into ruby red slippers. Witches were not without a sense of humor. The sparkly slippers were the last thing Aunt Lily had given her.

She slapped light switches on as she hurried downstairs. From the noise level she half expected the guys to be tearing down a wall or dragging dangerous things out of the basement, but apparently they'd gone to bed *and* gone deaf.

Those bastards better not have eaten all the lasagna!

It took her a moment to realize the pounding came from the front door. Visions of reporters crowded into her imagination. Her brief flash of boob in the parking lot probably wasn't worthy of television news coverage, though. Sarah stalked to the front door and yanked it open.

The woman pounding nearly fell inside.

"You'd better be drunk," Sarah told her.

The tall blonde straightened, adjusting a fringed pink scarf. "Not a day in my life. I'm Kathleen Karrie. I'm here to see my fiancé, Henry Longfellow."

The sentence rendered Sarah speechless.

Kathleen shifted impatiently from one long leg to another.

Sarah remembered to close her mouth and drew herself up to her full height. It wasn't very impressive next to Kathleen Karrie.

"Do you mind if I wait inside?" The tall blonde crossed her suntanned arms, shivering in the sixty-degree temperature.

"I think you have the wrong house," Sarah lied.

"I tracked his phone, and I can see his shoes." Kathleen pointed at a pair of loafers next to a jumble of Sarah's shoes. She put one hand on a slim hip and tugged her roller bag closer with the other. "I know he's here, sweetheart."

"Henry's asleep. You'll need to come back later."

"I don't think so," said Kathleen. She pushed past Sarah, wheeling her roller bag over the toe of a witch slipper. The woman looked around the spacious entry for a moment before turning back. "Where is he? I'd be happy to wake him myself."

Sarah put a hand on her own hip and looked Kathleen up and down, determined to ignore the mean girl attitude. Kathleen looked like a Victoria's Secret model, complete with big perfect blonde hair and artfully drawn eyebrows. It made Sarah aware of her own frumpy sweats and braless sag. Unconsciously a hand flew to her hair and she remembered she'd gone to sleep with it wet. It now stuck up far bigger than the Texas fiancée's. It didn't take a mirror to know she looked like a witch. She dropped her hand without trying to change the truth.

"What's going on?" said a male voice from the kitchen.

Both women spun to see Paul crossing the foyer, barefoot in only his gym shorts, his horse tattoo more visible than Sarah had ever seen it. "Sarah, what are you pounding on?" he asked, rubbing his eyes.

"Hello, Paul," said the fiancée with a serious Texas twang.

"Kathleen!" Paul seemed to wake up quickly. "Uh, I didn't know you were coming."

Henry appeared right behind Paul in striped cotton pajamas. He smiled at Sarah. "Hey, kitten! You're up!"

Kathleen whipped her head around to stare at Sarah, her jaw dropping. Apparently she hadn't put one and one together to come up with Henry and Sarah as a couple. Disbelieving eyes examined Sarah from head to foot, pausing on every flaw—unkempt hair, imperfect skin, breasts hanging around town without support, slight belly bulge, and soft thighs in baggy sweats.

Kathleen arched a flawless brow and drawled, "All right, so *you're* his *someone else*? That didn't take long. And he calls you kitten too? How nice."

Henry froze. "Kathleen?"

Avoids confrontation, except with lawyers. Always sleeps in pajamas.

Kathleen turned her attention back to him. "Henry. I hope you don't mind my stopping by without calling. It's just that after four years I think I deserve more than a text that says, *Sorry, I met someone else.*"

"Oh," said Henry. "Ah." He nodded. "Yes."

"Dear Lord! What happened to your face?"

Henry didn't answer, but Paul chuckled. "You might want to start with something less combustible." He crossed his arms over his bare chest as silence descended.

Kathleen shot one accusatory glance at Sarah and waited, her long fingers clenching and unclenching the handle of her bag. Henry's gaze flitted between both women, settling at last on Sarah. Kathleen's fingers froze in their clenched position until they turned bone white. Sarah's stomach snarled, and she had to pee. She knew whoever spoke first lost. She understood power plays, and she'd piss herself before losing this one.

"So, awkward," said Paul. "Anyone want a glass of wine? Some midnight lasagna? I know you do, Sarah." He turned and shuffled back toward the kitchen, and Henry hurried to follow.

After another brief moment of silence and a short staring contest, Kathleen went too. Sarah stopped in the half-bath off the hallway. She peed, but left her hair and face alone. Even if her mascara looked like Marilyn Manson's, there was no way she'd fix anything for the ex-fiancée. She had her own version of mean girl and she called it *bitch witch.*

All the kitchen lights were on, and Kathleen's roller bag sat next to the island. She sat perched on the edge of a kitchen stool. Sarah watched her adjust diamond jewelry and smooth her hair like she was putting the finishing touches on an art exhibit.

"Are Mom and Dad okay?" asked Paul as he dug food out of the refrigerator. Henry hid behind him.

"Your mom and dad didn't believe it when I told them. They assumed Henry's text was some sort of mistake or a really bad joke, which is a reasonable assumption. I thought so too until I realized Henry had *blocked* my number." Kathleen hooked her heels over the bottom rung of the stool, glaring at Henry. He now shadowed Paul, feigning helping him carry a plate of lasagna to the microwave, as though it took two men in their thirties to carry a single slice of lasagna.

Obviously I'm going to have to take care of this myself.

Sarah took the stool right beside Kathleen. Mockingly she adjusted the cuffs of her sweatshirt and smoothed the front so that the green glitter letters of the word *Wicked* laid flat against her plentiful breasts. She made exaggerated motions patting her snarly mess of hair. Paul rolled his eyes at her.

"I'm Sarah Archer, by the way. Henry's *new* girlfriend."

Kathleen turned to her and offered her hand, clasping Sarah's smaller one warmly and smiling a gracious southern smile. "Kathleen Karrie, Henry's *fiancée*." Her smile vanished on the last word and she let Sarah's hand drop, turning her attention back to the men.

"Would you like some lasagna too?" Henry asked, not quite meeting Kathleen's eyes as he pushed silverware and a napkin across the counter for Sarah.

"You know I don't eat this late."

"Uh, that's right. How about a glass of wine?" Henry slid an empty goblet in front of Sarah and held the second one while he awaited Kathleen's permission. He seemed incapable of making direct eye contact.

"That would be nice."

Paul walked up behind his brother with an armload of wine bottles. "Is it okay if we open these, Sarah? You have enough bottles around the house. I don't know much about wine, but based on the years I think the best we can hope for is a glass of vinegar."

Kathleen leaned forward, eyeing the bottles. "Henry! Did you look at these? Good gracious, there's a Vino Nobile di Montepulciano from Tuscany!"

"Really?" Henry plucked a bottle from Paul's arms as his brother unloaded them onto the counter. "This one is a Brunello from the eighties! Sarah, you'll want to save these. They're valuable!"

"Might as well open them tonight. It's not every day your *fiancée* meets your girlfriend," she said.

"Uh," said Henry, his confidence going from investor to intern. "Um. Yes. Wine would be nice. You know, I'm uncomfortable wearing this and drinking those though. Excuse me while I go put on something more appropriate." He scampered out of the kitchen in his striped pajamas.

Paul grabbed a corkscrew and went to work on a bottle. "So you must have gotten a flight this morning, Kathleen? How long after that text did it take you to get to the airport?" His grin couldn't have gotten wider without hurting something in his jaw.

"Don't you want to go put on a shirt, Paul?" replied Kathleen.

"I'm comfortable." He eyed Sarah's hair and added, "And I think I fit right in." Somehow the grin grew wider as he fumbled with the corkscrew and bottle. Sarah reached over the counter and nabbed both off him as the microwave beeped.

Paul moved toward it. "By the way, we did try to wake you at dinner."

Sarah curled her toes in the sparkly slippers over a chair rung and set to work opening the wine bottle. "You must not have tried too hard because I sure didn't hear you, and I'm not exactly a deep sleeper."

"I even texted you. About four times. Did you leave your phone on mute?"

She almost dropped the bottle. "Crap. I left my cell phone on my desk at work!"

Paul set the plate of lasagna in front of her, his smile fading. "Don't worry. We'll get it. You're going back soon enough anyway. I promise."

Thankfully he didn't elaborate in front of Kathleen. Sarah yanked the cork out of the bottle and attempted to pour into Kathleen's glass.

The woman stopped her with a bejeweled hand over her goblet. "You have to let it breathe!"

Sarah poured herself a glass and handed the bottle to Paul. He poured it into his and Henry's glasses and left the bottle to breathe next to Kathleen.

Raising his goblet toward Sarah, he said, "May you live in interesting times."

Sarah clinked her glass against his. "Fuck you, Paul."

Ignoring Kathleen's startled gasp, Sarah gulped the wine. It had been three years since she'd had anything to drink. *No, longer than that. I was afraid to drink or eat for months before they died.* The memory of why sent a shiver up her back and she polished off the entire glass, not sure if it was good or not. It tasted like dark memories.

Paul watched her beneath raised brows. "Impressive. You must have been fun in college."

Sarah burped against the back of her hand and picked up her fork, ignoring the look she sensed Kathleen giving her.

Henry returned, dressed in khakis and a pinstriped button down shirt with his hair artfully arranged. Five o'clock shadow made him look like a cover from a dreamy romance novel. The black eye only added a dash of pirate. Sarah frowned when he filled Kathleen's glass before hers. Apparently it had breathed enough, because she didn't object.

Polite. Has never ridden a roller coaster. Doesn't like women who swear.

"You do drink, don't you, kitten?" he asked Sarah as he poured her a second glass.

"Quite well," Kathleen murmured beside her, reaching for her cut crystal goblet. "Heavyweight contender potential."

Vinegar. The spell slid out of Sarah. *Sheath your claws, catty bitch! Enjoy a glass of vinegar!* It didn't take more than a drop of dark matter to accomplish.

Not an ounce of remorse followed the cast. Sarah hacked off a piece of lasagna with the edge of her fork and jammed it into her mouth. It tasted delicious. *Paul shouldn't be an EMT; he should be a chef at some Italian restaurant.*

From the corner of her eye Sarah watched Kathleen lift her goblet, sniff appreciatively, and take a large sip. She held it in her mouth a moment before swallowing.

Across the counter Henry did the same, closing his eyes. "This is fantastic! It reminds me of Venice. Remember that bottle of *Frá a Broli* we had that time at Osteria Bancogiro on the Grand Canal?"

Sarah shoveled lasagna into her mouth, glaring.

Kathleen took another sip and seemed to consider. "That was a lovely trip. Of course I remember. We stayed at that little pension on Murano." She smiled at Henry and took a third sip of wine.

What the fuck? I know it worked! Sarah grabbed her own glass of wine, fully expecting it to taste like vinegar now. The aftershock of the little cast hovered over her like a fart, but her wine tasted fine. After several uneventful gulps, she set it down and shoved another huge mouthful of lasagna into her mouth.

Cat food.

It tasted like a slimy hunk of solid, warm cat food. Sarah's eyes watered. There was no way she could swallow it. It took every ounce of self-control to keep her gag reflex under control. She leaned forward and let it fall out of her mouth onto the plate. Henry and Kathleen were smiling over their shared memories of Venice, but Paul put a hand on the counter and leaned forward.

"What's wrong with it?"

"Nothing. It was too hot," Sarah lied, wiping her tongue off with a napkin. Paul narrowed his eyes at her and glanced at Kathleen as she took another sip of wine.

Bitch! Sarah couldn't believe the woman could drink it. Something like admiration stirred within her. She stuffed it down and kicked it a few times, refusing to appreciate anything in the snooty picture perfect ex.

"Henry?" Sarah asked.

"Hmm, kitten?" he replied, still smiling at Kathleen.

"Is there any more chocolate lasagna?"

"I don't know. Is there, Paul?" Henry passed the chore to his brother without even looking at Sarah.

Paul grinned at Sarah. "There is, kitten. You want to have it in the living room with a couple bottles of wine?"

Sarcastic self-satisfied bastard.

chapter fourteen

Human Sacrifice

Henry sat next to Sarah on the sofa. With Kathleen on a wing-back chair behind him, out of his direct line of vision, he had eyes only for Sarah again. She sat cross-legged, working on her second glass of wine and annihilating a huge slice of chocolate lasagna as Henry stroked her knee through a hole in her sweat-pants. Kathleen sipped her wine and reminisced about Venice.

"Remember we rode a gondola? You sang *La Donna e Mobile* to me, and proposed under the Rialto Bridge."

Sarah almost choked on her dessert. "You proposed?" she said through a mouthful of chocolate and whipped cream. "You said you'd never officially proposed!"

Henry's dark eyes widened and he wiped a bit of whipped cream off Sarah's lips with his thumb. "No, no, kitten. I said I never gave her a ring, so it wasn't official. I wouldn't lie to you!"

"Maybe it wasn't official, but Henry has proposed to me—hmm—three times," Kathleen said. "He used to say he was practicing for the real thing, once for every year we've been together, until he got it perfect."

"You proposed *three* times?" Sarah whispered against his thumb.

"There were going to be four, total," he said, looking guilty. The Jack Sparrow eyes had turned Edward Scissorhands-sad. "The fourth would have been the real one. But I never got to that one!"

"And the theme of each proposal was our first four dates! The first proposal was in the Grand Canal in Italy, because on our first real date we had Italian food. I actually went out with Paul that time. He'd made me eggplant parmesan, and Henry crashed our dinner. We always considered that our first date."

Henry grinned, nodding in agreement. "I crashed their date and stole the girl. Paul was so mad."

"I was not! I knew she was better for you!"

"No, you didn't!" Henry said, laughing at his brother. "You just gave in graciously! You knew Kathleen didn't want you."

"I knew you two belonged together," he corrected.

Sarah jutted her lower lip out. Henry quickly leaned in to kiss it, tucking a strand of hair behind her ear. "Sorry! You know you're my kitten, don't you?"

"Yeah, your second kitten," muttered Paul.

"The second proposal was beneath the Eiffel Tower at night," Kathleen continued, "because our second date was for French food. You gave me these diamond earrings from Tiffany's in Paris, to go with the drop necklace you'd given me in Italy."

Sarah couldn't stop herself from looking at Kathleen. The woman tugged her earlobe out from beneath all the perfect hair to show off. The ostentatious earring looked like something Aunt Lily would have worn. Even in the lamplight of the living room the diamonds in the matching necklace were blinding.

Henry fingered Sarah's bare, unpierced earlobe. "Hey," he whispered. "There's a Tiffany's in Boston. I'll get you anything you like. Everything you like." He smiled and Sarah's heart sank. She thought of Aunt Lily's never-ending incoming gifts from besought men, of the way both Lily and her mother had used men, and her heart sank lower. Jewels and gems gathered dust in boxes and drawers all over the house. Why did she feel jealous of Kathleen's? In a house full of treasures, why did she suddenly want more diamonds? She would never wear them.

From the other sofa Paul watched her, his brown eyes intense. Sarah knew exactly what he was thinking. He'd said it often enough. *It's the spell, Sarah. He doesn't love you. He loves Kathleen.*

A suffocating band of pain squeezed Sarah's heart.

It's the spell. It's all just a spell.

"Do you think it will be the same?" said Kathleen in a low voice. "If you give her diamonds and call her kitten, do you think it can ever be the same as what we've had, Henry?" She took another sip of her vinegary wine without a shudder and met Sarah's eyes.

Sarah's witch senses told her exactly what Kathleen was thinking. *"Do you? Whatever hold you have on him isn't real."* She turned her eyes to Henry's and saw his confusion.

"Chi su quel seno non liba amore!" sang Kathleen, the Italian quite poor with her accent and lack of talent.

Whatever the words meant to Henry wiped confusion from his eyes. They crinkled at the corners as a smile lit his lips. Henry's hand worrying the knee of Sarah's pants moved as he twisted around to look at Kathleen.

Sarah's spell spewed more facts. *Kathleen understands him like no other woman ever has. She drinks the exact same wines he does. He knows she thinks wine tastes like vinegar, but drinks it for him.*

Chi su quel seno non liba amore!

Who on that bosom does not drink love!

Jealousy torched through Sarah. The pain in her heart turned to fiery anger.

No! She's doing her own type of casting!

Regular bitches weren't without their own kind of magic. Sarah refused to allow Kathleen's poison words to affect Henry. *Drink love? Drink poison, you bitch!*

A furious spell sizzled from Sarah's heart and she pushed it free with a pleasured sigh, shivering from the thrill of it. A faint whistling sound cantered around the edges of the room, as if a demon had been released. It sounded similar to the sound in the Target parking lot weeks ago.

Sarah turned her eyes to meet Paul's alarmed ones. Hot dark matter shot through the floorboards to help with the spell, warming the soles of Sarah's feet right through the couch, snaking along her legs, touching her *there* and *there,* offering delicious rewards of approval as the spell circled the room.

"The third proposal was in Dubai, and Henry gave me a platinum bracelet that looks like jack-up rigs studded with diamonds. Our third date had been to meet his parents. We'd known then that we belonged together. We're both from oil families, so we understand each other like a pair of jack-up rigs." Kathleen swirled her glass of vinegar wine, once again meeting Sarah's gaze.

She raised her glass to drain the last of it and both Paul and Sarah shouted as the spell hit, "Don't drink it!"

Too late. She downed every drop.

MAYBE IT WAS the fact that both Sarah and Paul rushed her, or maybe it was the spell acting that fast, but Kathleen toppled backward with the chair, clutching her chest.

"Ah, Lord, Sarah. What did you do?" whispered Paul.

I didn't mean it!

Like hell.

"What's going on?" asked Henry, rising from the couch slowly.

"Call 911," demanded Paul. Kathleen's breath came in short gasps. Foamy spittle gathered in the corners of her lips.

Memories crashed over Sarah. The last months that she'd tried so hard to block, the months before they'd died. Dark matter had demanded complete sacrifice and complete obedience from both Aunt Lily and her mother. There had been so many innocent victims.

Strange men, lured into a hotel room and left almost lifeless, immobile and staring as the three of them packed to leave before anyone noticed.

Angry young wives at the front door, shouting into Aunt Lily's laughing face. They hadn't been so young when they left.

The little girl. Sarah put her hand over her heart as she remembered. She'd been clever and bright, wearing a Batman shirt, waving a school form selling candy and wrapping paper. She happened to knock on the door when they needed her. *"Fate,"* Aunt Lily had laughed. *"Dark matter thinks of everything!"*

"She looks like you did," said Sarah's mother.

"The coloring and everything!" said Aunt Lily as they leaned over her, petting her as they'd once doted and loved on Sarah.

*But...but...*A shiver rippled through Sarah. *But when she left, she wasn't clever and bright anymore.*

She squeezed her eyes shut, trying to shut out the memory.

Paul's voice intruded. "Henry! Listen to me. Call an ambulance! Now!"

Sarah opened her eyes. Paul knelt beside Kathleen, trying to force her mouth open.

"I don't understand! What's going on?" asked Henry. He sounded half-asleep. He sounded bound into a spell.

Sarah dropped to her knees, staring at Kathleen. *She's not clever and bright anymore.*

"Sarah cast a spell on her! Dial the goddamn number now!" Kathleen's body spasmed, her arms and legs rigid as her torso trembled beneath Paul's hands.

"There's no such thing as a spell," said Henry, but he sounded doubtful and Sarah heard the clicking of his cell phone as he dialed.

Beneath her she sensed dark matter stirring. It stretched throughout the entire length of the house, like a languorous dragon waking.

Henry spoke into the phone in a wooden voice. He moved closer and bent over to peer at Kathleen, speaking into his phone. "Oh, dear God, something is wrong! What kind of poison? They want to know what kind?" he asked.

Paul looked at Sarah, but she couldn't answer. Dark matter called to the night sky for more, licking her hands and feet with approval, distracting her.

"Kathleen Karrie, she's twenty-nine, and I'm certain she's not on drugs," said Henry.

"Sarah!" Paul shouted at her. "Look at me! Is this who you are? You have a choice. Right now you have a choice. It will be gone soon, and too late. But right now, you still have a choice."

She shook her head at him. There was never any choice. Not really. She'd been so stupid.

"Look at her! She won't be okay. Is that what you want?"

She won't be clever and bright anymore.

"Is this who you are?"

No.

"No," Sarah whispered, still shaking her head. She did not want this. She did not want to be this.

"No!" she said it louder. "I don't want this." The heat licking its way over her skin turned sharp; beneath her, dark matter growled. *Too late. You've chosen.* "I changed my mind!" said Sarah, pushing to stand as the sharp touch on her skin heated, flaming over her like lit matches. "I said I changed my mind. It's my right! I rescind and claim it for myself times *ten*! Fuck you!"

"Sarah, what are you doing?" said Paul. "What does that mean?"

The entire house shook, and a low rumble moved through it.

"What the hell?" said Henry.

Too late. It growled through Sarah's bones. *You've chosen.*

Yes, I have, and I haven't chosen you. Come what may. Bring it.

The house rumbled again, and the sound of glass falling and breaking echoed through it.

"Sarah! What's going on? What does this mean?" Paul shouted at her. He held Kathleen across his lap. Henry sat beside them with tears streaming down his face.

Love of his life. Mother of the children he'd hoped to someday have. The only woman he ever wanted to marry.

Something inside Sarah, somewhere in the vicinity of her heart, twisted with new pain and broke. "It means I'll never be clever and bright again."

THE YOWLING OF cats in heat woke Sarah. She opened her eyes as they batted against her bedroom window, trying to get in. *I threw the food away. Why are they back?* She reached for her cell phone to call animal control to come take away strays again, but she couldn't find it.

No, wait. She couldn't reach for it because she didn't have any arms.

Aunt Lily shoved open the bedroom door and peeked inside.

"Lazy bitch," she teased in her deep voice. "Stop reporting the cats. You don't even like them. Would you rather I used some*one* instead?" Lily put the emphasis on *one*, her slanted feline eyes glittered but she grinned when she said it. The smile stretched the skin tighter across her face, and Sarah could see the way dark matter flowed beneath her flawless skin, writhing like snakes.

She tried to answer her aunt. She tried to open her mouth but she couldn't find that, either. It had gone with her arms.

Lily opened her lips; they were puffy from far too much filler. She opened them wider and dark matter flowed out, looking like a giant snake. It shot across the room with its maw open and swallowed Sarah. Without a mouth she couldn't even scream.

She lived inside the belly of dark matter. Its stomach acid burned her.

It lit her on fire and gnawed on her bones, turning her to charcoal.

Mother sat next to the pilot inside a cockpit, wedged into his seat. Sarah kept her eyes on the view of the Grand Canyon below, refusing to see what was happening to him. Refusing to know she had no body. Behind them in the main cabin, Aunt Lily straddled the co-pilot's lap. Sarah knew what was happening to him. His happy but pained grunts echoed through the small plane.

"Mother, you've taken enough," Sarah heard herself say.

"Go sit in the back," Mother replied.

Sarah could see their reflection in the windshield. The pilot's head looked limp between her mother's hands. "No, Mother. His heartrate is too high. Someone has to land the plane. I can't!" Even if she had hands she didn't know how.

"Tell Lily to stop! Why does it always have to be me?"

Despite the fact that she had no body, Sarah knew she sat in the co-pilot's seat. "Mother, you've lost control. You're acting worse than grandmother did at the end!"

That got through. Mother let go of the pilot. He slowly shook his head, trying to reorient himself. Relief shot through Sarah.

This is the last time I flew with them.

The realization came sudden and she tried to look down, to see herself as the memory returned, but she couldn't move. She recalled this day like a memory even as she sat there. This was the day she'd begun to wonder if dark matter really wanted the energy or essence it demanded. Did it actually consume a decade or two of a man's life, or a woman's youth? Or did it want to detach a witch's soul by forcing her to make such offers? Maybe it was both. Lily and her mother had gone from hurting animals to people in the bat of an eye.

Somehow the plane landed. Somehow Sarah now sat inside the little terminal of the private airport, still without a body. Aunt Lily and Mother sat beside her, watching her with guilty eyes and apologizing.

"It's so hard to tell anymore."

"Sometimes we lose ourselves."

"That's why we need you to remind us."

They waited for an answer. Sarah couldn't reply. They were gone and she was at home with her body again. It worked fine.

SARAH APPLIED FINISHING touches to her face; a bit of eyeliner made ice-blue eyes pop against black lashes. She ignored the doorbell echoing up the stairs. Someone must have come early. Tonight the entire coven would gather. The autumnal equinox was a big deal for some. The Archers weren't particularly devoted, or into ceremony. *Or company much, anymore.*

Sarah hoped no one would comment on Aunt Lily's looks.

She grabbed a tissue and wiped the makeup off.

No reason to upset her. Besides, who cares?

From downstairs came the cackle of mother's laughter and Sarah glanced at the clock. She slipped into her heels and hurried downstairs.

Gray rushed past, her arms loaded with linens for the dining room. Sarah barely glanced at the ghost of a woman. Gray cleaned the house and cooked, and rarely said a word. Like the rest of her family, Sarah often forgot she was there.

Sarah headed for the kitchen to see if any food was ready. Before she got to the archway, Gray stepped in front of her and Sarah nearly plowed into her. Their eyes met, and for a moment

Sarah wondered if she'd ever looked at Gray's face before. She had ruddy, windburn cheeks and droopy brown eyes. The woman swallowed and nervously chewed her lip.

"What's wrong?" Sarah asked.

Frightened eyes stared meaningfully back at her before glancing in the direction of the doorway. Sarah could hear a faint childish giggle, her mother murmuring, and the rustling of Aunt Lily's silk skirts. Slinky dresses and bare midriffs had given way to old-fashioned gowns and occasional cloaks. They hid the cost of a lifetime of casting.

"Is that your Halloween costume?" a little girl's voice asked. "I'm going to be Batman. Daddy thinks I should be Catwoman, but I'm going to be Batman anyway."

Sarah moved past Gray and the large bureau near the entryway and stopped. Mother knelt beside a little girl, a scrawny arm around her shoulders as if hugging her. An expression of wicked glee made her look almost as bad as Aunt Lily. Lily stood blocking the open door, a fake smile plastered on her skeletal face. Thick makeup and perfect hair did nothing to hide the monster inside. She moved forward until her gown touched the child, and reached a bony hand toward her. Blood-red fingernails glistened.

"Do you want to fly, little one? Like Batman?"

"Batman doesn't fly!" said the girl. "But if I sell five hundred dollars in candy and wrapping paper, I can get his mask!"

"I can make you fly!" said Aunt Lily, clearly not listening to the child.

Sarah saw dark matter oozing from her mother's arm and Aunt Lily's hand, drifting over the little girl. Perspiration beaded across the child's unwrinkled forehead and her fine skin grew paler by the second. The trusting smile didn't waver.

"What's going on?" asked Sarah, stepping into view. "Are you selling something for Batman?"

The smile grew wider, and the girl waved a form with one hand and a thin glossy brochure with the other. "No, silly! For school! But I can win a real Batman mask if I sell enough!"

"We'll take it all," said Aunt Lily, running chicken bone fingers through dark waves of thick hair. "Everything!"

The little girl stiffened and her eyes widened. "For reals? Goody!" she squealed, and jumped up and down, fading right before Sarah's eyes.

"She reminds me of you!" said Mother, squeezing the girl closer, making motions like air kisses with her lips.

Sarah knew she was consuming her, and her stomach dropped. She barely heard Aunt Lily's murmurs of agreement.

Sarah tried to keep her voice calm. "Mother, go get your pocketbook. You're going to need it if you're going to buy enough for her to win a Batman mask! Aunt Lily, will you nab mine, too, when you go upstairs to get yours?" Sarah needed only seconds alone to send the kid safely packing.

They saw right through her. Both the women frowned as the girl looked up at them expectantly.

"Grab my checkbook, Sarah," Mother said. "It's in the desk right there."

Lily beamed at her sister.

"My tummy hurts," said the little girl.

"No, it doesn't," said Aunt Lily.

"No, it doesn't," echoed the girl, but her papers fluttered to the floor as she hunched over and clutched at her stomach.

"She's a neighbor!" said Sarah. "Where are her parents?"

Both women leered. Lily answered, "Our clever girl snuck out."

"Gonna. Surprise. Daddy," the child whimpered, her pallor turning quickly from white to grey. Mother supported her as her legs gave out.

"No," said Sarah. "Stop it. You're really hurting her!"

The little girl's eyes went wide, locking on Sarah's with the first trace of fear in them.

"You stop it, Daughter!" said Mother. Her lips reached the girl's cheek like a kiss to whisper, "We're not hurting you. We're your friends."

The child smiled faintly, a hand grasping Aunt Lily's gown. "Um, kay." Her head rolled loosely on her neck, dropping forward.

"I said no!" Sarah stepped forward and wrapped her arms around the limp girl, wresting her from them. She backed away, holding the girl to her.

Both women turned on Sarah, shoving her and the little girl against the wall with a flick of their wrists. "Who do you think you are? Who do you think provides for your needs? We do! We always have! Why do you think we need so much?" said Mother.

Aunt Lily growled, reaching for the girl. "Let go of her!"

"Gray! Call the police!"

Both women laughed. Sarah held the limp child tightly, trying to protect her from their reaching hands. For a moment they grappled; Lily attempting to pry Sarah's hands loose and mother tugging on the girl. Something changed though, and they both stopped fighting Sarah at the same instant. For a second Sarah thought her mother had regained some sense. Her lips pressed against Sarah's cheek as though to offer a token of gratitude. Then she noticed Lily's mortified expression.

"Sissy, no," said Aunt Lily. "She's your daughter."

Mother turned her head to respond, her fingers now running down Sarah's cheek. "Dark matter flows through her. It's intoxicating. Taste."

Lily licked her lips.

Despair ripped through Sarah's heart, taking her breath, and she squeezed her eyes shut. She didn't want to see what they'd become, and her strangled words came out with angry sobs. "Go ahead then, both of you, if this is what you've become! If you're going to kill children, you might as well have your own too! I won't fight! You don't have to waste a cast on me!"

"Open your eyes," said a man's voice. "Sarah, I know you can hear me. Open your eyes. Kathleen is going to be okay, don't cry. Do you hear me, Sarah? It's Paul."

Sarah's body disappeared again, along with her mother, Aunt Lily and the little girl.

It took time for Sarah to know anything. It took time to really feel the pain, to feel dark matter again gnawing on her blackened bones as she floated in lava. Between those times she disappeared without a conscious thought. Nothing was the bearable part. Everything else tried to kill her, searing heat through her bones and icy sharp pain into her stomach. The memory of Paul's disappointed dark eyes scorched her. Henry's didn't, but they were focused on someone else. Somehow that was worse. Sarah didn't struggle as she vanished again.

chapter fifteen

Power and Light

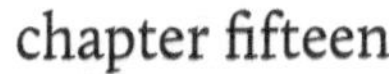

Dark matter roosted inside Sarah, so much she thought the bed would collapse from the sheer weight of it. *Where am I?* She tried to remember what had happened. Memories came with a wave of remorse. She'd cast against Kathleen. Big time.

Big time? You tried to kill her.

No, she argued with herself. *I never meant to kill her. Not for a second.*

You cast poison. You wanted to annihilate her.

No. Not really. How often do people say drop dead without really meaning it? I meant it like that.

Lie to yourself if it helps.

Sarah tried to move but couldn't. She couldn't feel her body, yet the mass of the planet seemed to weigh her down. Her eyes wouldn't open. She wasn't certain how they functioned anymore.

"No change?" an unfamiliar voice asked.

Sarah tried to locate her mouth to answer. All lines were down.

"None." Paul's voice sounded close by.

"Hmph," said the other one. An older woman with a wicked South Boston accent, all misplaced *R's* and jumbled words. "Yanno yaneed to take care of ya-self too, Mr. Longfella. Go home, get some sleep. Maybe take a shower." She pronounced it *sh-ow-wah*.

"I will, after she wakes up."

"Sometimes it takes a while. Have pity on the nursing staff, or at least me. If ya don't care that we have to smell ya, consider that it's entirely possible that Ms. Archa can smell ya." Possible came out *par-sable*.

"Do you think so, Doctor Shaw?" Paul sounded hopeful. If Sarah could have rolled her eyes, she would have.

"It's absolutely par-sable."

The doctor was lying. At least Sarah thought so. She couldn't smell a thing. She couldn't figure out where her nose was or how she was breathing. A rhythmic hissing and beeping in the background offered a horrible clue that she chose to ignore.

"Is it true that the longer she's in the coma, the more unlikely it is that she'll come out of it?"

"You're not getting on the Google, are you? Stay off the Google. Ms. Archa will do what Ms. Archa does. I see some amazing grace in my practice. We're going to get some of that for your friend here."

"Two weeks is a long time though, isn't it?"

"Depends on what you're talking about. I can tell ya that two weeks is too long to go without a shower. You're in a hospital. We keep things sanitary. Your underthings must have disintegrated by now."

Sarah could hear Paul shift uncomfortably in his chair. She would have smiled if she could have found her mouth controls. The doctor was embarrassing him.

The squeak and rattle of a metal tray table with wheels scraping across the floor followed the shuffling of many feet. More people must have entered the room.

"We need to swap out some of these tubes. Are you staying again?"

"Yes."

"Maybe I'll have you do it then. We could leave this stuff here and go take care of another patient who has visitors that bathe regularly."

There was a clacking sound as the bedrails dropped and a low *wup-wup* as blankets were spread. Someone hummed low in their throat, a tune Sarah recognized from church. Dark matter writhed inside her, clawing in protest, and Sarah dropped into a fiery inferno again.

"THERE ONCE WAS a dude from Pawtucket who caught some kelp in a bucket. It tasted like crap, so he threw it all back, and ordered some pizza saying fuck it. That, in a nutshell, is why I'm overweight, Sarah. Just in case you were wondering."

Mindy Millerton!

"I would have brought flowers, but you let the last bunch die. Like you couldn't get your lazy ass up and water them? That's inconsiderate. I spent almost ten dollars on those. Well, not quite ten. I took up a collection at work so technically I made close to a hundred dollars profit. Maybe I will send you some more. At least as long as people keep falling for it—I mean, contributing. You're boring the fuck out of me. Not as much as when you talk, but close. Give me that remote."

A moment later the television clicked on. Sarah listened to an entire episode of Survivor before it abruptly shut off.

"I thought you were going to keep her company!" Paul sounded angry. "You said you'd talk to her the whole time I was gone!"

"I did, but then she wanted to watch some TV."

"She said something?!"

"I could sense it," Mindy said. "You do know she's faking. I could see her eyes moving under her eyelids."

"Even when she's herself, Sarah doesn't watch TV," Paul said, his impatience obvious.

"She could have said."

"You're not funny, please go. I'll find someone else to stay with her next time I have to leave."

"Avery Gross would do it. He'd probably feel her up though, if you left him alone. He's a total perv I heard. Hey, are you the one he punched in the face?"

"No. That was my brother."

"He's still bragging about it at work, like every day. Says you were attacking Sarah in her car and he rescued her and kicked your ass."

"My brother and Sarah were making out in her car. Avery jumped inside uninvited and sucker punched Henry in the face. Once, I think."

"I can't believe you let him get even one punch in. He's kind of a pussy."

"He punched my brother, not me!" Paul said in exasperation.

"Why were you attacking Sarah in her car anyway? I'm pretty sure she puts out fairly easy."

"Mindy, I thought you were her friend."

"She wants more, but I'm really not into her like that. I mean look at her. She just lays there. That doesn't do it for me. I'm guessing it does for you though."

"Maybe you should go," Paul said without humor.

Mindy heaved to her feet. Sarah heard something creak like she'd grabbed onto the bed to pull herself to stand. "Yeah, I've got to get up early tomorrow anyway. Hey, can you think of anything that rhymes with Crapstone?"

"What?"

"Crapstone. It's a town in England. I'm working on a poem for Sarah, but all I can come up with is twat-bone. Not only does that not really rhyme, I don't even know if a twat-bone is a thing. I think

I invented it. In my head, I mean. I don't know. Maybe we could ask one of the doctors about it. Hey, whoa, whoa, mister-mister."

Sarah had a distinct impression Paul had taken hold of Mindy to drag her out of the room.

"Let's not get all handsy," Mindy insisted. "I hardly know you. Is this why Avery punched you? You're making me highly uncomfortable. I could get into it though, now that you smell better."

"Mindy, I can't tell if you're joking around or if you're being serious."

"That's probably why Sarah's dating your brother."

"Goodnight, Mindy."

"Hey, you're going to throw me out now that we're getting to second base? You should see me slide into home."

Sarah heard the door shut, and thought Paul stood there for a moment holding it closed. She assumed Mindy had left when he chuckled and crossed the floor. Although she couldn't feel it, Sarah heard Paul lean over her and adjust blankets.

"You know she claims to be your best friend. I don't know whether to believe her hands-down, or call security when she shows up."

Believe her. The thought warmed Sarah. Dark matter didn't like it. As the feeling waned, searing heat blasted her away from consciousness once more.

"MOM, THIS IS awk-weird. Are you sure she's alive?"

Sarah didn't recognize the young voice.

"Of course I'm sure."

That voice she did recognize. *Jackie Hamilton from Human Resources. What on earth is she doing here?*

The flush of a toilet sounded from nearby, followed by the scrape of a door opening.

"Hello!" Paul sounded surprised.

"Hello, I'm Jackie Hamilton from Mass Power and Light." Sarah could almost see them shaking hands, extra firm and brief, the way Jackie rolled. "This is my daughter Mary Elizabeth. We just stopped by for a moment to pay our—visit."

"It's good of you to come. I'm Paul Revere Longfellow."

Mary Elizabeth snickered and Sarah wondered not for the first time why Paul didn't drop his middle name when introducing himself. *Who does that?*

"Yes, I recognize you," said Jackie.

"From the parking lot? No. That was my brother, Henry. We're twins."

"What's his middle name?" Mary Elizabeth asked.

"You probably guessed it," Paul said, a smile evident in his voice. "Wadsworth."

"Does Henry Wadsworth Longfellow write poetry?" giggled the girl.

"Mary Elizabeth," Jackie admonished her. "You and your brother don't talk like you're from here."

"We're not, although we both went to college up here."

"You did? Where?" asked Jackie, incredulous northern superiority in every syllable.

"Henry went to Harvard, and I went to Bowdoin up in—"

"Really," interrupted Jackie, "your brother went to Harvard? Maybe it's not so tough to get into with your last name."

Sarah just knew Jackie winked as she said that.

"My mom wants me to go to Harvard," explained Mary Elizabeth. "But it's not looking good."

"How's our patient?" asked Jackie, changing the subject.

For a moment Paul didn't answer. When he did, his voice sounded determined. "Fine. Sarah will be fine. She only needs time."

"Yes." Jackie didn't sound like she believed him. "Well, we only stopped by for a minute. If there's anything we can do—"

"There is. You can make sure Sarah has a job to go back to."

"Well, now—"

"That Avery fellow still does, doesn't he? He didn't get fired, and the way I understand it is he went after Sarah uninvited."

"Now, no. I spoke to Avery. Sarah asked him to meet her in the parking lot."

I did not!

"I find that hard to believe. It doesn't make sense that she'd have any interest in another man. Sarah and Henry were rather—close."

Paul sounded uncomfortable saying it, and Sarah appreciated him defending her. *Wait. Were close? Past tense? At least I know how to break a love spell. Go in a coma.* Other than residual surprise that information didn't bother Sarah, but neither did the unpleasant click and hiss of nearby machines she chose to ignore.

Jackie slipped into professional mode. "Mr. Longfellow, I personally saw Ms. Archer and Mr. Gross in an embrace right before the incident."

You did not! You saw that ape manhandling me!

"If that's the case, why is Sarah's job in jeopardy and not Avery's? It sounds like sexism, and frankly I'm surprised you'd allow that."

For a moment the room got so quiet Sarah wondered if she'd passed out and come to after everyone had gone.

"I wouldn't," Jackie said at last. "You can be assured of that. I'm not free to discuss Mr. Gross's situation with anyone outside the company. Suffice to say he was acting in Ms. Archer's best interest as he understood it at the time."

"Which wasn't the case at all."

"Is there any chance that Ms. Archer's medical condition might have affected her judgement during the incident in the parking lot?"

Paul exhaled loudly. "There is every chance of that."

He's thinking about the spell.

"Because if there was a pre-existing medical condition—"

"There definitely was a pre-existing condition."

"I see. I don't know Ms. Archer well, but now that I think on it there was another incident where she came to work acting rather oddly. It was just a matter of a strange choice in clothing for the workplace, but from what I heard at the time it was unusual for her. I'm glad we had this conversation. I'm going to take care of this."

Sarah groaned inside at the memory of the blue dress she'd thought she looked so hot in, but something in her lightened knowing Paul had gotten her job back for her.

"That would be great. Sarah loves working at Mass Power and Light."

"Does she?" Sarah could hear the smile in Jackie's voice. "I do too. Well, I'll do my part for her. You make sure she gets all better now. We've got to get going. I've stayed far longer than I planned."

"Thanks for coming, and thanks for the flowers. Sarah loves flowers."

"One of her co-workers has been taking up a collection for them every week. I've never seen this many flowers anywhere outside of a florist shop."

What? Sarah tried to force her eyes open, desperate to see them. *Dammit! The one time I get flowers from other people!* Inwardly she grinned, falling a bit more deeply in love with Mindy. *That booger is such a liar! If there's that many, she's spending her own money too!*

Dark matter grabbed Sarah somewhere around her middle and yanked her away.

"UT CUSTODIANT TE et seducam te et Dominum nostrum Iesum Christum in vitam aeternam."

The droning words in Latin roused Sarah. Dark matter rocked as though laughing. Even barely conscious, she recognized the monotone chant of a priest. *It lulls me back to sleep even now.*

"What are you doing to her?" Paul asked. He sounded tired.

"It's the Viaticum," answered an old man. Sarah tried to place his vaguely familiar voice.

"What's the Vita—viata—what's that?"

Paul's accent made Sarah smile inside as she attempted a translation of the Latin word "viaticum." *Money for a journey? Something like that...money for provisions?*

"It's commonly called the last rites."

Oh, great! No!

"Isn't that for when people die? Don't do that to her. You said you were going to pray over her. She's not going to die."

"Son, just because I speak the words doesn't mean she won't live. That's in God's hands."

Why is his voice so familiar? All the priests from Our Lady of the Light sounded the same to Sarah.

"But if she hears you, she might believe you. She probably understands Latin. Don't say that prayer just in case."

The priest sighed. "What did you have in mind when you called me?"

What the hell did Paul call a priest for?

"I don't know. Except—do priests really perform exorcisms?"

Don't you dare! Sarah tried to move, but her body wouldn't respond. The rumbling of dark matter increased. It felt like glee.

"Not on witches, Mr. Longfellow. It wouldn't be a good idea, and I'm not altogether certain there'd be anything left of your friend after I was done."

It's Father McCloud! Thank heavens! She recalled the knowing look in his faded eyes.

"You know she's a witch?"

"Yes, I've had the pleasure of meeting Sarah once before."

"You did?" Paul sounded incredulous.

"Yes, I did. As I recall she owes me a shingle."

"Oh, um. Yes. I'm sorry, I'd forgotten about that."

"I hadn't."

"Father, can you tell if she's going to be all right?"

Sarah thought she heard the priest move closer to Paul and pat his shoulder.

"Paul, I'm a priest, not a doctor. What do the doctors say?"

"Doctor Shaw tells me not to give up hope. She says miracles happen all the time."

"I would encourage you to follow her advice."

"It's been a month now. Look at her."

A month? I've been in the hospital for a month? It seemed like moments.

"What's a month to a young life?"

"Can you tell—I mean, do you think the dark side has taken her?"

"That's her decision, not yours or mine or even the other side's," said Father McCloud. "Likely she was promised to the darkness before conception. It's hard for human beings not to do what's expected of them, even when they don't like it."

"She doesn't want to be a witch."

"That's ridiculous. She is a witch. I don't want to be old. But here we both are."

"So there's no hope? She's doomed to evil?"

"I didn't say that. Of course there's hope! There's always hope."

"But what can we do? How can I help her?"

"You're doing it, Mr. Paul Revere. Just don't give up. I'm afraid the rest is up to Sarah."

chapter sixteen

Gotta Go

The harvest moon lolled fat in the sky and October air blew leaves through the night. Sarah couldn't see it, she couldn't see anything, but she could feel it with her witch senses. It was the first thing she'd sensed with them since the night Kathleen had showed up at her door. According to the moon, that was six weeks ago.

Dark matter wrapped around Sarah like Smaug snuggling gold in his lair. Yet for the first time since that night, Sarah could distinguish between herself and dark matter.

That has got to be a good thing, a good sign!

Dark matter shifted, like an enormous snake wrapping tighter, its scales rippling over Sarah's skin. After several moments it stopped and sighed, as if content and comfortable.

That, not so much.

What did Father McCloud say?

"I'm afraid the rest is up to Sarah," echoed through her mind.

That's not very helpful. What exactly is up to me?

Explicit instructions would have been useful. Sarah knew instinctively how to draw dark matter closer; repelling it didn't come naturally. For the past three years all she'd done was ignore it and try to leave it alone.

The piles of books in the attic came to mind, but she knew they'd be of no use even if she could access them now.

Still, I know how to draw dark matter in. Logically, what would chase it away?

I could tell it to go. Sarah considered that for a while. Outside her body she could hear the beeping of that machine and the mechanical hiss of her breathing. *And I can't just do nothing. I have to try something!*

Maybe it is as simple as telling it to go away and leave me alone.

Maybe I've been keeping dark matter nearby just in case I need it, like the crap in the basement.

Maybe that's all Father McCloud meant when he said it was up to me.

Maybe Paul was right when he said I have to find other ways to get what I need.

Permanently.

Could it be as easy as a choice?

The memory of the night she'd rescinded her spell against Kathleen returned.

Other than a few brief moments of lucidity when she could hear what was happening in the outside world, all she'd been aware of had been pain.

There was pain, and then there was dark matter fiery *pain.*

Sarah did not fancy another go of what had already transpired. There would be nothing easy about another battle against dark matter and likely it would all be for nothing. She doubted she could survive it again. *It always wins.* All witches said that. *Why did I think I could be any different?*

Somewhere near the hissing machine, a voice whispered. "Sarah, sweetheart, if you can hear me, do something. Do *anything.*"

Fear vibrated through her, followed by what felt like dark matter licking her entire body with a massive tongue. For once that wasn't a pleasant sensation. It scared her. She wanted it to go away.

If Paul is calling me sweetheart, I'm in trouble.

I'm dying.

I'm really dying. Dark matter is just waiting for me.

Sarah knew it. She hadn't been privy to anything the doctor had said for a while, but judging by the moon it had been about six weeks since the incident.

The thought of telling dark matter to go frightened her. *It's not the pain I'm really afraid of. I'm afraid it will really go away.*

What would she be without dark matter?

What was a witch with no power?

She'd have no defense against the world. *Like everyone else.*

I have two choices. Die with it, or live without it.

Do I want to die and join it?

"*Go,*" Sarah said mentally.

Nothing happened.

"*Go,*" she repeated inside herself, struggling to find real words, certain that dark matter slept around her, content and confident it had her. "*I don't want you! I'm never going to want you again! I don't care what happens to me. I can survive without you!*"

Or not.

Still nothing happened.

Gathering every ounce of strength she could muster, Sarah attempted to shout. It came out a weak breath of stale air as she choked on a tube lodged inside her throat, "Go."

Like a waking volcano, dark matter exploded to life around her. In the midst of being consumed by fiery hot lava, Sarah heard Paul shouting for a doctor. *He heard me!* A mental image of her ears floating and sizzling in a field of molten rock and magma came to mind, and once again darkness descended.

I HAVE TO pee.

Sarah stood knee deep in the Aegean Sea with every intention of getting into deeper water and going. Aunt Lily stood beside her, topless and suntanned, one hand shading her eyes and the other clutching Sarah's.

"You could swim here with us if you hadn't decided to waste your life," Lily said. "But you made your bed. Good luck sleeping in it."

Sarah heard her mother comment from the beach, "Doesn't look like all that schooling helped much."

The beach vanished and Sarah sat alone inside her cubicle at Mass Power and Light, her hand aching with loneliness. She still needed to go something fierce, but now Father McCloud blocked her from exiting the cubicle.

"After you bring my shingle back," he said.

It occurred to Sarah at that point that this was all a dream.

I need to wake up and I can go anywhere I want.

Father McCloud and her cubicle at Mass Power and Light vanished. Red light scorched beneath her eyeballs, shooting pain into her brain like lightning strikes. Sarah lay prone under a blanket that seemed to weigh as much as a building. It held her tightly against the mattress, and she couldn't cast to escape it. Somehow it even held her eyelids closed.

Uselessly she told the blanket, "I want to get up."

"If you cast me off, you can do what you want," said the blanket, the top edge of it forming into a strange dark wrinkle that looked like a mouth. Sarah wondered how she could see it with her eyes closed.

"No," she told it. "I can't cast anymore."

"You can. Just choose to and all will be as it should be."

"I don't want to."

"Yes, you do."

Sarah considered her options until chills rippled through her. She needed to get up, but refused to cooperate with the creepy captive.

"I *have* to get up."

"You know the price."

"I don't need your permission," she said.

"But you do need my help," it told her. "You always will."

Sarah tried to prove that wasn't true. It didn't work. The effort to escape her paralysis made her chills worse, and she shivered miserably beneath the blanket that gave no warmth. The blanket's smile grew wider and darker. Sarah thought she saw dark matter shifting and swirling inside the toothless mouth.

"Get away from me! I told you to go! I'm done with dark matter!" she growled at it. "You're part of it. I know you are. Go away!"

The smiling dark wrinkle grew wider, as if laughing. "You can't make me leave. You can never make me leave. No one can."

This made her mad. "Maybe not, but the light can make you move. I've seen it."

"You are not the light."

"That doesn't mean it won't make you leave me alone!"

"Why would it do anything for you?"

Sarah considered that. Why would it? She had nothing to bargain with. Nothing to offer.

"Do you think light is a better master?"

"I don't care. I would choose light over you."

The blanket snapped up into the air far above her, almost reaching the ceiling, and floated down lightly, landing softly and gently over her. The mouth looked like a smile, but not the dark one. This smile looked like a beam of sunlight.

SARAH OPENED HER eyes. Blinding bright light made them water. The light hit somewhere behind her eyeballs and she sneezed. It ripped through her body with such intensity it felt like her lungs exploded. For a moment she lay motionless and tried to recover, certain she'd at least broken a rib and sneezed a couple teeth loose. Pain spread from ribs to lungs and clawed up to her throat. Sarah willed it away, but it didn't go. Opening her eyes again, she blinked against searing light and swallowed.

Dry agony attacked her aching throat like fingernails cutting flesh. A cross dangled in her line of vision. Henry's necklace. The one Paul always wore.

She stared at the necklace, trying to determine if the thick neck supporting it was really Paul's. Through blurry vision she saw the fine lines of his horse tattoo, the ends of the tail flared against his neck. Tears slipped from her eyes.

I'm alive! I'm awake!

Paul pressed his hands against her cheeks as his thumbs wiped the tears away. "Hey, there you are! Welcome back. Lord, witchy woman, I've missed those wild eyes of yours. You've been out a very long time."

A fresh flood of tears covered his fingers.

"You're going to be okay, Sarah." He leaned forward, pressing his head against her forehead and tenderly patting her shoulders.

Sarah reached to hug him, but her arms wouldn't come. It felt like her weeks of wild dreaming had returned, and for a brief moment she thought she'd lost her body again.

"It's okay!" Paul said. "They have your hands tied down so you couldn't hurt yourself. Hold on."

Fear shot through Sarah, and she yanked on her restraints, attempting to cast herself free. The area in her center that she'd cast from all of her life, felt dry and empty, like a hose filled with nothing but air. *I have no power. Nothing.*

"Don't panic. Come on, you're pulling your IV out."

"Untie me!" Sarah struggled, kicking her legs which were wonderfully free. She focused on the restraints on her hands, willing them off, willing the pain away from her body. Nothing changed.

"Sarah, please. Trust me. I'll get you loose," Paul whispered, his cheek now pressed against hers.

Her chin wobbled with emotion. It wasn't about being tied down. It was being helpless. It was the pain. *I feel everything.* She tried again to will her pain away. *I don't like feeling everything!* "I hurt," she whimpered. *I'm scared!* Saying that out loud would make it worse, but Paul knew. Sarah saw it in his eyes. His brown eyes were every bit as beautiful as Henry's, but there was a sadness in them Henry's didn't have. A few more errant tears slid down her cheeks. *Is this what it's like for people? I don't know how to do this.*

Paul went to work on the band of a leather cuff wrapped around Sarah's left wrist. "If the doctor walks in and catches me doing this, you'll have to bail me out of jail again."

Sarah smiled through her tears, but it trembled.

"There was a big car wreck or they'd be in here already. Actually they thought it would take you longer to regain consciousness. You've only been off the ventilator since yesterday. Does it hurt to breathe?"

"Everything hurts."

Paul got the buckle loose and rubbed her wrist. It erased the feeling of the horrible cuff. Sarah lifted her freed arm and gave Paul a one-armed hug.

"Thank you for being here," she cried, feeling like a baby. She wished she had some pride left, but it was gone. She'd never been so afraid in her life.

"Where else would I be?" He looked from one eye to the other. "You're going to be okay. Don't be afraid."

Sarah shook her head but didn't say anything. She didn't want to tell him she couldn't cast.

He turned his attention to her right wrist. "Do you know you were in a coma?"

"Yes."

"It's been awhile, Sarah."

"I know. Six weeks." More tears slid from her eyes.

"They can give you something for the pain. It doesn't have to hurt. Let me hide the evidence and I'll hit the call button." Paul lifted her right arm to show her it was free and straightened.

"No, don't. I can't take drugs," her voice rasped, like Aunt Lily's barfly one.

"Not even if it makes you stop hurting?"

"Witches don't take drugs."

"Is there a fine if you do? Because pain isn't going to help you any."

"It messes us up. We have to be able to feel everything around— uh, I've been given drugs, haven't I?" *Of course I have.* Maybe that's why she couldn't push pain away. Maybe it had nothing to do with chasing away dark matter. *Keep telling yourself that.*

"You've been given *all* the drugs."

"Help me up? I need to get out of here."

A whispery chuckle escaped him. "You're not going anywhere, at least not anytime soon. Meds have been keeping you alive. I don't think you should rule them out just yet."

Now that Paul mentioned drugs, she could feel them sluggishly moving through her system. Anesthetic numbed the inside of her mouth, and ammonia made her nostrils cold. Although Paul leaned close, she couldn't smell his body wash or tell if he was still brushing his teeth with kid toothpaste. Bright light reflected off the icon dangling from his neck and it hurt her eyes. Maybe the light hurt because of the medication, too. "I can't stay here."

Paul dropped into a chair beside her bed. "Listen to me. You nearly died! I'm not just saying that. You haven't moved in ages. I doubt you can sit up, much less stand."

"Don't be ridiculous, of course I can." Sarah tried to prove it by sitting, but her muscles ignored her and her insides screamed in protest. She squinted against the scorching light at Paul. A very important question entered her mind. *If I'm this bad, what happened to Kathleen?*

Suddenly more afraid, she asked, "What happened after I passed out that night?"

Paul stood again, checking the wires and tubes attached to her body. "They had no clue what was wrong with you. At first both you and Kathleen had the exact same symptoms, only she didn't get worse and worse! They've been calling in doctors from all over. You don't have a doctor, you have a team! It's going to take your entire Archer fortune to pay for this."

Kathleen didn't get worse and worse? Tears of relief filled her eyes this time.

Apparently satisfied, Paul stopped fiddling around with her wires and leaned against the bed railing. "About a week ago they decided both you and Kathleen had ingested some sort of rare bacteria that supposedly formed once in some wine somewhere. They're calling the fact that both Henry and I drank from the same bottle with no problem 'a decanting fluke.' An entire team of world-renowned doctors came up with that theory, but not one of them figured out you were actually a bitch witch having a jealous meltdown because of a love spell. Such is the state of medical care today. Blame it on your HMO."

Sarah didn't laugh. "She's out of the hospital though? With Henry?"

Paul glared. "If you're going to start on Henry already, I'll have you sedated."

"I'm trying to know what happened!"

"Of course she's with Henry. He's taking care of her."

Sarah nodded. "He has to take care of her?"

"He wants to. He loves her! He always has."

Sarah closed her eyes. To a small degree that hurt. Even knowing her attraction to Henry was a love spell, she'd been so certain it had also been real. "The spell broke for him then? That night?"

"Obviously," said Paul without pity.

Sarah nodded, opening her eyes. "Me too."

Paul crossed his arms. "Don't you lie to me."

Memories of how she'd mooned over Henry came back and shame warmed her cheeks. She'd run into that love spell with eyes wide open. *Aunt Lily would have laughed her head off.* The groping incident in the basement came to mind, followed by the parking lot fiasco. Sarah couldn't quite meet Paul's eyes. "I don't blame you for not believing me."

"What's going on?" Paul narrowed his eyes at her. "You never give in this easily. I thought you'd start ripping tubes out of your body and head back to Henry."

Sarah jutted her lip out and fisted her hands. She could feel some of the tubes dig deeper into her veins and her bladder seemed to be pressing against her lungs. More tears filled her eyes. She shoved away the humiliation of being a love-sick moron and focused on the fact that Kathleen had survived. Even after rescinding the spell and claiming it ten-fold against herself, she'd had no way of knowing how Kathleen would end up.

In that respect she'd been fortunate.

So what if she'd never have a chance to meet Henry and find out if there was anything real between them. He had Kathleen, and she was un-witched, neutered, and useless. Being alone was a small part of her troubles. No matter that it suddenly felt like the biggest.

"Talk to me, Sarah."

Her entire face trembled, but she still couldn't bring herself to tell him she'd lost the ability to cast so much as a spark in the palm of her hand. A sob bubbled up.

"Are you in that much pain?"

"I need to get out of here!"

"Oh, Lord." Paul took a step away from the bed and rubbed his hand through his hair. "Shoot, Sarah! I can't just take you out of here. They're going to want to keep you for observation for a couple of days at least."

"Please! I want to go home."

"I can't believe I'm doing this." Paul moved closer and pulled electrodes out of the top of her gown. A machine behind the bed beeped. He leaned over and shut it off. "They won't even put me in jail. They'll put me back in the psychiatric hospital." Paul tugged a metal needle out of the back of Sarah's hand that looked as big as a nail. Sarah tried not to pass out.

Paul pressed his thumb against it to stop the bleeding. He tugged a stray piece of tape off a tube and stuck it over the wound. "You've got a urine catheter in your bladder too."

"A what?"

With his other hand he lifted a clear tube with some yellow liquid in it. "This is how you've been peeing."

Sarah closed her eyes as a wave of nausea moved through her.

Paul chuckled. "You're such a baby."

"It's not funny."

"After all the bitch witch stuff I've seen you do, it kind of is."

"Can you take it out?"

"Unless you want to."

Sarah turned her head away and tried not to moan. She was not cut out for this kind of a life.

chapter seventeen

That Hurt

Sarah screamed into her pillow to muffle the sound. Paul was lucky she couldn't cast, otherwise he'd be nailed to the ceiling.

"Sarah, I'm sorry. Was it really that bad? It came out fairly easily. Textbook even."

Taking a breath, she aimed a punch in the general direction of Paul's voice. He managed to duck it.

"Look, if you want to go we'd better get moving. Things are quieting down out there, but if someone comes by, we'll never get out."

Sarah wiped her tears on the pillow and sat up with a little help from Paul. The position made the burning from the catheter's removal worse. Paul took a wadded up ball of clothing from a narrow locker near her bed and handed it to her. It took a moment for Sarah to recognize her sweats.

"They're dirty," she said, shaking them out. Something white flitted to the floor like dandruff.

"Sorry. I never thought to bring clean clothes. It didn't look like you were going home—uh—anytime soon."

"Is that dried barf?"

Paul took the sweatshirt and shoved it over her head, right over her hospital gown. "Don't be a princess." He helped her get her arms through the sleeves, and pushed her feet through the pants. Within moments she had her sequin ruby slippers on her feet and Paul was tugging her to the door.

"Hold on." He peeked out. "We're going to have to use the elevators. There's no way you'll make it down the stairs. You look like you're going to pass out on me."

It felt like it. All Sarah's blood seemed to be draining into the lower half of her body, and she held onto Paul's waist with a death grip. This pain was nothing compared to what dark matter had put her through, but weakness was new. She couldn't recall a time in her life when walking felt like climbing a mountain with not enough oxygen.

"Come on, all's clear." Paul hauled her into the hospital corridor. The lights seemed even brighter than her room, and her head swam as she did her best to keep up with his long stride.

"Wait," Sarah warned, sensing the approach of people. Judging by her second sense, they were dressed in scrubs. "Someone's coming."

They ducked into the room of another patient and Paul closed the door. He put his finger to his lips and motioned to an elderly man asleep in his bed. Sarah sensed the people move past the door. It was a foggy sense with meds coursing through her veins, but it might be the only witch skill she had left. "It's good now." She closed her eyes and leaned against the door.

"You know we could make your great escape tomorrow," Paul whispered. "I'd stay with you tonight." He pushed hair off her face and tucked it behind her ear.

"No. I'm not staying here!" *I can't!* The temptation to call out to dark matter and cast away her misery was too strong. It would come back if she called, she knew it. With the help of dark matter she could shove this misery away and skip out of the hospital.

She needed her house. She needed quiet. She needed Meg Ryan and Tom Hanks and *Outlander*. She needed to figure out what the hell witches did without dark matter.

Paul wrapped an arm around her and pulled her from the room. "This escape better not be about your obsession with my brother."

As they made their way with stops and starts, Sarah spotted dark matter in the hospital hallway, crammed into the usual spots. It thrived in cracks and corners and vents, like mold and dust. Wearing the dried vomit-encrusted sweats she'd worn to the hospital, Sarah forced her legs to move down the empty corridor and held tightly to Paul's warm hand. When they reached the elevators, Sarah stumbled inside and clung to the wall.

How often have I relied on dark matter without realizing it? No wonder it stayed.

But how am I going to function without it?

Inside the elevator dark matter dusted the control panel. "There's barely any dark matter on this floor of the hospital, and there was none in my room." *It literally left when I told it to!*

"Is it in here?" asked Paul.

"Yes." Sarah motioned toward the control panel of the elevator without thinking about the fact that Paul couldn't see it anyway. The smudges of dark matter dotting the buttons for the basement and lobby melted away, as if hiding from her reach by going deeper into the control panel. "Holy shit."

"What?"

"It just moved."

"Doesn't it always?"

"Well, sure, but I mean it moved *away* from my hand! All of it!"

Paul looked from her to the control panel and back again. "It doesn't usually?"

"No! If anything it runs toward me." Leaning on the railing circling the elevator, Sarah took a deep breath and scooted closer to the errant bits of dark matter. Dark matter slid away with every step closer she took, moving down the closed elevator doors and vanishing into the crack beneath them. "It's avoiding me!"

"What does that mean?"

"I have no freaking idea, but I like it."

Paul smiled at her. "Maybe it'll make it easier to resist using it."

"I don't care if it climbs into my panties and hosts a party; I'm never using it again. I can't allow myself to, and I won't." *I can't! This is my only chance. If I fail now...*

"So the temptation is gone?"

"I've never wanted to use it more. This pain stuff is bullshit. Every part of my body hurts like a mother fu—"

"I get the idea."

"Sorry."

"So you're chasing away dark matter now?"

"Apparently." Sarah moved her hand and watched dark matter scurry away like opposite polarity chasing magnetic dust. "Huh."

"That's a good thing, Sarah."

"I know. I just feel so—powerless without it."

"There's nothing powerless about you."

There is now.

She tried to shove that thought away. "Do you have a car here?" Even with Paul's help, her legs trembled from the strain of walking.

"Ah, yeah. Henry's rental."

"He didn't go home?"

"No. Kathleen can't make the trip yet. I've been running back and forth so he gave me the car."

The knowledge that Kathleen was still in bad shape further drained Sarah's energy. She leaned against the wall and closed her eyes. "I thought she was better."

"She's better than you are."

Unable to hold herself upright, Sarah slid down the back wall of the elevator. Paul grabbed her before she hit the floor. She opened her eyes and mouthed, "Sorry."

More than a couple days growth of beard showed on Paul's face, and dark circles ringed his eyes. Sarah swallowed. Part of her wanted to ask why he'd stayed at the hospital with her all of these weeks, but she didn't. Paul was the kind of guy who didn't leave his friends behind and that was that.

"You've gone above and beyond. I know you stayed with me when no one else did. I—I, don't know what to say."

"'Thank you' is tradition."

Leaning all her weight on his supporting arm, Sarah used the last of her energy to smile. "You're the best friend I've ever had. Thank you, Paul."

Paul wrapped his arm tightly around her back in a half-hug. "You're welcome. Let's get you home before you collapse."

DARK MATTER WHISPERED to Sarah in her sleep and she jerked awake. They were driving on the Mass Pike.

Paul handed her a bottle of water. "How do you feel?"

"Like I've been beaten with baseball bats." She unscrewed the lid and took a sip. It was the best thing she'd ever tasted.

"If you weren't so stubborn, you wouldn't have to be hurting."

"I had to get out of there."

"If you don't eat, drink—a lot, and pee in the next few hours, you're going back."

"No. I'm not going back. I'm tough. I'm a witch." *I think.*

"Pfft." Paul frowned. "Apparently that doesn't make you impervious to plain old human frailty. Trust me. I had a front row seat the last six weeks. Just do me a favor and cooperate the next few days, okay?"

"If you'll do me a favor first. Paul, would you mind taking me to see Henry before we go to the house?"

"That's what this is all about!" Paul cried. "So that's why you had to get out of the hospital! Sheesh! I can't believe I fell for it. Dammit, Sarah! No wonder people used to burn witches at the stake."

"Don't be mean."

"No, I guess mean is your job." Paul shot her a dirty look. "Anyway, you'll see Henry soon enough."

"I will?"

"He's at your house."

"Henry's at *my house*?"

"Yes. The better to keep his *Big Brother* eye on me."

"Oh. Hmm."

"Try not to swoon. Kathleen's there too."

"So they're *both* at my house?"

Paul groaned. "If you need to obsess about Henry, you're going to have to find another friend to do it with."

"I'm not obsessing."

"Obviously."

"Paul, I'm not in love with your brother."

"Right."

"Apparently a six-week coma will break even a love spell."

"Good to know. But you're not acting like it's broken. Anyway, the thing is Kathleen can't recover in some hotel. Try to remember you owe her. You tried to *poison* her!"

"I did not! I mean, not really," Sarah protested lamely.

Paul turned a withering look on her.

"Fine. For a nanosecond I wanted to annihilate her, but I never wanted to or really planned to poison her!"

Paul rolled his eyes. "I was there."

"I didn't! Not really!"

"You should have seen your face. I couldn't believe Henry didn't see it coming. He was too busy simpering over you, blindly wallowing in that stupid love spell."

"It was just an impulsive thought—haven't you ever told someone to drop dead?"

"Pretty much not since I saw my friends actually dropping dead around me in Afghanistan."

"It was reactionary. I didn't actually want her to die! I'm not saying I was innocent, you saw what happened. I'm just saying I didn't plan—"

"Sarah, stop. I've seen the look on people's faces right before they kill. I know what it looks like."

Sarah bit her lip. *He's right. Don't gloss it over. You meant it when you cast, even for a moment. Then you were afraid to pull it back because you knew the cost. Just because you did the right thing eventually doesn't negate your original intention.* "I'm sorry, Paul. I really messed up."

"That's an understatement."

"Thank you for calling me on it." Her eyes filled with tears.

Paul reached over to pat her on the head a couple times. "Hey. My point was that Kathleen wouldn't be sick if it weren't for you. You can be gracious and let her stay in your house, in your mother's room if that's what it takes."

"My mother's room!" *That is not a good idea!*

"Sarah."

"Fine." Sarah crossed her arms. "Where's Henry sleeping?"

"Oh, Lord. Here we go." Paul's hands tightened on the steering wheel. "The only thing I can imagine worse than watching the two of you slobber on each other, is watching you make an ass of yourself while he's trying to make amends to Kathleen."

"Bite me, Paul. Wait. What do you mean make amends?"

Paul rolled his eyes and chuckled. "I'll admit I've been enjoying it. I guess you will too, for different reasons. It'll probably put some hope in that black heart of yours—once Kathleen knew Henry had returned to his senses, and she'd finally quit vomiting things I think she'd ingested back in high school, she did an about face. She went all, '*I don't think so, Henry. You can't cheat on me and come crawling back.*'"

Sarah laughed. "I guess you can't blame her."

"Of course not. I blame you."

"Why? I got caught in the same spell. I didn't even cast that love spell." Sarah took another sip of water and glared out the window.

"You really looked like you were suffering. Do you think I didn't realize what you were doing when you made him coffee? And not just some drip-type thing after all your lectures to me about how you can't cook without casting. You practically danced beneath a full moon waving a wand the minute he walked in the door!"

Sarah turned her glare on him. "I did not! I know I completed the circle of the spell, binding us—"

Paul took one hand off the steering wheel to make an open handed gesture at her. "Thank you! At least you're admitting it!"

"Look, I never denied that! But the thing is, Paul, I knew after I'd touched Henry I was in deep. So I cast another spell with the coffee. It helped me see the truth about Henry. That way I could keep my head."

"Apparently that didn't work very well." Paul put both hands back on the steering wheel.

"It worked fine. The problem was that Henry's a pretty great guy. Even without a spell I would have been interested in him."

Paul snorted. "I call B.S. on that."

"Why?!"

"Because I know both of you."

Sarah lifted her short legs to press her ruby red slippers against the leather dashboard of the car. She frowned out the window, blind to the setting October sun as she considered Paul's comments. They were easier to think about than the dark matter beckoning in the distance or the anxiety churning in her gut.

"How bad is Kathleen?"

"Bad enough. You're going to need to stay away from her."

Paul exited the highway and Sarah relaxed against the leather upholstery as the car moved over familiar back roads. "Bet you anything Kathleen has witch blood somewhere in her past."

"What are you talking about?"

"That night before I cast the poison spell, I made her wine taste like vinegar and she drank every drop. Who does that?"

Paul chuckled low in his throat. "Kathleen has the fortitude of a monk, and she hates wine. She once told me it all tastes like vinegar, but when she started dating Henry she was all over it because he is."

"That's stupid."

"Look who's talking. I've had a front row seat into your shenanigans, Miss *My Car Uses Oil*."

Sarah laughed, remembering. "That was pretty bad."

"You were both ridiculous."

"I'm not blaming the poison thing on her, but Kathleen was trying to provoke me that night." Sarah sucked the rest of the water out of the bottle and forced it into the cup holder.

"No kidding! Did you expect her to be friendly? Henry dumped her by text message for you, and you were rude and mocking from the second she walked in the door. She's a good person, and she deserved better than that."

"She's a catty bitch."

"Don't you have any empathy? She hopped a plane to come see what happened to the man she loves, and you started poking pins into her!"

"*She* was being a snoot and a snob."

"Yeah, well so was Henry, and you gave him a lap dance." Paul parked in front of Sarah's house and clicked open his seatbelt. "You ready?"

Sarah looked toward the house. The morning glory had died. Heaps of October leaves were blown against the porch steps. She swallowed and whispered, "Yes."

"Say you'll be nice."

"You know what, Paul? I'm not nearly as awful as you seem to think I am. I have no intention of hurting Kathleen."

"You mean this time?" He opened his door.

"Just shut up."

chapter eighteen

Exes and No's

Light illuminated the doors under the porch roof in a golden glow. Sarah froze halfway up the front steps.

Paul stumbled at her sudden stop, his arm still around her. "What are you doing?"

Sarah's mouth had gone so dry she couldn't form words. She pointed at the front doors. The glass in them that had crackled three years ago after the death of her family had changed again. Instead of the familiar crackly cobwebs etched into frosty glass, colorful vines and flowers gracefully flowed over crystal clear glass. Most metaphorical dark matter messages had a basis in the laws of physics. This glass had healed itself. It wasn't possible. It now looked like the Morning Glory that grew around the house in the summer.

A shiver ran up her back.

"What?" Paul said. "The doors? They're new. Kathleen picked them. We had to have a lot of the windows replaced too. When you had your little hissy fit you blew out half the glass in the house. Henry took care of it."

"Oh." Sarah laughed a dry exhalation of relief. "That was nice of him."

"Hardly. It was getting cold. He left a stack of receipts for you. Make sure you pay him back. He can be a real jerk about money. I was afraid to offer him some of your piles of cash. I didn't want him to think you're a drug dealer or something. He's pretty down on you." Paul fished in his pocket for the key, and then took Sarah's elbow to escort her across the threshold. All the blood in her head felt as though it drained down, and she could hear her pulse beating inside her ears. Automatically she reached further than Paul for additional help. Even knowing she'd rejected it forever, Sarah's mind and heart swept through the old house, looking for dark matter like the drug it was. It surprised her that she couldn't sense it even in the basement.

It really left the house! It was both a relief and a disappointment.

Sarah didn't make it any further than the sofa in the living room. She let go of Paul's arm and dropped face first onto the old gilt-edged couch. It occurred to her that she hadn't eaten in weeks. Maybe Paul had been right. She should have stayed in the hospital. Sarah pressed her face against the soft material, breathing in the familiar dusty scent of old jacquard silk. She closed her eyes to protect them from the light. The house seemed far brighter than she remembered.

Paul tossed a warm blanket over her back and turned on *You've Got Mail*, putting her laptop on the coffee table near her head. Meg Ryan was missing her mom.

What must that be like?

Sarah slept as though she'd fallen back into a coma.

When she woke, Paul watched her from the opposite sofa.

"Feel better?" he asked.

Sarah sat up, pulling a pile of warm blankets closer. They were the thick white ones from her bed, and even her pillow had been tucked on the end of the sofa. "Some. Thanks, Paul."

"No problem," he said, pointing at a cup of tea, a bowl of steaming soup, and crackers set on the coffee table. "You've been asleep for over twenty-four hours. I was beginning to think about taking you back to the hospital. I will if you don't eat and drink and pee. The soup isn't much more than broth. I don't think you should start with much else. But it's from that Wegman's supermarket. It's good, I had some."

Sarah pulled the bowl closer and picked up a spoon. Her stomach snarled as she spooned soup into her mouth. "You're a good friend," she said between bites. Her stomach roared in appreciation or protest. She couldn't tell which, and didn't care. The soup tasted warm and too salty and wonderful. "You know I don't expect you to cook for me, but hell I do appreciate it."

"You're letting me stay here, not to mention my brother and his *fiancée*."

Sarah shot him a dirty look. "Where are they?"

"Henry took some soup up to Kathleen a few minutes ago. He's been trying to feed her something every few hours. She's not really eating well."

Sarah looked in the direction of the staircase.

"He said he was going to go back to bed," Paul added.

"What room is he in?"

"Please. Would you *please* try not to be nauseatingly jealous? I don't think I can take it again. Henry's not sleeping with Kathleen if that's what you're worried about. Not that he wouldn't be if she felt better, or if she didn't currently hate his guts."

Paul's tone made her smile.

"You're doing it," Paul accused. "It's not very attractive."

To hide her eye roll Sarah gulped some of the hot tea, holding the mug between her hands to warm them. "Does Kathleen know about me?" At his blank look she added, "That I'm a witch, Paul."

"Of course not. She wouldn't believe that if we told her anyway."

"I have ways of making you believe." It hit her with sudden horror that she didn't. Not anymore. She put down the mug.

"You can really be a you-know-what," Paul said.

Sarah plopped several crackers into the soup and jammed them into the bottom with her spoon. "But Henry knows I am. I mean, he believes it now, doesn't he?"

"Yeah, Sarah, he does. He also believes you tried to kill Kathleen."

"Does he know I'm here?"

"He could hardly miss you snoring in the middle of the living room. You sounded like a pack of San Francisco sea lions."

Sarah straightened, spoon in hand. "Did I really?" Witches didn't sleep deep enough to snore. "That's odd."

"Are you more embarrassed by the fact that your crush heard you snoring than the fact that you tried to kill his fiancée? Because that's messed up."

Scowling, Sarah scooped soggy crackers onto her spoon. "He's not my crush, and I wish you wouldn't say I tried to kill her."

"This is the part where I'll again point out the facts. You *almost* killed her. I suppose everyone has those brief flashes of anger, but most people aren't witches. You're like a loaded gun."

When he put it like that, it made her new lack of ability a little less terrible.

Except now I have no defense against even a loaded gun.

"After your warning shot, she vomited for weeks. The medical community tortured her trying to figure out why. She lost close to twenty pounds, weight she couldn't afford to drop. Kathleen barely weighs more than a bag of bones and hair anyway."

Despite a guilty shiver, Sarah gave him a self-satisfied smile. "You don't like her either."

"The way I feel about Kathleen has nothing to do with her size, and I didn't say that I didn't like her!"

"You didn't have to. Why'd you ever go out with her? Isn't that how Henry met her? When she was on a date with you?"

"It was a blind date, and I think she's perfect for Henry. They get each other. They're both as deep as the kiddie pool, and as pretentious as lip filler. Don't take that wrong. I love them both."

"I don't think Henry's like that." Sarah stuffed another spoonful of soup into her mouth.

"Well, you don't know him, or you would."

"She is, though she is beautiful in that big hair suntan way." Sarah ran a hand over her mess of dark hair. It felt greasy. "Shit! I need a shower!" Lifting an arm she sniffed. "I smell like a horse!"

Paul shrugged. "You smell better than you would if you'd have died. Barely, though. Good lord, Sarah, you were in a coma, and they did wash you. Besides, you seem to forget that Henry doesn't care what you smell like anymore. Homicidal tendencies are a real turn off for some men."

"Shut up. This has nothing to do with him!" Though she sure didn't want to come face to face with Henry like this. "What room is he sleeping in again?"

Paul leaned against the back of the sofa with a sigh and scratched the backside of his horse tat on his bicep. "You're just never going to stop asking about him, are you? Your near death experience taught you nothing. I don't know why I'm making jokes about Henry and Kathleen. Maybe you are shallow enough for him. Henry is sleeping in your bedroom. I knew you didn't want us to use most of those rooms upstairs. I wasn't sure if it was worse to use your room or the room you keep all those clothes in—"

"Paul! Deal. I was only asking because I didn't know if I could go upstairs to use my shower! Do you care if I go take a shower in your room? And would you mind bringing me some clean clothes from upstairs?"

"It's your house, so of course I don't mind. What do you want? It is three o'clock in the morning. Pajamas or clothes?"

"What day is it?"

"Friday."

"I guess it doesn't matter. I got fired so I'm not going to work—wait," Sarah said, remembering. "Did someone named Jackie come visit me in the hospital?"

Paul's somber expression vanished. "How did you know? Could you hear what was going on? Doctor Shaw said maybe you could!"

"I remember bits and pieces." Sarah thought back. "Mostly it was darkness—and not good stuff. I'm trying to remember the semi-conscious bits. You asked her about my job!"

He grinned at her. "Yep, and you didn't get fired, although I suspect they didn't really think you were going to make it. Still. They can hardly rescind it because you lived."

"They sent me flowers!" Sarah banged her soup spoon against the low table, disappointed to realize she hadn't noticed them. Remembering what else had happened, she smiled and leaned back on the sofa. "You got me my job back! What day did you say it was?"

Paul shook his head. "No way. I helped you sneak out of that hospital, but I am not taking you to work any time soon. How can you think about going anywhere right now? For starters Sarah, and don't take this wrong, but you look half-dead—no, you look mostly-dead. For another thing, *nobody* pops out of a coma overnight and goes to work."

Sarah rubbed a hand up and down her arm. "I don't have the energy to do anything yet. But it's hard not to cast if I don't keep myself busy. If I backslide now, Paul, I'll never be able to get to this point again. Ever."

"Ever try jogging? It's repetitive and soothing."

She stood. "Don't be ridiculous."

Paul laughed. "Too soon? You have a pile of bills, if you're looking for paperwork. For now you need to eat and sleep. And shower."

"All right," said Sarah, heading for the room she thought of as Paul's. "What did Henry say when he saw I was home from the hospital?"

"Just get in the shower. You smell like a zombie looks. Wait. You look like one too."

Sarah flipped him the bird as she hurried toward his bathroom.

"WHAT KIND OF flowers?"

Freshly showered and bathed since only one hadn't cut it, Sarah sprawled across Paul's bed waiting for him to finish his shower. She examined her pruney fingers, a side effect of falling asleep in the bathtub. She felt much better now.

"What?" Paul yelled back, and she heard the shower door slam shut behind him. "Hey, did you use my razor? This is gross!"

"Maybe. What kind of flowers did my work send to me at the hospital?" Sarah ran her fingers through wet hair, fanning it around her head on top of Paul's pillow. It needed to be cut. She squinted in the glare of the overhead light, determined to drink a couple gallons of water that day or whatever it took to wash the meds out of her system.

"I don't know. The kind in a vase," came the muffled reply. "It looks like you shaved a chimp in that shower."

"But what color were they? What kinds of flowers? What kind of vases? Were they small or big?"

"Big and flowery and lots of them. Get out of here. I need to get clothes out of my dresser." Paul peeked around the corner of the bathroom wall at her.

"So get them," Sarah said. "I've always wanted to see all your tats anyway." She sat up and her wet hair ran rivulets down the Snoopy sweatshirt Paul had chosen. Her pants were too loose, and she recognized them as from her too-small pile. It was a heady feeling sliding into jeans two sizes smaller than usual, but she defi- nitely hadn't lost twenty pounds like Kathleen. *Maybe five. After six weeks in a coma I lost maybe five pounds. Life is so freaking unfair to short people.*

"Don't think I won't march right out there," Paul said, hover- ing behind the wall.

"Waiting," she taunted.

Paul stalked around the corner with a towel wrapped tightly around his waist. Sarah's eyes widened. She hadn't taken the time in a while to appreciate how beautiful he was. For some reason it had never occurred to her that Paul would look every bit as good as Henry; perhaps even more so soaking wet and wrapped in a nice fluffy white towel, with all of his tats gleaming and slick against lean muscle.

Paul stopped at the foot of the bed and put his hands on his waist. "Well, at least you look like a clean zombie now. You do need to eat a bit more."

Sarah dropped back onto the bed and put her hands over her stomach. "Maybe not just yet."

"You'll have to force yourself at first. I'm serious. You look like a vampire heroin addict between fixes. Your eyes are freaking me out."

"Don't sugarcoat it."

"They're like a strung out rabid raccoon. You look hungry. Feral."

Sarah sat up. "Shut up, Paul! I am hungry, but not for food! I want dark matter. I want to fling open the doors and run naked into the woods where it lives and beg it to take me back and make me feel better!"

"You'd pass out before you got halfway across the yard." He crossed to the dresser and grabbed a crumpled t-shirt off.

"I think you might be missing the point."

"I got the point, but I figure since dark matter spent the last six weeks torturing you, you're smart enough not to do it."

"Let's hope so."

"And smart enough to have some more soup, so you don't weird me out with your hungry predator eyes." Paul sniffed his shirt, shook it out, and pulled it over his wet body.

"Speaking of weird," Sarah said evenly.

Paul grinned at her. "At least it's not witch weird. I am glad you're all better and home, even though you should have stayed in the hospital. I missed having someone to freak me out and argue with."

"I'm here for ya."

"It was weird sitting next to your hospital bed. I hardly got any grief, and no one swore at me."

"Well, the witch is back." Sarah hugged her knees. "At least partially. Did you bring my toothbrush from upstairs?"

"There's a bunch in the drawer in my sink."

She shook her head. "I want my ultrasonic one. Obviously you've never used one. If my house caught on fire it's the only thing I'd try to save."

"Don't be so picky."

"That's not being picky. I haven't brushed my teeth in six weeks."

"Now there's a pleasant thought." Paul grabbed jeans off the floor and fled to hide behind the wall by the bathroom, peeking around the corner as he tugged them on. "Use one from my drawer, but please don't use mine." He threw his towel onto the sink and moved into view as he zipped his pants. "After six weeks I'm picky too."

Sarah scrambled off the bed, knocking pillows to the floor. "Yeah, I can tell by the way you don't even wear underwear."

"Hey!" Paul held his hands up. "I haven't done laundry since you went in the hospital. I ran out! Cut a guy some slack! Where are you going?"

Sarah didn't turn. "To my room for my toothbrush."

"Look!" Paul called, and Sarah heard him rooting in the sink drawer. "There's like two dozen different kinds. You'll have to make do with a manual toothbrush, princess. You're not allowed upstairs."

"Pfft," said Sarah, and darted out of the room, slamming and locking the bedroom door behind her.

"Sarah!" Paul shouted from inside the room.

Sarah laughed as she hurried through the brightly lit kitchen. Paul pounded on his bedroom door, and his usual PG-13 swearing went up a couple notches. In seconds Sarah had zipped through the living room and hit the stairs. She made it halfway up before noticing Henry standing frozen at the top. He held an empty breakfast tray.

Sarah stopped in her tracks. "Hi. Henry."

He shifted the tray and nodded, one curt jerk of his head. Even at five o'clock in the morning he wore khakis and a button down shirt, his hair slicked back with just a bit of an Elvis curl happening on his forehead. He looked every bit as beautiful to her as he'd looked under the love spell. *'You go together'* bobbed into her mind, and despite everything she wondered if the logic spell could have been right.

Sarah listened, half expecting to hear random facts about him flitting through her mind, but nothing came. "Uh, how's Kathleen?"

Holding the tray defensively against his body, he bared his teeth and hissed, "You leave her alone."

"Of course. Look. I wanted to talk to you about Kathleen. I want you to know I don't mean her any harm, and I'm sor—"

"Don't you lie to me, you witch! You could have killed her!" Henry took a step down, looking like he might throw the tray at her.

Sarah fought her instinct to take a step backward. "Henry, I am sorry. You don't need to worry. It was a bad situation and I wasn't myself because of the sp—"

"What did she ever do to you, you soulless bitch?!"

That hurt. Sarah put a hand on the railing. "For what it's worth I took the bulk of that spell to protect her. But I know I made her sick, and I am sorry I did that. She didn't deserve it. It's no excuse, but I got mad and—well, it's really easy to do. One impulsive flash of anger got away from me. I was so jealous because—"

Henry took another step closer. "I don't want to hear your excuses, and you'd better be sorry! She's worth a hundred of you. Kathleen wouldn't harm a fly, and you—you—*witch*! No wonder your ancestors were burned at the stake. As far as I'm concerned you should join them!"

"Wait a minute. For one thing that's not true. If Kathleen had the same abilities I had, she'd have eviscerated me on the spot! She was doing her best to provoke me, and that's partly why it happened!"

"You're blaming Kathleen? You foul evil *bitch*!"

"No, I'm not! I'm trying to apologize, but if you recall—"

"I don't want to hear anything you have to say! After what you've done, I can't believe you have the nerve to speak to me. If it had been up to me, you'd have been disconnected from life support a month ago!"

"Whoa, Henry!" Paul had caught up, and raced up the stairs to stand beside Sarah. Putting a hand on her shoulder, he squeezed it. "Name calling and blaming won't change a thing. Let's break this up for now. I'll take that tray downstairs for you."

"No! Don't try to smooth it over. And don't you dare defend that witch. Are you afraid to rile her? I'm not!" He descended another step.

Sarah recognized the look blazing in his dark eyes: hatred. The smallest bit of dark matter writhed inside his irises, and sudden tears welled in hers. *Love spell or not, I never expected to see hate in his eyes. This is my fault, and he's right. Even if I was under a spell too, it was my fault. There's no excuse for what I did to Kathleen.*

Henry held her gaze like a circling hunter and she knew he'd meant every hateful word. She'd hurt the woman he loved and he wanted to destroy her for it. It pressed against her as a real and palpable danger, as though she could burst simply from Henry's anger pressing against her. Something hit her then, cutting across her arm like a razor blade. It burned and Sarah glanced down to see blood trickling from the sleeve of her sweatshirt.

What?! The first explanation that came was that her IV wound had reopened. But then another razor sharp pain slid over her arm. Automatically Sarah tried to shove the burning sensation away. It was no use. That ability had gone with dark matter, and somewhere deep inside she knew nothing would bring it back.

Paul grabbed her around the waist as Henry took another step. "Back off, Henry!" He dragged her roughly down several stairs. "What are you doing?"

"I'm going to make sure she doesn't touch Kathleen!"

"Sarah, you're bleeding!" Paul held her close. "Henry, just what are you planning to do to her? She's not well." He extended her bleeding arm. Red stained the sleeve of her white sweatshirt and thick droplets of blood fell, landing on his jeans and bare feet. "Hold your arm up," he said, forcing it into the air. Blood splattered across the front of her shirt. It looked like Snoopy had been shot.

"It's just a trick," said Henry, but he sounded doubtful.

"She wanted her toothbrush. She wasn't coming for Kathleen."

"I wanted to apologize," said Sarah, ignoring Paul's warning hush against her ear. Ignoring the fact that she'd also wanted to see Henry again, to see if there was anything real between them. Warm tears filled her eyes. He was lost to her now, and it was her fault.

"Save it," Henry bellowed, and turned and stomped back up the stairs. He paused at the top to bang the tray onto the landing. "I swear to God, Paul. You told me she wouldn't even get out of the hospital for another week, and then, oh, miracle cure here she is!

I want her out of this house!" He stormed across the landing and slammed a door shut behind him.

Sarah did her best to blink her tears back and sniffled. "It's my house."

"Ignore him." Paul bent her arm, squeezing hard near her elbow in an attempt to staunch the blood flow. It surged over his hand. "You must have popped a vein. Let's get to that bathroom before you ruin the carpet." He gestured with his chin to the half-bath near the entryway.

Upstairs a door banged open and Henry shouted over the banister, "Here, and if she goes near Kathleen, I'll have her arrested—or worse." Something whipped over the railing, and Sarah sensed her electric toothbrush falling. A split second before she could grab it, another razor sharp pain sliced into her. The toothbrush clattered down the steps. Upstairs the door to Henry's room slammed again.

"What the hell!" Sarah bent her right arm against her chest. Blood was already seeping through the sleeve. "Henry's casting!"

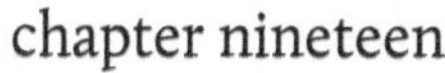

"Don't be ridiculous." Paul tossed Sarah's bloodied sweatshirt onto the floor and pressed a gauze pad over one of her wounds.

Sarah sat on the toilet lid in her bra and sweatpants, one arm propped on top of her head to slow the bleeding. She watched Paul's face to see if the blood bothered him, but arguing seemed to distract him.

"If my brother could cast, I'd never have survived adolescence. You can't imagine what a couple of unsupervised boys on a ranch can get into. I thought you said all witches were female anyway." He bit off the end of a bandage and glared at a deep wound. "That one needs stitches." He crouched in front of the cabinet under the sink, searching.

"I said dark witches like me are female. It's a gene we inherit. But we hardly corner the market on dark matter!"

"In this house you do."

"So what's your theory then?" Sarah averted her eyes from the deepest cut. It made her stomach drop out like on a roller coaster. "Separation of otherwise healthy tissue for apparently no reason? Is that a thing, Doctor EMT?"

Paul emerged from under the sink with a bottle of alcohol and a small paper packet. "Dang, Sarah, I can't begin to formulate a theory about what goes on around this house."

"Liar." Sarah saw guilt flicker in his eyes. "You notice everything. Are you going to pretend you didn't haul me down the stairs away from Henry to protect me?"

For the third time Paul scrubbed his hands in the sink, using an excessive amount of anti-bacterial soap. "Were you born without any sense of normal self-preservation? Did you not hear what he said to you? One thing he and I do have in common is meaning what we say. You need to stay away from him, not because he suddenly learned how to cast spells, but because he's scared of you, and he's protecting the woman he loves. A frightened man is a dangerous thing."

"This was a cast. Not one, but three. If it wasn't Henry casting, it was Kathleen listening up in my mother's room and doing something." Sarah could tell from his expression he didn't believe her. He poured alcohol over his hands and tipped the bottle over her wound. She almost shot off the toilet seat. "Ahh!"

"Come on, this is nothing compared to what you've been through." Paul stretched her arm over the sink basin and poured more of the liquid.

"You're doing this on purpose you bas—"

He covered her mouth, his hand still dripping rubbing alcohol. Sarah shut her mouth. "That's better. Now this will pinch a bit, but it won't be as bad as you're expecting."

Sarah felt a needle jab into her skin, followed by a thread as Paul pulled. She shivered and kept her gaze on the striped wallpaper. "I'm not saying that your brother and Kathleen are witches! I'm saying they've been alone in this house for—how long? A month or more? Did you tell them the rules?"

"Henry can't cook and Kathleen is in no condition to leave her room. I've been bringing them food that Henry nukes."

"Cooking wasn't the only rule! Did you clean up the spell books that were lying around?" She winced as Paul tugged the string more firmly through her flesh.

"No matter what they found, they wouldn't fool with it, and for some reason I haven't had much time for cleaning," he said, sarcasm evident.

"Don't take this personally, Paul. You know I appreciate everything you've done. But who knows what they might have found or gotten into? You've got Kathleen holed up in *my mother's room!*" Sarah shivered, trying not to think of dark items they might have come across. *Although as angry as Henry is, if they'd found something that bad I'd be dead already.*

"I get the feeling you think of your mother as the wicked witch of the east—or was that the west? I can never keep those two straight. The green one."

Sarah moved her arm off her head to grab his shoulder. Blood dripped onto her jeans. "Is that your gold standard for evil?! *The Wizard of Oz?*"

Paul stopped sewing, turning his intensely sad eyes on her. "No, Sarah. It's not. My gold standard for evil used to be having to go through excessive airport security because of 9-11. That's how sheltered my life was, until I found myself in the middle of sand and blood storms in the desert, watching good men cut to shreds because people can't get along."

"Paul," she said, unsure what else to say.

"It changed after watching you fight the temptation to have anything your spoiled little heart wants, and watching what evil did to you when you finally had the good sense to tell it to go to hell. I went from thinking nothing mattered to the terrifying realization that maybe everything matters."

Sarah held his gaze, her eyes watering with his. She let go of him, suddenly a few flesh wounds and her inability to cast meant little.

PAUL'S CLEAN SWEATSHIRT fell almost to her knees. Sarah stood in front of his bathroom mirror brushing her teeth with her toothbrush for the third time. Cleaned, stitched, and wrapped, the wounds on her arms still burned. She had to hold her elbows out at awkward angles and was stuck using Paul's disgusting grape-flavored toothpaste, but feeling clean was heavenly.

Part of her wanted to march upstairs and see what Henry and Kathleen had gotten into. Another part of her worried that Paul was right. It wasn't them. Maybe this was what happened to witches without dark matter. A sudden image of the green witch melting in the *Wizard of Oz* came to mind. Goosebumps rose over her skin. Maybe this is why she'd never heard of a witch sending dark matter away. Maybe it would kill her. She wished there was someone she'd dare to ask about it. She looked at Paul in the mirror, standing next to her and scrubbing his teeth like they were the floor. Foam trailed down his arm and dripped off his elbow.

Sarah rinsed her toothbrush off and said, "I can't believe how much I'm sleeping."

"You did just get out of a coma," he said around his toothbrush.

"Yeah, but witches don't ever really sleep. Earlier you said I was *snoring!*"

He rinsed his brush off and dropped it onto the counter. "Sounds like someone's going to get their witch card revoked."

Sarah's chin wobbled and Paul frowned. "What are you really worried about?"

"I'm tired again! I napped all day! That's not normal." She felt teary, hormonal. *Terrified.*

He wiped his mouth on a towel. "Have you ever known another witch to go into a coma?"

"No, but I'm sure it's happened. Not for long though. If we get hurt that badly, dark matter takes us."

"But it didn't take you."

"It tried."

"I know. But instead of worrying, why aren't you glad it didn't take you?"

"I am! It's only—I'm not sure I'm a witch anymore."

Paul grinned. "Sarah, you'll always be a witch to me."

"It's not funny!" Her eyes filled with tears and she moved toward him, motioning him to bend down so she could whisper in his ear, "I can't cast." She didn't understand why, but she didn't want the house to hear. She didn't really think it listened to her. It was just a house, but still.

Paul stood there a moment, examining her face. He bent down again and whispered back, "You're still who you've always been, Sarah. Only now you're free."

Sarah leaned against him and he hugged her for a long moment, then Paul announced in a normal voice, "Sleep. It's healing you, and I'll make you pancakes for breakfast."

She nodded, crossed the room and climbed into his bed.

"Hey, make yourself comfortable."

"I know you're policing me. You spent your day watching me sleep on the couch," she pointed out with a yawn. "I'm just not sure if you think I'm hell bent on reuniting with Henry or poisoning Kathleen. It doesn't really matter as long as you use pancakes for bait."

"Good, because the reasons are too numerous to list."

"Fair enough. Just shut the lights out when you're done. They hurt my eyes."

Sarah climbed under the blankets and closed her eyes. A couple minutes later she heard Paul reclining the big chair next to the bed. She wanted to tell him to shut the damn light out, but fell asleep before she could muster the energy.

A light at the end of the tunnel beckoned to Sarah, calling her by name. Dark matter whirled along the sides of the vortex, but soft beams of light kept it at bay. *"It's safe here, Sarah Elizabeth Archer,"* the light whispered.

She pretended she couldn't hear it. She was too warm and comfortable, and some part of her worried that if she went to that light, she would die.

Dark matter laughed; it had no form, and came to her only in sound. *Come back or you will die,* it whispered.

Sarah jerked awake, her heart hammering. The standing lamp behind the recliner was on and all three lights were pointed at her. For a moment she was tempted to whack Paul in the head with a pillow, but he sprawled on the chair with an open book resting on his chest, his head tipped back, and his mouth wide open. The strangest snores issued out of it, like the open mouth inhalations and guttural exhalations of a roomful of meditating yogis. Sarah wondered when he had last had a decent night's sleep.

Quietly she pushed her blankets down, climbed out of bed and tiptoed to the door. It was locked. She sighed, knowing she'd never find the key. *He probably swallowed it.* Crouching down in front of the door to examine the lock, Sarah wished that the Harry Potter *alohomora* spell worked in the real world. *I probably could have made it with dark matter.*

She jiggled the handle, wanting to throw a temper tantrum from the frustration of being powerless. Paul would be angry if he caught her trying to get out. She pushed and pulled a few more times, her mind racing for a way to open it that didn't involve dark matter.

She gave it a final jiggle, and the old door opened as the ancient lock gave way. Sarah covered her mouth to stifle a giggle. Paul always said the locks in her house could be picked with a pen. *Or apparently enough jiggling.*

SARAH STOOD AT the sink and drank two glasses of water, then unplugged Paul's phone from the charger in the kitchen and took it with her. She found her purse sitting on the dresser in the entryway, dug out her credit card, and started rooting through the pockets of coats looking for a pair of earbuds. All she wanted to do was curl back up in bed, stream a movie on the Internet, listen to some music—hopefully Paul had something besides country—and fall asleep without tunnels of light and dark matter talking to her.

A cabinet door opened in the kitchen and Sarah froze. It squeaked closed. The refrigerator door opened. Sarah's bare feet slid over cold tile as she crept to the doorway and peered into the kitchen. The narrow frame of a skinny blonde woman silhouetted in the light of the fridge was unmistakable.

Sarah pulled the neck of Paul's sweatshirt over her nose to muffle her breathing. She watched Kathleen out of her peripheral vision, afraid the woman would sense a direct stare.

Kathleen tore the wrapper off string cheese and stuffed two tubes into her mouth as she continued to loot the fridge, gathering items. Her arms already loaded, Kathleen balanced two sodas between her chin and the top of the stack and kicked the door shut with her foot. She emptied her treasure onto the counter, popped open a can of Dr Pepper and shoved a spoonful of peanut butter followed by jam into her mouth.

Sarah couldn't believe it. Kathleen didn't look like the type of woman who grazed for food in the middle of the night. Sarah was that type of woman. "I thought you didn't eat this late," she said.

Kathleen whipped around with the faintest squeak. "I didn't know you were out of the hospital!"

"Surprise."

"Well." Kathleen flipped a switch under the cabinets and the lights beneath them illuminated the countertop along the wall. "I'm glad you're better, but I hope you know Henry proposed to me for the fourth time."

"Then why aren't you wearing the ring?"

"It's too big," said Kathleen, unwrapping another string cheese and popping it into her mouth. She studied Sarah as she chewed. "You don't look like you should be out of the hospital."

"Neither do you." The cabinet lights illuminated Kathleen's rail thin body in her sheer white nightgown. Sarah glanced at the food littering the countertop. "You have an eating disorder."

Kathleen glared at her. "Look who's talking."

Sarah put her hands on her hips. "Does Henry know?"

"Mind your own business." Kathleen put the jar of peanut butter back into a cabinet, and gathered the rest in her arms. "What Henry knows or doesn't know is no longer any of your concern." Opening the fridge, Kathleen tossed the rest of her stash inside, empty soda can and all.

"I didn't sleep with him for what it's worth," said Sarah.

"Liar."

"I'm telling you the truth."

"I don't believe you. Why else would he have—have *wanted* you?"

Sarah sucked down the angry urge to swear at the woman. "I wanted to, but it was only a couple days after we met that you showed up."

"A couple days is plenty of time for the kind of woman you are."

Don't, don't, don't. You owe her and Henry this. Sarah took a deep breath. "Paul was always there too, and I had to work. The night you showed up you *saw* them both come out of Paul's room!"

Kathleen bit her lip as she studied Sarah's expression. "Why are you trying to be nice?" she asked at last.

"Six weeks in a coma can change a person." *Even her head looks skinny! She needs help.*

Kathleen crossed her arms. "You know if you're planning to switch your gold digging to Paul, you can forget it. Henry will make sure you never see a penny of his money."

"Fuck their money! I don't need money!"

Kathleen laughed. "Oh, honey, you might want to work on that line." She waved a hand at the cabinets and appliances. "It's obvious you do. This place is practically falling apart."

"It is not!" Sarah got a brief mental image of what mother would have done if she'd heard someone say that. She grimaced.

"Please. The taxes alone have got to be killing you. You're a clerk!"

"My finances are none of your business," Sarah growled. The taxes were killer, but she paid them out of the Archer fortune. It killed her to touch it, but she'd lose the house otherwise.

"Actually, they are."

Sarah said nothing, waiting, trying to talk herself down and ignore the faintest glimmer of dark matter she sensed in the woods behind the house.

"My hospital bills alone are over a hundred and fifty thousand dollars. And then there's the lawsuit."

"You have got to be kidding me," Sarah shouted. "You're suing me?"

"Sorry. When you serve a drink to someone you should make sure it's not going to poison them."

"I drank the same damn drink, and I got a lot sicker than you did!"

"That's pretty much your problem now, isn't it?" Kathleen said as sweetly as could be. She smiled the most saccharine smile Sarah had ever seen.

"You bitch! You're staying in my house. I will wipe that smirk off your face." As the last word left Sarah's lips, a scalding hot burning sensation blasted up the middle of her torso.

Footsteps thundered down the staircase. "If you touch her I'll kill you!" Henry roared.

The kitchen lights all flicked on. Blinking against their brightness, Sarah reached for the counter, trying to stay upright and breathe at the same time. It felt like she'd been gutted with a sword.

"Shit! You couldn't leave well enough alone," came Paul's voice from the far side of the room.

Sarah dropped to her knees and collapsed onto the ceramic tile.

"WHAT WERE YOU thinking eating cheese and peanut butter so soon?" asked Paul.

Sarah opened her eyes to the bright bedroom lamp again. She closed them and curled into a ball, protecting her middle. Paul sat beside her on the bed.

"I told you to eat soup, not get up in the middle of the night and binge, you nincompoop."

Sarah tried to catch her breath to tell him it had been skinny bitch bingeing, not her, but she couldn't get enough air. Outside dark matter whispered to her from beneath the skeletal branches of the October trees. *"Ask me. I can make the pain go away."* She shook her head, blinking against the blinding light, searching for the strength not to do it.

Paul awkwardly patted the top of her head. "You'll feel better after it gets through your system."

Sarah glanced at him, and the light made tears overflow from her eyes.

He leaned closer. "If it hurts that bad, I can take you to the emergency room. Actually, that's probably not a bad idea. It'd keep you away from your lover boy for a few hours. I know this is a bad time, but I'm so mad at you right now I'm almost glad you have a stomachache!"

Sarah ran a hand over her knees to the edge of the heavy red sweatshirt. "No hospital," she whispered in a strained voice. "Promise."

"Fine," Paul relented. "Maybe Tums will help."

"Swear it."

"I said maybe. I don't know if they'll help or not. I'm an EMT, not a gastroenterologist."

Sarah grabbed the bottom of the sweatshirt and tugged it up over her hips and belly. She rolled onto her back.

"Oh, dear God!" Paul jumped off the edge of the bed to stand and covered his mouth with shaking hands. He looked terrified.

"It's okay," she said. "Don't be afraid. I'll be okay. I promise."

"Sarah, what the hell happened?" Paul bent over her. Up close he looked as white as the blinding light.

"I told you," she managed. Lack of oxygen was making the room sparkle around her. "She's a witch, or she found something bad. Remember, you promised. No hospital."

She slipped from consciousness with the thought, *Please, please, I don't want to go back. Please, please, help me not cast again!*

chapter twenty

Light Up Your Life

By the time daylight shone in through the narrow window beside the bed, the wound in Sarah's stomach no longer felt fatal. Paul lay asleep in the recliner. Sarah sat up tentatively, wincing. Cautiously she stretched one short leg toward the far end of the bed.

Paul woke in an instant. "Don't you dare."

"Dude, I have got to pee."

He rose and leaned over the bed, perfunctorily lifting her sweatshirt to look. Sarah gazed down, expecting to see she'd been gutted. Paul lifted the gauze pad an inch to peek and dropped it with a sigh.

"Ah, Sarah. You used dark matter, didn't you?"

"I did not!" Sarah lifted the gauze to look, her stomach dropping in anticipation. A wide red wound stretched up her belly a good eight inches. She dropped back onto the pillow and closed her eyes, feeling woozy. "Maybe I should go to the hospital."

Paul laughed.

Sarah flipped him the bird without opening her eyes.

"Tell me the truth. You owe me that much. Did you cast to heal that?"

Sarah opened her eyes. "No!"

"How did it heal? I nearly called 911 last night."

"You promised!"

"I thought by now you'd be delirious with infection, but it's closed. The tissue looks healthy."

"You're serious? It's disgusting."

Paul ran his hand over his messy hair. "No, but it sure was. So how did it heal so fast if you didn't use dark matter? How did you sleep through me bandaging it?"

"Well, I'm not sure, but I think I passed out. I really do need to get up."

Paul bent over the bed and helped set her onto her feet. "Would dark matter heal you even if you didn't ask it to?"

"Like a freebie?" Sarah took tentative steps to the bathroom and snorted. "That happens."

Paul followed.

"Get out." Sarah went into the little toilet cubicle. "We're not that kind of friends."

Muttering under his breath, Paul turned away and flicked the light switch. Sarah slapped it back off. He leaned against the sink, his back to her. "I think whatever happened to your stomach and arms is dark matter."

"Well, duh."

"Maybe that's even why light bothers you."

Sarah didn't respond as she hobbled out of the toilet closet and made her way to the sink. She'd been intimate with dark matter for a long time and light had never bothered her before. But he was right; the wound wasn't bothering her much. It felt tight, but not painful.

"I don't think any of your problems have anything to do with Henry or Kathleen."

"It only happens when they're around," she said, washing her hands.

"It happens when you're agitated and arguing with them." Paul picked up his toothbrush and smeared his grape toothpaste onto it.

"I'd know if I was using dark matter. I'm done with it."

Paul didn't say anything as they brushed their teeth. Sarah discretely changed into her bloodstained jeans while Paul shaved at the sink.

"You might be done with dark matter, but that doesn't mean it's done with you," he said at last.

Sarah grabbed her bra and one of Paul's t-shirts and marched back to the sink. "I realize that, but it's a choice. I discovered that in the hospital. Not just a choice not to use it every day, but a choice to send it out of my life."

Paul arched a brow. "Are you trying to tell me you no longer have access to it?"

"It's not even in the basement anymore."

"Really? Huh." He rinsed shaving cream off his face.

Sarah turned her back on him and yanked the big sweatshirt off. "It's not like I can't access it. I can sense it outside and it's hopeful I'll call, but I'm stronger with it so far off. I managed not to cast on Kathleen last night and she was being a royal bitch." She grabbed her bra and hooked it on backwards around her waist, careful to avoid her newest wound.

Paul grabbed a towel and dried his face. "But it's still inside of you," he said.

"What is? Dark matter? No it's not. Not any more than it's inside you or anyone else."

"Why'd you go after Kathleen last night? Or was it Henry you were after?"

Sarah scowled at him in the mirror. "Would you drop the Henry thing? I was just getting a glass of water!"

Paul tossed the towel aside and looked at their reflections. His jaw dropped. "Put your top on!"

She twisted her bra around and pulled it into position. "Geez. Don't look."

"I thought we weren't that kind of friends! Though you sure don't mind when you want me to remove your catheter or give you stitches! But I draw the line at topless! I'm not your gay best friend, Sarah! Try to keep in mind that I'm a thirty-year-old man who hasn't had a date since before I went to war."

Sarah grabbed her shirt off the sink. "Sorry! I'm having some trouble here."

Paul took the t-shirt from her, bunched it up and thrust it over Sarah's head. He shoved one of her arms through the appropriate hole and then the other, and gently pulled the shirt down over the healing wound. Sarah glared at him, feeling like a kindergartener. He'd put it on backward.

"You're welcome," Paul said between clenched teeth.

"Thank you, but I was not going after Henry last night. I'm not stupid."

"That remains to be seen." Paul turned and marched across the room. "I'll make breakfast." He left, slamming the door.

IT TOOK SARAH almost twenty minutes to tug a pair of dirty socks on. By the time she finished, the wound on her stomach felt like it might pop back open. She might have lain down to recover from the exertion of getting dressed, except Paul was frying bacon in the kitchen. It smelled like she needed to eat it all.

"That smells wonderful," she said as she entered the kitchen.

Paul didn't reply, his brows drawn low over his eyes in a thundercloud of a frown. A tray with a stack of pancakes and glasses of juice sat on the counter. Sarah assumed it was for Henry and Kathleen.

"Do you need any help?" she asked, pouring a glass of water from the tap.

Paul didn't reply.

Sarah downed the entire glass, poured another, and went over to the stove. There was little she wouldn't do for Paul, but putting up with the silent treatment wasn't in her makeup. "Did you put butter on them while they're hot?"

The sight of the meager remains of a butter stick was the only answer she received. Sarah reached over the bowls and pancakes to shut the bright kitchen counter lights off. Paul paused in his task of turning bacon with tongs to flip the switch back on. He looked at Sarah and flipped on a second switch, illuminating the kitchen in scorching light.

Oh, good. Passive aggressive anger. Everyone's favorite.

Sarah took a clean plate from the counter and tossed a pancake onto it. She reached for the bacon cooling on paper towels and Paul moved it away from her reach.

"I can eat bacon!"

Paul ignored her.

"Fine." Sarah rolled the pancake up with her fingers and ate it as she continued to stand next to him. "This is good!" she said, and meant it. "You're the best cook."

Paul dropped more bacon into the pan, carefully using the handle to dip and turn the pan so the splatters didn't hit either of them.

Sarah watched it splatter over the front of the oven door and thought about criticizing just to make him talk. Instead she tossed her half eaten pancake back onto the plate and said, "I don't understand what your problem is!"

Paul turned his head to glare at her. "Think hard, and don't freaking lie to me!"

"I don't effing lie to you!" Sarah shouted at him.

Paul, still jiggling the handle of the pan, twisted his body to better shout back at her. He carelessly moved the pan with him, nearly sloshing the grease out and onto Sarah. He yanked it back and shouldered her out of the way as it splashed down in a scalding wave, headed right for him.

Hot sizzling grease rained down toward Paul's bare stomach and legs.

Everything slowed.

Sarah saw it happening as though she had all the time in the world. The hollow place in her middle where she cast from, where dark matter liked to nest, filled—but not with dark matter. It filled with light.

Not Paul. Please.

The light responded to her plea with colors. They moved from Sarah's middle to her consciousness and she understood them.

Time seemed to have been suspended as Sarah rushed to Paul, wrapping her arms around his middle. She grasped his hips and pulled him backward, away from the splash of hot grease. To be safe she moved him across the kitchen into the far corner, well away from the spill.

She looked toward the stove where the wave of bacon and hot oil hung suspended in the air, like bacon-filled bubbles. Adrenaline flowing through her, Sarah tugged the pan out of Paul's hand, raced across the space and caught the mess inside the pan. She shut the stovetop off, set the pan on it, and turned to look at Paul. He still stood in the same position, his hand clutching a non-existent pan.

Sarah waited, but he never moved.

"Paul?" she said, "are you okay?" She couldn't hear her own voice. "What the hell?" That didn't come either. "What the fuck!" she said loudly, frightened. She could feel the colors continuing to move gently in her core. "Is he okay?" she asked the light.

It heard the words she couldn't, and responded in colors she understood. *No, but you are helping him.*

"Whatever that means," she whispered, and still didn't hear it. The light moved away then, not leaving her entirely, but dimming the awareness of so many colors from her mind. Sarah blinked. The light in the room seemed normal now. She looked to Paul and waited.

"Noooo!" Paul shouted at last from across the kitchen, jumping backward and ramming against the kitchen counter. "Ooof! Ow! What the—?!" He looked up and down, then up again and across the room at the pan safely situated on top of the stove. Once more he looked down and ran his hand down his bare chest to his legs, and bent to examine them more closely. Slowly he looked up at Sarah. "What the hell did you do?"

"I'm not quite sure. Something strange happened."

From out of nowhere her voice sounded again, although her mouth was closed. "Paul? Are you okay?"

Paul frowned at her, clearly noticing the discrepancy but he answered, "I don't know. I think I blacked out."

Sarah shook her head. "No. The light did something to me." More disembodied words followed, echoing across the kitchen, "What the hell!"

That's what I said when time froze. Those are the words I couldn't hear!

Paul frowned at her, and once again Sarah's voice sounded when her mouth wasn't moving. "What the fuck!"

He reached back and held onto the counter, eyeing her warily. "Hell. I'm hallucinating."

"Is he okay?" asked the ghost of Sarah's voice.

Paul twisted to look around the kitchen, his complexion paling rapidly. Sarah ran to him. "No, Paul. It's not you. That is my voice. I hear it too."

Their eyes met as her voice whispered, "Whatever that means."

Paul covered his face with his hands and moaned.

Sarah wrapped her arms around his trembling torso. He was slick with sweat. "Listen to me. You're not going to hear it again. That's the last thing I said."

"Oh, my God, I'm hallucinating!"

"No you're not! Listen, you spilled the pan of bacon grease. It almost hit me and then you, and time froze so I—oh, no!" Sarah let go of Paul and sank to the floor.

"What is it?" Despite his own fear, Paul stooped down beside her. "Are you hurt?"

"Yeah, oh, man! It kills!" Her stomach felt as if it had been torn open, and tears of pain leaked out the corners of her eyes. "Listen, Paul. It's just my stomach again. I strained it. When that pan started to pour down your front—I don't know—I guess I cast. But not with dark matter! I used light!"

"Sarah, I'm not following."

"I don't know how to explain," she gasped, pressing her head against her knees and swearing mentally. "But I saw that you were going to be hurt and burned badly. I reached for help and the light came. It told me to help you. So I pulled you out of the way. I dragged you across the kitchen—it didn't hurt. Not then, but shit, now it does!" Sarah looked up. "Everything moved so slowly. I had time to drag you across the kitchen, take the pan out of your hand, and go back and catch all the grease before it got anywhere near the floor. I caught every bit of it, and the bacon. I put it back on the stove, but you were just standing over here, frozen in position like you were still at the stove. I talked to you, but I couldn't even hear myself. After a while—like five minutes later I think, at least it seemed that long—you finally moved. And then my words came!"

Paul sank to sit on the floor beside her. "Sarah, that doesn't make any sense."

"IT'S IMPOSSIBLE TO turn back time. There are universal absolutes," Sarah said, uncertain how long they'd been sitting on the floor rehashing what had happened.

Paul rubbed a hand over his face. "It sounds like you only slowed time down, but that's impossible too."

Sarah leaned her head against the cabinet door. "No. I didn't slow it down. I think maybe *I* sped up, and everything seemed slow to me."

"That sounds like a crazy theory—although, light *can* move far faster than anything, even hot grease. But we're not just talking about light. The human body can't move that fast. It'd disintegrate. It's not possible for you—or me—to move that fast and survive."

"I can't explain it, Paul. I don't know how it works either."

"Do you think you can do it again?"

Sarah tried several times to make time slow again, or speed herself up, but couldn't.

"Hold on. However this works, do you realize what this means?" A smile lit his face, erasing the worry from his eyes.

"You're not going to need a skin graft?"

"Besides that, which I appreciate. If you can cast with light, you're never going to have an excuse to use dark matter again."

"Paul?" Henry's voice called from upstairs.

Paul put a hand on Sarah's arm and a finger to his lips. She rolled her eyes, but nodded in agreement. Paul stood and pushed the trays across the counter as his brother approached the kitchen.

"Hey, I was going to call you. Breakfast is ready."

"We're leaving. I got us flights."

"Is Kathleen okay to travel?" Paul pressed his bare leg against Sarah's arm as though warning her to stay down. She wondered if he thought she'd pop up and beg Henry not to go.

"I'm fine," Kathleen said. Sarah could hear the sound of her dragging a suitcase over the hardwood floor as she joined Henry at the kitchen island. "I'm sure I can handle sitting in a plane. I could use some help with my suitcase, though."

"I'll get it for you," Paul said. "Do—do you want to have some breakfast before you go?"

No one answered. A minute later Sarah heard the bathroom door slam in the entryway. *Awkward.*

"Why did you mention food?" asked Henry. "Dammit, Paul! That's insensitive."

"I'm sorry. She doesn't look good at all. I don't think she should be traveling."

"Well, we can't stay here!"

Sarah tried to stand. Paul pressed his leg harder against her and reached a hand down, trying to cover her mouth.

"What about a hotel? Or even a hospital, Henry?"

"That's where we'll go when we get to Dallas. She was in a hospital there years ago when she had this problem. I thought this was behind her, but either the stress of what I put her through, or maybe even all the vomiting—I'll never forgive myself."

"It's not your fault."

"I know it's not, and we both know whose fault it is! Grab your suitcase. The airport is a bit of a haul from here. We're racing the clock."

"What are you talking about?"

"You're coming with me. I'm not leaving you here alone with that crazy wit—woman."

"She's a witch, Henry. You can say it," Paul said evenly. "Try to remember she's also my friend. I'm not leaving her yet. She needs me."

Sarah leaned her head against his leg and resisted the urge to hold onto it.

"Bullshit," said Henry.

"It's not. I'm not downplaying what Kathleen went through, but remember what Sarah went through for six weeks. She paid the price for what she did."

"Paul, I will drag you out of here."

"No, you won't. For starters I'll be home when Dad's car is done—which if you can believe, is finally in the painting phase of repair. You have no idea how many excuses they've come up with for the delays. But for another thing, I don't need you to drag me out of here. I can take care of myself. Lastly, if you try to, I'm going to have to kick your ass."

Henry laughed. It made Sarah smile. It was different than Paul's laugh, deeper and briefer. She'd never heard Henry genuinely laugh before. Everything she knew about him had been spell-induced and that made it all seem like a lie.

"Fine, but if you don't call me every night I'm calling the cops."

"Deal."

"Help me with these bags while Kathleen is in the ladies."

Paul didn't look down at her, but pointed a finger as though ordering a dog to stay. Sarah resisted the urge to bite it.

No sooner had the men shut the front door than Kathleen returned. Sarah stayed down as Kathleen's shoes echoed across the hardwood and came to a stop at the far side of the counter. She heard the clink of a glass and the sound of someone swallowing.

"I know you're there," said Kathleen, setting the glass on the counter with a soft thud.

Sarah popped up. "How did you know?"

Kathleen shrugged. "I don't know. How did Henry not? I'm sorry I lied about you last night. I told the guys you'd been bingeing."

"I don't care," said Sarah, "that doesn't bother me."

"I do. It was a lie. I was embarrassed that I was doing it."

Sarah chewed on her lip. "I'm sorry if something I did made you have this problem."

Kathleen let out a humorless chuckle. "It's hardly your fault the wine was bad."

"That's not what you were saying last night. Aren't you suing me?" *But it is my fault. There was no bad wine, just a bitch witch.* A few strands of color—blues and violets—whispered their message into Sarah's head: *Fix it.*

"What? How?" Sarah asked out loud.

Kathleen ignored that. "Henry's going to sue you, not me. I'd prefer to put this all behind me, and that includes you."

Color gathered in Sarah's center and she shoved it out in her words, trying to get this spell of light right. "It's okay to eat good food, Kathleen, and hold it in your body. You don't have to be perfect. You already kind of are." She added the last bit a bit resentfully. *But it's true.*

Kathleen blinked as the spell blew over her. Sarah could swear she saw the colors alight on the woman's skin and sink in. "I-I can't control it. My stomach just does what it does."

Sarah wove another wave of color into her next words. "It won't anymore. You're free of it."

Kathleen put one painfully thin hand on the counter. "Henry doesn't like—uh—soft women. That's why I was surprised he was with you. Not that you're too soft, you're normal. But that's not his type."

The information shocked Sarah, not that she wasn't Henry's type, but that Kathleen would kowtow to what was. She heard the front door open and rushed her next words, although they contained no spell. They were simply her words. "If Henry doesn't like the way you are, Kathleen, find someone who does. You're beautiful."

"Sarah!" Paul bellowed.

"What the hell are you doing to my fiancée?" Henry shouted at her.

The force of a spell shoved Sarah so hard she fell onto her backside and slid several feet across the kitchen floor.

Henry and Paul both hurried Kathleen out of the house and away from her, leaving Sarah alone to tenderly check her face for broken bones. She was pretty sure there weren't any, but she had a swollen lip and a black eye.

That bastard is dog meat! When I can stand I'm going to kick his ass!

chapter twenty-one

Warlocks and Family Treasure, Oh My!

Paul slammed the front door so hard when he came back inside the whole house shook. Sarah remained sitting on the floor against the sink, her head bent and her hands on her knees. She didn't look up.

Paul didn't say a word.

He slammed around the kitchen cleaning up the breakfast mess, keeping his distance from Sarah. She waited, clenching and unclenching her fists, wondering if the light would let her cast one of Aunt Lily's spells or if there were nice rules she didn't yet know.

Dark matter would have never allowed me to help Kathleen with her problem. There are definitely different rules.

I could heat up the bacon pan and smack him with it. That wouldn't require any casting with light or dark!

After nearly an hour, during which Sarah's anger didn't abate but her butt bones grew sick of sitting on the hard floor, Paul stopped in front of her. "He's gone and he's never coming back. Deal with it. You'll survive."

"Fuck you, Paul," Sarah growled.

"I have no sympathy for you! What the hell did you do to Kathleen? Did you learn nothing from your six weeks in a coma?"

Sarah repeated the phrase, not looking up.

"I have no idea why I stayed here. Henry is going to sue you, and if you're lucky he'll stop there. You should have heard him. I've never heard him talking like that. I don't know if he really has access to corporate assassins, but if he does, I can't blame him." Paul slammed something onto the counter and the floor vibrated. "Look at me when I'm talking to you!"

Sarah looked up.

Paul's mouth dropped open and he took a step backward. His entire demeanor changed. "Holy hell! Did Kathleen do that to you?"

Sarah staggered to her feet. "No, she didn't. You did."

Paul opened and closed his mouth. "What do you mean? I've never hurt a woman in my life."

"Actually, you have. Let's tally it up, shall we? You virtually knifed me three times." Sarah held her arms out to display the bruised and scabbed wounds. The one with stitches looked particularly nasty. "You gutted me, and as I am a woman and both knifing and gutting hurt, I'd say you probably don't need to make that statement again. At least not in front of me, not if you don't want to suffer the same." She lifted up the big grey t-shirt to expose the two-inch wide by eight-inch long glaring red wound on her stomach, and dropped it. "And today you slapped me in the mouth—knocked a tooth loose too. It's a back one, or I'd probably have called in dark matter by now. From the way it feels, I think you punched me in the eye too."

Paul gaped at her.

"What did you take?" she asked, hoping it was nothing, but knowing better. *There's no way he found it. I've looked so many times.*

"What?"

"What did you take from this house? I'm assuming it was something from my mother's room." *Please let it not be that!*

"What on earth are you talking about? I never took anything from your—wait." Paul reached into his back pocket and tugged out his wallet. "I did take your picture. Right after Kathleen got out of the hospital and I put Henry in that room, I saw this. I thought he'd flush it or something." He opened his wallet and displayed an old picture of Sarah. She recognized it and her heart sank.

He found it.

It couldn't be worse. The picture had been taken right after she'd finished college and Aunt Lily had taken her to Greece on vacation. Like most dark magic, it looked harmless. Paul had no idea what he'd done.

Sarah fought to keep her voice calm. "You took it out of a frame. What did you do with it?"

"I threw it out. It was just some old twigs. No glass or anything."

Please, no. "Are they still in the trash in the house somewhere? Or did someone throw it out?"

"I'm not sure. Do you want the picture?"

Sarah put her hands behind her back. The picture was covered in dark matter and she didn't dare touch it. "Not until it is back in the frame. Can you do me a favor and put that picture on the table in the dining room? Or somewhere you don't go?"

Paul didn't ask or argue. He headed for the dining room. Sarah went back to his bedroom and crawled into bed, trying not to think about what might happen if they didn't find that frame.

PAUL WOKE SARAH sometime after dark and turned on the lamp by the bed. The light made her blink, but it didn't hurt her eyes. He set a tray with a bowl of soup on the edge of the bed and sat on the recliner.

"It's probably better if we don't talk, until we find the frame for that picture," Sarah said.

"It got thrown out. I'm sure of it. I searched everywhere. I remember tossing it into the trash in your mother's room. Henry took the trash out every evening I think. Smells made Kathleen throw up more."

Tears welled in her eyes as she looked at Paul. *After all of this, old dark matter is going to claim me?*

Paul looked like someone had told him his dog died.

Sarah sniffled, grasped the tray, and slid it onto her lap. She picked up the spoon and plunged it into thick potato soup.

Paul slid off the chair and onto his knees beside the bed. "So it's when I yell or get mad at you?"

She nodded.

"I won't get mad."

"Have you met me?" She managed a smile, but he didn't.

"Can we make another frame? Were those twigs anything special?"

"I don't know what they were, but they were made using dark matter. I got rid of most of the stuff that could be bad—after my family died. My mother and aunt drowned themselves in the grist mill pond about three years ago."

"Oh, God, Sarah. I didn't realize."

"They'd been getting really bad. They were casting awful things, and using people to pay for it. There was a little girl..." Sarah's voice trailed off and a few tears rolled down her cheeks, landing in the soup. She put the spoon down and wiped her eyes. "She's in a wheelchair now. It could have been worse. I made them stop. And they...and they...used me instead."

"Sarah, what?" Paul reached for her. She leaned away.

"Don't touch me. It's not a good idea." She took a deep breath. "They only did it that once. Used me, I mean. They were mad that I'd interfered. Anyway, I was out cold for a while afterward, and

I could tell when I woke up that they'd cut me, so I knew they'd made a spell with my blood." Sarah picked up the spoon and stirred the soup, watching bits of bacon and cheese swirl.

"Eat a couple spoonfuls, Sarah," Paul urged.

Sarah was lost in her thoughts. "Of course you know me, I confronted them about it. Mother told me about the picture and said I'd stay out of their business from then on. Aunt Lily came to me later that night. She told me about the frame, and said it would contain the spell and keep me safe. She said not to worry too much, and behave myself. So, I told them I was leaving, to go ahead and do whatever they wanted with the fucking picture." She looked at Paul again. "I honestly didn't care. After what they'd done. It didn't matter anymore."

"I can feel that," he whispered.

"I didn't think they could hurt me any more than using me as a human sacrifice. But they could." Sarah stopped there, unable to talk about the police coming to the door. She didn't want to remember the ride in their patrol car to the mill pond. Blinded by a sudden onslaught of tears, Sarah jammed the spoon into her mouth.

Paul moved his hand so it was close to where her leg lay beneath the blanket and left it there, not quite touching.

Regaining control, Sarah pulled the spoon out. "I looked for the picture. Spells are really weird. They can make you walk past something you see every single day, and not be able to see it. I thought maybe Lily—my aunt—had destroyed it. I hoped. Where was it?"

"It was on the dresser next to the jewelry box."

She had looked on the dresser countless times and never been able to see it. "I wouldn't have known how to get rid of it anyway. I think I could have burned it as long as it had the frame on it. Maybe."

"We'll make a new frame."

"I can't without using dark matter."

"Could we just bury it in the attic?"

"No. The spell's got you now. It's not as strong as when you have the picture on you, but it's there. I can see it in your eyes."

"I hate when you say you can see dark matter in me. I feel like I'm being invaded."

"That's because you are."

"Can you touch my eyeballs and chase it away?"

Sarah smiled briefly. "It'd only go deeper." She studied Paul's eyes. There was very little dark matter in them, only a few grains dotting the golden sparks in his brown irises. Her scrutiny seemed to make him nervous and he moved his hand to toy with the pendant on his necklace. The dark matter shrunk so small she couldn't see it. She moved closer. "Let go of your necklace a minute."

Paul obeyed.

It came back.

"Now hold it."

It vanished.

"That pendant chases away dark matter too. I wonder why."

"What if I make a frame for your picture out of this?" He tugged the pendant out and fingered the heavy pewter chain.

"I'm not sure what good that would do."

"It's worth a try, isn't it? Come on, Sarah. We can't do nothing."

"Nothing might be the smartest thing to do." She didn't want to tell him it was only a matter of time. Without the protection of Aunt Lily's frame it was inevitable that type of spell would get her. Somehow she'd gone from furious at him, to the reality of what she faced. There was no anger in her, not even for her family.

At least when it does get me my soul won't be consumed by dark matter in the end.

"Do you want me to leave, Sarah? Is that what you're not saying? If I go, will you be safe?"

"It'll just follow you, or rebound. It could even go after Henry. The love spell did. I told you before that dark matter is smart. It's found a way back into my life, and yours. It's not going to give up easily."

Paul frowned. "Come on."

"Where?"

"We're fixing this. We're not letting it win. Get out of bed. Come on. Now, Sarah."

SARAH TUGGED ON the ends of her long t-shirt as she entered the dining room for the first time in years. Dust coated the surface of the dining room table, and thick cobwebs hung from the chandelier. Even Paul had avoided cleaning the room. This room held echoes of generations of Archers. If they were going to battle dark Archer magic, it was best done right here.

The picture lay on a corner of the table, inches away from a long tapestry embroidered by her grandmother's grandmother, Susannah Archer. A thick candle, handmade by Aunt Lily, sat in the middle of the table. A hand blown glass hurricane lamp covered it. Sarah's mother had been the glassblower, Lisha Celeste, known as "Sissy" to both Lily and their mother. Sarah had no pleasant memories of her grandmother, Blair Nisha, and she doubted that her mother or Lily had either.

Sarah darted her eyes around the room. Hand painted wallpaper—Kalonice Archer. Paintings—Ruby Archer. Thrown pottery—Sarah and Daisy Archer. Sarah quickly turned her eyes from the exquisitely decorated bowls. She knew who had made every item in the room and didn't want to remember a single one of the witches.

Paul leaned across the table to reach into the glass lamp and light the candle inside. The flame burned low and dark. Sarah averted her eyes. Paul glanced around the room and picked a shallow bowl. It was painted yellow and black with white calla lilies decorating the rim.

"This?" he asked, and tossed it onto the table without waiting for a reply. The faint dark specks in his eyes answered the question for him. He took the photograph of Sarah and dropped it into the wide bowl, pausing only to swipe a gentle finger across the face in the photo. Sarah could swear she felt it and shivered.

"Do you think you could invoke your new skills and cast with light to do this?"

Another shiver rippled through Sarah's body. "I don't see how. I don't even know how to use it really." She glanced at the chandelier casting a faint, shadowy light around the room.

"Sit down." Paul gestured toward a chair.

Sarah hesitated. It was her chair. She knew the stains on the cushion: berry cobbler from one summer when she was nine, and red wine spilled the night she'd lost her virginity in that very chair. She knew why the right front leg of that chair wobbled a bit.

Paul waited until she sat. The right front leg wobbled slightly.

Sarah crossed her arms and squeezed them.

Paul nodded approval and slowly unclasped his necklace, leaning his head over the bowl as he did. Dangling the chain over the bowl, he closed the clasp on it and slowly lowered it in, taking care to center the photograph inside the chain. "You're my friend, Sarah. Of all my friends living on this earth I would call you my best next to Henry." He glanced at her. "And only next because tradition demands I put him first."

A lump formed in her throat and she wondered if he had any idea how much those words meant to her.

Paul poked a finger into the bowl and moved the pendant over her face in the photograph. "I would give everything to protect my family and friends."

Sarah watched as he picked up the bowl and balanced it on top of the hurricane lamp. He walked around the table, tugged the chair out beside hers—Sarah tried not to think of whose it had been—and sat down in it. He laid his hand in her lap, palm up, and Sarah relaxed the death grip on her arms and put her hand in his.

Paul leaned back in his chair, stretching his long legs under the table, and waited.

For a moment Sarah thought that the flame would go out on the candle. Surely the bowl covering the lamp kept oxygen out of it. Universal laws had to be obeyed, even by dark matter. A wisp of color drifted through her mind, a wordless rainbow thought. Sarah squeezed Paul's hand, inhaling and exhaling slowly out her mouth.

The flame inside the glass shot up to touch the bottom of the bowl.

Sarah felt a flash of heat on her neck. She squeezed Paul's hand tighter.

Fire spread along the bottom of the bowl, and Sarah knew she wasn't imaging the heat against her back. She leaned forward. Paul tightened his grip on her hand and elbowed her to sit back against the hot chair. She looked into his eyes.

They were black with dark matter.

Sarah tried to let go of his hand but he held hers in a death grip.

"Trust me," he said, and turned his attention back to the candle.

I trust Paul. I trust Paul. I trust Paul. Sarah repeated the mantra to herself.

Inside the hurricane glass the flame burned hot and soot blackened her view.

Beneath her the chair grew warm, as if the back legs rested inside a campfire. The backs of her calves were too hot and she moved her legs further under the table. The heat followed.

Smoke curled out of the bowl, and Sarah could taste the acrid smell in her mouth.

"I'm afraid," she said.

"You should be," Paul answered, not looking at her.

Within seconds the glass of the lamp turned lava red, like it had been scooped from the glory hole by a gaffer. The table runner around it caught fire and ran the length of the fabric. In the kitchen the smoke detector, the one Paul had bought and installed a couple months ago, went off. Sarah felt the back of her arms burn.

I trust Paul. I trust Paul. I trust Paul.

Bravely she looked down, certain it was in her head. It wasn't. Her too-white arms looked sunburned and small blisters dotted her skin.

"Fuck that!" she shouted, attempting to wrest her hand from Paul's.

He responded as though he'd been waiting for it. He threw a long leg over her and grabbed her other hand, partially sitting on her chair to hold her down. Sarah struggled and swore, but it wasn't until she smelled and felt her hair burning that she panicked.

Kicking and screaming she swore at Paul. She bit his shoulder and arm and head-butted him until she saw stars. The table in front of them flamed like a bonfire and Sarah sobbed and thrashed under his iron grip. Like a wild animal trapped and terrified she couldn't even think to try and summon a spell with light to help.

I'm going to die. I'm going to die. I'm going to die.

Seconds later she could no longer draw breath. The smoke in the room clogged her lungs and the fire ate her oxygen. The wisps of colors in her mind bloomed into a rainbow that grew bright, filling her with light. Sarah slumped forward in her chair.

LIGHT FILLED SARAH'S mind, but she couldn't locate a colored strand to make sense of it or to cast with. It reminded her of looking into the sun. *Help me.* She sensed the power, yet the ability to use it escaped her.

"Help them." The words reverberated inside her head like thoughts, but they weren't her own. *"Help the ones you can, the ones you've harmed. The ones they harmed."*

The light slid out of her head, cooling her body as it escaped.

"Sarah. Hey, Sarah. Sarah? Let go of me."

She opened her eyes. They burned from smoke, but there was none in the room. The middle of the dining room table now resembled a charred log. The far side leaned toward them as though it would collapse in half. The bowl and candle and hurricane shade were gone, along with the old family tapestry. Paul's necklace—the one that belonged to Henry—dangled partially down a hole burned through the middle of the table. But all Sarah could smell was stale bacon from Paul's uneaten breakfast.

"Let go of my arm, please," said Paul.

Sarah looked down. The fingernails of both hands were digging into Paul's flesh, and trickles of blood dripped down his arm and hand. She was impressed considering the hospital had kept her nails trimmed painfully short. It took her a moment to unclench her fingers and let go. Her arms were sunburned and blistered. The skin on her face hurt, so she knew it had burned too.

Sarah turned almost fearfully to face Paul, uncertain what she would find.

The skin on his sharp nose was peeling on the end. The rest of his face looked more tanned than burned, although his eyebrows were scorched. The front of his hair had shriveled in places and dropped off, leaving his bedhead style looking a bit homeless. The spots where she'd bitten him left bloody marks on his shirt and bruises ran up and down his right arm. But Sarah smiled when she looked into his eyes. Not a hint of dark matter remained in them.

"I think it worked," he said, "but we need to work on your interpretation of the word trust." He stretched across the table and picked up his necklace, tossing it from hand to hand for a moment before setting it back down to cool on the table. "Who knew it'd be hot?"

Sarah shook her head. "You scared me. How'd you know what to do?"

"My best friend is a witch. I picked up a couple of things."

Sarah eyed the pendant on the table. "I think that's how the love spell transferred from you to Henry. It's really his, and the night I touched it as penance it bound the three of us into a love spell *together*."

Paul's crunchy-looking brows drew together. "But it broke for us. Why?"

"I have no idea."

Paul stared at the icon, running a finger back and forth in the air over it as though attempting to tug answers out of the object.

Sarah shivered. "You might not have any witch in you, but you've definitely graduated to dabbler."

"Dabbler? Where I come from that's a duck."

"Not where I come from, but I'd suggest retiring today. Nothing good can come of it."

"Only if you call me a retired warlock. That sounds way cooler than dabbler."

chapter twenty-two

Here, Kitty Kitty

 ou know sometimes I don't know quite what to make of you. You waffle from being mean as a snake to hiding in the closet next to the vacuum cleaner, crying your heart out like a little kid." Paul leaned into the broom closet, smiling at her. "Which are you, Sarah?"

"The mean one." Sarah couldn't quite meet his eyes, embarrassed at being caught.

"Hon." Paul crouched down to brush a hand over the top of her head. He tenderly smoothed the crunchy, dried up strands that no amount of conditioner could repair. "I'm not going to argue that. I know you."

Sarah's chin wobbled.

"Hey, come out of here. I was teasing." Paul grasped her hands and tugged her out. "I bought all the groceries for your favorite meal, including chocolate lasagna. I've got to put some weight on you before I go. I couldn't live with myself knowing you were wasting away on Popsicles and take-out this winter." He headed down the hallway to the kitchen.

Sarah followed. "I tried all morning to summon the light to fix my burns, but it's like it didn't even hear me."

"Well, it worked good on me," said Paul, displaying his perfectly healed arms. He'd slept like a baby last night while she tossed and turned, covered in the sap from an Aloe Vera plant. "Thanks for that. Too bad I'm a *retired* warlock. Maybe I could have fixed you up if I hadn't given it up after—what was it? Forty-five minutes? I was good, too."

Sarah was learning when to tune him out. Glaring at his arms, which weren't pink or peeling but nicely tanned for October, she said, "I think I can only help other people when casting with light. With dark matter I could only really help myself."

"Hey, seems like you're figuring it out fast," Paul said as he began unloading groceries from the dozen bags on the counter.

"That totally sucks! Even some of the places where tubes were jammed into me in the hospital haven't healed all the way, and I look like hell!"

Grinning, Paul shot a look back at her. "Poor baby, you actually look worse than hell." He paused and turned to her, his smile gone. "Please don't tell me that's why you were crying. You never struck me as vain."

"Well, I don't want to look like shit! That's not vanity! I can't go back to work looking like Night of the Living Dead!" It wasn't why she'd been crying, but she'd rather he thought that.

"You do realize you only have to go back to work if you want to, right?"

Sarah walked around the kitchen island and took a seat. That hadn't occurred to her. She no longer had to occupy her mind with the mundane. "But I have to work. I need income."

Paul walked around the kitchen as he put groceries away. "You have plenty of time to think about it while you recover. That Jackie Hamilton lady got you on company disability. You have a pile of checks in your mail, which you should open because I'm pretty sure you have bills due too." His phone buzzed on the far counter and he picked it up. "Hey. What's up?" He glanced at Sarah. "I'm fine. I forgot. I will." Paul clicked the phone off and set it down.

"Was that Henry?"

"Yep."

"How is he?"

"No idea."

"How's Kathleen?"

"Not a clue."

"Did they get back to Oklahoma?"

"Probably not, since they were heading for Dallas."

"I can't believe you didn't ask him how they were!"

Paul narrowed his eyes at her. "Why do you care how Henry is?"

Sarah rolled her eyes. "Because I'm madly in love with your slightly misogynistic, narcissistic, asshat brother."

Paul laughed. "*Now* I believe the spell is broken! Sounds like you finally met the real Henry."

"You know when you two came howling at me yesterday, I was actually trying to help Kathleen."

Paul leaned across the counter. "Now how was I supposed to know that?"

"I don't know, maybe you could listen when I tell you stuff," Sarah suggested. "How many times did I have to tell you that the spell with Henry was broken?"

"You still wanted him after you got out of the hospital."

"Only because I couldn't believe the attraction had been all love spell. When we did the logic spell, it told me something. So I thought there was something real there, but then I met him."

Paul laughed, but it sounded forced. He moved to the cupboard to get two glasses. "What were you trying to help Kathleen with?"

"I cast trying to help with her medical condition."

"I *knew* you cast on her."

"With light! Because it's probably my fault she'd had a recurrence with her eating disorder, so I was trying to help. But then I said if Henry doesn't like the way she is, she should find someone who does."

"Why would you say that? Henry adores her."

"She said she has to watch her weight because Henry doesn't like fat chicks."

Paul sighed, sliding a glass of water across the counter to her. "Wow. Man, if she leaves him he's going to sue you blind. Henry doesn't fight fair."

"Did you know I'm a witch? Same thing."

"You're a reformed, good-ish witch."

"Is that a thing? And did I mention I once got accepted into law school? I didn't go, but still," Sarah said, feeling the need to defend herself.

"Now that is a scary thought. Here." Paul dropped a box on the counter. "These are bath salts. Go upstairs and soak your aches and pains away. By the time you're finished, dinner will be ready."

THE BATH SALTS smelled so good Sarah wanted to put her nose under the water and breathe them in. She wallowed in the bath until the water coming out of the tap ran cold. For the first time in ages she used her blow dryer, and applied lemon oil to the burned bits of hair until it fell shiny and smooth. She felt presentable despite the bruises on her face and the dark circles under her eyes. A moment of standing inside her closet staring at sweat suits and jeans led her to impulsively scoot down the hall to Aunt Lily's closet.

It seemed silly to dress up, but she wanted to. As bad as Lily had been in the end, her best childhood memories were of her aunt. Sarah grabbed a long-sleeved silk tunic. It fit her shorter frame like a mini-dress, but her legs were the only part of her not bruised, and her burns looked way better than they felt. She slipped on a pair of red flats to match the dress and headed downstairs.

At the entrance to the kitchen Sarah stopped short. Henry stood by the kitchen table wearing the suit he'd had on the day she met him. "You caught the celebratory vibe," he said in Paul's voice.

Sarah smiled. "Where did you get that suit? For a second I thought you were Henry!"

"He left it." Paul turned in a circle to give her a better look. "I can do G.Q. too." He pulled her chair out. "I broke all your rules, by the way. I figured it was safe now. So prepare yourself for the best meal you've ever eaten."

One glance at the table set with vintage dishes, the Archer silver, crystal, and fresh flowers told Sarah he'd put extra effort into the meal. She resisted the urge to tell him he'd long ago made her the best meal she'd ever eaten. Sarah noted every detail, from the fresh herbs mixed into the salad to the crockery that the lasagna had been baked in.

Paul joked as they ate. He talked about funny things her friend Mindy had done while she'd been in the hospital, and how Father McCloud had demanded he leave the hospital and come by the rectory to replace his stolen shingle.

"I told him I took it from the overhang in the back where they keep their bikes. Boy, he gave me what for. Told me stealing was stealing and get my backside there and fix it. That was the longest I left you alone at the hospital. When I got back, Mindy was in the bathroom with an orderly and a bucket-sized tub of petroleum jelly. I think I'll end that story right there."

Sarah wanted to tell him not to leave out the good parts, but her heart ached and she worried if she started talking she might cry. All she'd ever wanted was to escape dark matter. Now she had that and she wanted more. Far more.

Paul dished out dessert as he told her about going to college in Maine and how he hated snow. "Which is why it's good my dad's car is finally ready. The only thing worse than walking in snow is driving in it. I wasn't looking forward to driving a rear wheel drive sports car in bad weather clear to Oklahoma."

"It's only October," she managed.

"You can't fool me. I know how early it comes, and it's nearly November already."

The chocolate lasagna might as well have been sawdust.

"Timing-wise this worked out great. Now I don't have to worry about you, not too much anyway."

Sarah didn't look up.

"My only worry was that you'd be lonely here."

Sarah looked at him then, hope dancing in her chest.

"Nobody should be in this big house alone."

A faint smile quirked the edges of her lips. *Please, Paul, please!*

Paul stood up and took her hand. Leaning close he whispered into her ear, "How'd you like a permanent roommate?"

Yes! Blinking back tears, Sarah nodded her approval, not trusting her voice.

"Come here," he said, leading her a few steps to the little broom closet. Grinning, he opened the narrow door. A little black kitten meandered out.

Sarah's heart plunged somewhere under the basement. "A cat?"

"Yep!" Paul bent and scooped it into his arms. "I already named him. Revere, meet your mommy."

"I hate cats," said Sarah without heat.

He held it up so the animal was level with her face. "Look at his little face. You never had a chance to like cats. You're going to love him. He already went in the litter box!"

Sarah took the kitten.

Paul bent over and kissed it on the head. "The bad news is what my mother always says to my dad. I cooked, you clean. Goodnight, Sarah. I need a shower before bed." He smiled at her and walked away.

SARAH FOUGHT TEARS the entire time she cleaned the kitchen. It took forever with the kitten clutched in one hand. She covered the leftovers with wax paper and shoved them into the refrigerator.

I can't believe he's going to leave already!

"You'd *better* go in the litterbox," she told the kitten.

Just because dark matter left doesn't mean I don't need him!

"You're not sleeping with me." She lifted the kitten to look into its golden eyes. "Ever."

I just got out of the hospital! I don't know how to use light to cast! And how am I supposed to get the burnt dining room table out of the house? Plus, the light said I have to help the people my family hurt—how can I do that by myself? What do I know about helping people?

"And you're *not* getting on the furniture either, or the counters!"

The kitten meowed in her face. She kissed him in the same spot Paul had. *It's not going to snow for at least a month. He's such a baby!* "I hate pet fur. Don't you dare shed." *What kind of name is Revere for a kitten? I'm calling him Adolf.*

The sound of her ultrasonic toothbrush echoed down the hall.

Sarah marched down the hallway to Paul's room. "He'd better not be using that," she told Adolf. "It's mine and I want it back!"

Paul's door stood open. "You are not stealing my toothbrush," she announced as she deposited the kitten on Paul's bed and swung to face the thief.

The man in question leaned against the sink, freshly showered, brushing his teeth with her toothbrush and not wearing a stitch of clothing.

Sarah's mouth dropped open.

She'd never seen him run or work out once in the time since he'd moved in, but he obviously did something to deserve the long lean muscles rippling down his body. Despite his predilection for lasagna and other Italian food, Paul's body lacked evidence of all the calories. His hair had grown. Even combed back and damp it looked like it needed to be cut. He definitely needed to shave with a razor she hadn't been secretly using. Dark stubble trailing down his chin and throat met darker and thicker hair down the front of his body, all the way down.

He turned back to the sink, not batting an eyelash at her intrusion. Sarah dropped onto the end of the bed. Paul took his sweet time rinsing his mouth and drying his hands.

Finally he turned and walked toward her. "What do you think?"

It took a moment for Sarah to respond, and she opted for fake-sounding nonchalance. "About what?"

"My tats?" Paul turned around; displaying an impeccable back perched upon two globes of perfection.

What tat? Sarah bounded off the bed. "Nice. Uh, I need my toothbrush." *And to take a cold shower. Now.*

Paul moved in front of her, blocking her path. "That's a big cup of nope."

"What?"

"I gave you a cat. Now, you give me custody of the tooth-brush." He breathed the last two words against her face and she smelled the grape of his toothpaste, his clean body-wash, and the underlying scent of him, remembered from that first encounter in the Target parking lot.

Things in the Netherlands melted.

Sarah opened her mouth and, "My brush cat, yeah," came out.

"Is that a fact?" Paul put his hand on her shoulder, smoothing the silk of her dress. "Do you remember that night in the Target parking lot? The night we met?"

Sarah blinked at him, trying to focus on his words and not the fact that he was naked, and not just regular naked, but excellent, five-star naked.

Paul continued, "We got wrapped up in that love spell?"

Sarah's brain unscrambled. "We did."

"And the necklace pulled Henry in too—"

"Yes, I think it—"

"I think I know why the spell let us go."

"Why?"

"Because a love spell has nothing to do with real love, does it? Let's say, hypothetically, that one of the people wrapped in the love spell begins to genuinely have feelings for the other. Real feelings. Good feelings."

"Wait. Are you saying that you—"

"Fell in love with you?" Paul asked, his voice a whisper as he leaned close, too close. "No. But that day in the attic I suddenly cared about you. I wanted to help you. I friend-zoned you that day, deeply enough that dark matter either got uncomfortable, or bored with me."

"That might explain why it moved from you to Henry, but—"

Paul rubbed his thumb on her cheek, carefully avoiding her bruises. "It got bored with you too, when you started to like me. I think that happened the day you bailed me out of jail. Or maybe even sooner. You went from bitch witch to tenderhearted friend helping a wounded warrior."

"Paul, that makes sense!" Sarah exclaimed. "And it was so much stronger with Henry because it had gone unchecked for so long. It blindsided me. I couldn't think straight!"

Paul shook his head. "That's ancient history now. Remember the logic spell? Remember when it said, *You go together*?"

"Yes—wait. How do you know what the logic spell said to me?"

Paul leaned down to look into her eyes and waited.

"Did it say something to you?"

He nodded.

"It said "*you go together*" to you too?"

He nodded again.

"Wait. You mean it didn't mean me and Henry? It meant me and—"

"I have another theory, if you're interested."

The way he said it had Sarah's complete attention. She swallowed and nodded too.

"When you used dark matter you never needed to sleep much, and you couldn't really feel pain."

"That's true, but I'll have you know there's really no down side to not feeling pain."

"Maybe, but I think it's more about feeling anything. You feel everything now. You once told me that sex wasn't much fun for witches, but now I wonder if that's still true."

Sarah's mouth dropped open. "Oh, that's a really good theory." *What if that's true? Oh, my stars, what if that's true?*

"I think it's worth compiling some scientific data to find out."

"I think you're right." Sarah swallowed. "So, is that why you're naked?"

"I'm simply trying to get your attention, Sarah Archer." He leaned forward and kissed the tip of her nose. Sarah's heart slammed against her ribs. "It hasn't been easy with love spells and comas. My fabulous cooking and the little kitten were breadcrumbs you heartlessly ignored. You forced me to kidnap your toothbrush and show you the entire poem." He motioned with both hands to his tattoos.

It took effort to keep her eyes on his. "But you friend-zoned me. You said you wanted the blonde at the bakery more than me."

"That was before I really got to know you. Do you remember this part of the poem?" Paul turned his leg out and motioned toward his inner thigh.

"No," she whispered, staring.

Brushing his bristled cheek against hers, Paul whispered in her ear, "What is education in Massachusetts coming to? This is the part where it goes, *'Meanwhile, impatient to mount and ride, booted and spurred, with a heavy stride.'*"

Sarah turned her eyes to his again. "It sounds like you're trying to cast a spell, except there's no magic in it."

Paul lifted Sarah under the arms and sat her on the edge of the bed. "*Au contraire mon frere.* It's the real kind of magic." He leaned down and pressed a hand against her torso, carefully avoiding her scar. Gently he moved her across the bed, past the kitten, and crawled after her on his hands and knees, corralling her until her back rested against the pillows.

Paul stretched out beside her and smiled, saying in a normal tone, "I don't want to hook up with you, Sarah. To be clear, I want to make love to you without anything that has to do with spells or dark matter."

Sarah wrapped her arms around him and pulled him closer, until their foreheads touched. "You don't mind that I'm an evil witch?"

"I don't mind that you used to be," Paul whispered against her lips. "There's light in you, Sarah Archer." He brushed his lips over hers. "And that's only one of the things I've grown to love about you."

Sarah left Adolf on the front porch, safe from the snow coating the ground, and told him to stay. He listened. Paul stooped to scratch his ears and tell him goodbye.

"I can't believe Mommy renamed you after a fascist, genocidal maniac."

Sarah didn't have the heart to argue that one madman didn't get to own a name. She followed in Paul's footprints, not even trying to hide the tears streaking down her face.

"It's not safe to drive that car in this weather," she told him.

"It's nearly forty degrees. It's already melting. My dad's having a fit that by the time he gets his new car it'll be last year's model. I promised him, Sarah. But I'll come back in the spring for a visit." He opened the passenger door and tossed his backpack in.

"A visit?" Her chin wobbled. "After the last couple days?"

"I told you, that's up to you."

"Do you want to leave? Is this really even about your dad's car?"

He leaned down and kissed her cheek, whispering into her ear, "You know what it's about."

"I'm afraid."

"I know. Goodbye, Sarah." He kissed her on the forehead, hovered for a moment over her lips, then straightened. Without looking at her Paul walked around the car, got inside, and within seconds was driving away from the curb.

Sarah watched, her heart aching with loneliness already.

Don't go. Don't go. Don't go.

Please, make him come back! She watched as the car stopped at the end of the block and waited for another car to pass.

Light slid into Sarah's mind. Red light. A second later a whistling sound echoed over the snow, heading down the street. Adolf hissed from his perch on the porch. The whistling followed Paul's car, catching up with it and landing as he tried to turn onto High Street. It sounded like a meteorite dropped through the hood and tore the engine out. A sonic boom vibrated over the neighborhood and the percussion set off car alarms up and down the street.

Sarah gaped, reminded of her first encounter with Paul all those weeks ago. Adolf had hurled himself off the porch to tunnel under the snowy leaves.

The guy who cut the grass in summer came running with a snow shovel in hand. He bolted across the yard and around the side of the house heading in the direction of the greenhouse. Farther up the street Paul got out of the car and slammed the door shut with a bang. Sarah waited as he stalked up the street toward her, his expression furious. He'd barely gotten within earshot when he started yelling.

"Are you kidding me? Are you freaking kidding me? You do not do that kind of crap to a war vet! Woman, you have got to be out of your mind! I'm going to need to go back into therapy and take medication. Lord! Even my legs are shaking!" Paul stopped several feet in front of her. "What the *hell* were you thinking?"

"I'm thinking," Sarah admitted.

The thundercloud of dark brows over his eyes lifted.

Paul took a step closer. "Really?"

"Yeah."

He turned to look up the street at the car. Several people had gathered around it. He turned back to her. "You couldn't text me that? You know I would have turned around! I told you last night all you had to do was say you'd think about it. That's all I needed to hear. Did you really have to blow up my dad's car? *Again?*"

Sarah crossed her arms. "I didn't think it would work. I guess I *can* use light for bad stuff too."

Paul fought a smile. "That's not funny, or good."

Sarah shrugged. "Sorry. I don't think the light is happy with me either." The zig-zagging patterns of lightning dancing through her head lightened and faded away, now that she'd acknowledged it.

"Life is short and I'm old-fashioned, I told you. If I stay we'll have to talk about commitment."

"But I'm not old-fashioned," Sarah pointed out.

"You're very old-fashioned. You're not traditional."

"Yeah. That," she said.

"But you said you were thinking."

"I am, Paul, and I'm willing to talk about it if that's what you need. We can discuss it every day for years if you like."

"If you're going to be like that, I might have to bust my warlock outta retirement."

She smiled. "I love when you talk dirty."

"You're not the only bitch witch in town," he drawled.

"Pretty sure I am."

Paul moved the last few steps between them and wrapped his arms around her. "Don't be afraid, Sarah. A relationship simply means you're going to be with your best friend forever."

Dear Reader,

Thank you for reading *Bitch Witch*. Your feedback is important to me, so please take a moment and leave a review. It's the best way for me to know what you're thinking, and your reviews are instrumental in getting the next book published.

The idea for *Bitch Witch* hit me last summer during a night run to Target. As a full blue moon rose over the parking lot, I tossed paper towels, coconut yogurt, and a step ladder into the back of my little Jeep. Because I'm an introverted writer who spends most days wearing my workout clothes (because I *am* going to get to it *soon*) I tend to run errands after dark.

That spectacular moon deserved to be the opening scene of a novel. In my mind I could see Sarah Elizabeth Archer. The title *Bitch Witch* came immediately to mind and the entire story unfolded in several heartbeats. Sarah's house took form in my mind. Many moons ago I lived in Shrewsbury, Massachusetts. I knew she'd work at Mass Power and Light, because I once temped there, besides, what better name for a book about power and light?

That very night I pitched the story to my publisher, thinking surely *Bitch Witch* is a concept and title that's been taken. Yet it was as available as any title can be. I wrote as fast as I could, barely giving a thought to the fact that my mother would probably have to change churches after this book (sorry, Mom.) It wasn't until the book was out of my hands and in the capable hands of my editors that my publisher said, "This book will redefine you as a writer." *Uh-oh*, I thought, quickly followed by an uncooperative *whatever*.

My job as a writer is to write stories with honesty and fearlessness. I hope you enjoyed your time with Sarah as much as I did. Surely there's a little bitch witch in all of us, and even when we follow the light there's just no getting rid of her completely, is there?

With love and light,
S.R. Karfelt

Paul Revere's Ride

Henry Wadsworth Longfellow (1807–1882)

LISTEN, my children, and you shall hear
Of the midnight ride of Paul Revere,
On the eighteenth of April, in Seventy-five;
Hardly a man is now alive
Who remembers that famous day and year.
He said to his friend, 'If the British march
By land or sea from the town to-night,
Hang a lantern aloft in the belfry arch
Of the North Church tower as a signal light,—
One, if by land, and two, if by sea;
And I on the opposite shore will be,
Ready to ride and spread the alarm
Through every Middlesex village and farm,
For the country folk to be up and to arm.'

Then he said, 'Good-night!' and with muffled oar
Silently rowed to the Charlestown shore,
Just as the moon rose over the bay,
Where swinging wide at her moorings lay
The Somerset, British man-of-war;
A phantom ship, with each mast and spar
Across the moon like a prison bar,
And a huge black hulk, that was magnified
By its own reflection in the tide.

Meanwhile, his friend, through alley and street,
Wanders and watches with eager ears,
Till in the silence around him he hears
The muster of men at the barrack door,
The sound of arms, and the tramp of feet,
And the measured tread of the grenadiers,
Marching down to their boats on the shore.

Then he climbed the tower of the Old North Church,
By the wooden stairs, with stealthy tread,
To the belfry-chamber overhead,
And startled the pigeons from their perch
On the sombre rafters, that round him made
Masses and moving shapes of shade,—
By the trembling ladder, steep and tall,
To the highest window in the wall,
Where he paused to listen and look down
A moment on the roofs of the town,
And the moonlight flowing over all.

Beneath, in the churchyard, lay the dead,
In their night-encampment on the hill,
Wrapped in silence so deep and still
That he could hear, like a sentinel's tread,
The watchful night-wind, as it went
Creeping along from tent to tent,
And seeming to whisper, 'All is well!'
A moment only he feels the spell
Of the place and the hour, and the secret dread
Of the lonely belfry and the dead;
For suddenly all his thoughts are bent
On a shadowy something far away,
Where the river widens to meet the bay,—
A line of black that bends and floats
On the rising tide, like a bridge of boats.

Meanwhile, impatient to mount and ride,
Booted and spurred, with a heavy stride
On the opposite shore walked Paul Revere.
Now he patted his horse's side,
Now gazed at the landscape far and near,
Then, impetuous, stamped the earth,
And turned and tightened his saddle-girth;

But mostly he watched with eager search
The belfry-tower of the Old North Church,
As it rose above the graves on the hill,
Lonely and spectral and sombre and still.
And lo! as he looks, on the belfry's height
A glimmer, and then a gleam of light!
He springs to the saddle, the bridle he turns,
But lingers and gazes, till full on his sight
A second lamp in the belfry burns!

A hurry of hoofs in a village street,
A shape in the moonlight, a bulk in the dark,
And beneath, from the pebbles, in passing, a spark
Struck out by a steed flying fearless and fleet;
That was all! And yet, through the gloom and the light,
The fate of a nation was riding that night;
And the spark struck out by that steed, in his flight,
Kindled the land into flame with its heat.

He has left the village and mounted the steep,
And beneath him, tranquil and broad and deep,
Is the Mystic, meeting the ocean tides;
And under the alders that skirt its edge,
Now soft on the sand, now loud on the ledge,
Is heard the tramp of his steed as he rides.

It was twelve by the village clock,
When he crossed the bridge into Medford town.
He heard the crowing of the cock,
And the barking of the farmer's dog,
And felt the damp of the river fog,
That rises after the sun goes down.

It was one by the village clock,
When he galloped into Lexington.
He saw the gilded weathercock
Swim in the moonlight as he passed,
And the meeting-house windows, blank and bare,
Gaze at him with a spectral glare,
As if they already stood aghast
At the bloody work they would look upon.

It was two by the village clock,
When he came to the bridge in Concord town.
He heard the bleating of the flock,
And the twitter of birds among the trees,
And felt the breath of the morning breeze
Blowing over the meadows brown.
And one was safe and asleep in his bed.
Who at the bridge would be first to fall,
Who that day would be lying dead,
Pierced by a British musket-ball.

You know the rest. In the books you have read,
How the British Regulars fired and fled,—
How the farmers gave them ball for ball,
From behind each fence and farm-yard wall,
Chasing the red-coats down the lane,
Then crossing the fields to emerge again
Under the trees at the turn of the road,
And only pausing to fire and load.

So through the night rode Paul Revere;
And so through the night went his cry of alarm
To every Middlesex village and farm,—
A cry of defiance and not of fear,
A voice in the darkness, a knock at the door
And a word that shall echo forevermore!

For, borne on the night-wind of the Past,
Through all our history, to the last,
In the hour of darkness and peril and need,
The people will waken and listen to hear
The hurrying hoof-beats of that steed,
And the midnight message of Paul Revere.

Acknowledgments

The light.
  The night.
The muse.
  My amazing editor.
The *Bitch Witch* Launch Team.
  My Women Reading Aloud Kula.
Blue Harvest Creative.
  My stoic and astonishingly patient husband, and
The Blue Moon. You complete me.

Where in the brain or heart does story come from? I don't know, but I do know that it takes a team to make a book. *Bitch Witch* thrived thanks to my talented and insightful editor, and early story edits by Shieldmaiden for Hire.

My launch team's feedback proved invaluable. Thank you: Kim, Kelsey, Tom, Patricia, Colette, Jennifer, Laura, Bailey, Ashley, Mirdala, and Jan. I appreciate your feedback and your laughter as we shared far too many witch memes.

To my Kula who magically brings story to the surface, I love you ladies.

Blue Harvest Creative, thank you for answering my questions 24/7, letting me romp when I ran amok, and propping me up when my enthusiasm waned.

For my darling Dear Hubby, I love you—and I'm saying that during fishing season despite the fact that you at this very moment smell like fish. If that isn't real love, I don't know what is.

About the Author

An entrepreneur, wife, mother, and novelist, S.R. Karfelt enjoys spending time with her muse and living outside her comfort zone. She currently resides in the soaring capital of the world.